SHADOWS OF DEATH

The Dorothy Martin Mysteries from Jeanne M. Dams

THE BODY IN THE TRANSEPT
TROUBLE IN THE TOWN HALL
HOLY TERROR IN THE HEBRIDES
MALICE IN MINIATURE
THE VICTIM IN VICTORIA STATION
KILLING CASSIDY
TO PERISH IN PENZANCE
SINS OUT OF SCHOOL
WINTER OF DISCONTENT
A DARK AND STORMY NIGHT *
THE EVIL THAT MEN DO *
THE CORPSE OF ST JAMES'S *
MURDER AT THE CASTLE *
SHADOWS OF DEATH *

* available from Severn House

SHADOWS OF DEATH

A Dorothy Martin Mystery

Jeanne M. Dams

30653 4013

L

This first world edition published 2013
in Great Britain and 2014 in the USA by
SEVERN HOUSE PUBLISHERS LTD of
19 Cedar Road, Sutton, Surrey, England, SM2 5DA.
Trade paperback edition first published
in Great Britain and the USA 2014 by
SEVERN HOUSE PUBLISHERS LTD.

British Library Cataloguing in Publication Data

Dams, Jeanne M. author.
    Shadows of death. – (The Dorothy Martin mysteries; 14)
    1. Martin, Dorothy (Fictitious character)–Fiction.
    2. Excavations (Archaeology)–Scotland–Orkney–Fiction.
    3. Murder–Investigation–Scotland–Orkney–Fiction.
    4. Women private investigators–Great Britain–Fiction.
    5. Americans–Great Britain–Fiction. 6. Detective and
    mystery stories.
    I. Title II. Series
    813.5'4-dc23

ISBN-13: 978-07278-8280-6 (cased)
ISBN-13: 978-18475-1491-2 (trade paper)

All Severn House titles are printed on acid-free paper.

Severn House Publishers support the Forest Stewardship Council™ [FSC™],
the leading international forest certification organisation. All our titles that
are printed on FSC certified paper carry the FSC logo.

Typeset by Palimpsest Book Production Ltd.,
Falkirk, Stirlingshire, Scotland.
Printed and bound in Great Britain by
TJ International, Padstow, Cornwall

Acknowledgements

There are two real people in this book. Andrew Appleby, who kindly gave me permission to introduce him into my fiction, is a splended potter and a delightful person. He resembles my fictional character in both appearance and personality, though my character's thoughts, words, and actions are not to be imputed to the real Andrew.

I first met Roadkill (who counts as a person) at the door of the cat charity shop in Stromness. He demanded loudly to be let in, though the shop was not open. I tried to tell him I couldn't do a thing about it, but he was not impressed. He certainly did not give me permission to put him into the book, but I dared do it anyway. I should stress that not a hair of his ornery head was harmed in the writing of this book. So far as I know, he still roams Stromness terrorizing the human and animal population, and daring cars to run him over.

All the other characters are fictitious, especially members of the Orkney Area Command of the Northern Constabulary, and if they resemble any real persons living in Orkney or elsewhere, I didn't mean it. I have tried to use typical names, so if I have hit upon someone's real name, be assured that it was by accident. I have arranged ferry and excursion boat times to suit myself. Some of the shops are real and some are not, some of the Neolithic sites are real and some are not. In particular, the site I have called High Sanday is fictitious, as is the island of Papa Sanday, and though its resemblance to the marvellous dig now going on at the Ness of Brodgar can hardly be denied, I must state firmly that none of the characters involved in my dig are at all like the dedicated archeologists at the Ness of Brodgar site. I would strongly urge readers to look up the real one. It's awe-inspiring.

I owe so much to so many people it's impossible to list them all, but besides Andrew, I especially need to thank my friends Tuck and Janice Langland for insisting I must come to Orkney, and serving as my hosts there for several days. On the island of Shapinsay, which Dorothy and Alan didn't get to visit on this trip, I had a lovely time with my hostess Lesley McKeown at Haughland House and then at Balfour Castle with David McCowan Hill and his superb staff.

Orkney is a magical place, a place unlike anywhere else on earth. Visit it. You'll never be quite the same again.

ONE

'How much do you know about archaeology?'

I looked up, startled. I was deep in a new Alexander McCall Smith book, miles away in Edinburgh. Alan's question had come out of nowhere. 'Um . . . archaeology?' I said brilliantly.

'The study of ancient civilizations and so on.'

'I do know what the word means, dear. I suppose I know pretty much what everyone knows. What brought that up?'

'I wondered if you might enjoy a visit to Orkney.'

I shook my head to clear it. 'Alan, my love, I've barely heard of Orkney. I know where it is, more or less. Way north. What does it have to do with archaeology?'

'The whole island group is an archaeologist's dream. The oldest evidence of human occupation in all of Britain is in Orkney. There are stone circles that predate Stonehenge by a thousand years or so, and houses that were built long before the Pyramids. Helen and I visited briefly, many years ago when the children were in their teens, and I read just now –' he waved his newspaper – 'that they're doing new excavations that may prove to be very exciting. It might be worth a visit, if you're at all interested in that sort of thing.'

I wasn't, particularly, but I was extremely interested in Alan. Our marriage, the second for both of us after our respective spouses died, was rock-solid. But there's always a tiny residual jealousy of the first spouse. If Alan and Helen had enjoyed a visit to Orkney, then I would enjoy a visit to Orkney if it killed me.

Thus began our part in events that were to change many lives.

Alan emailed a friend in Orkney, a potter named Andrew Appleby whom he hadn't seen for many years. Andrew's reply was an ebullient phone call inviting us both to come and visit the dig and have dinner with him and his wife and stay in the islands for a few weeks. 'We can't ask you to stay here with us; the house is being refitted and isn't really liveable. But I know of a lovely holiday flat in Stromness that's available. It'll do you beautifully.'

'The dig is on Papa Sanday, I understand,' said Alan, on the speaker phone. 'I don't think I know that island.'

'You wouldn't. It's away up north, a tiny place and very nearly uninhabited, only three or four crofts. And there's no regular ferry service. Makes it a bit difficult for the crew – they've had to build a tent city – but they're turning up some amazing stuff. Come see for yourself.'

'Andrew's very active in the Friends of Ancient Orkney,' Alan said when we'd ended the phone call with vague promises. 'He'd give us a tour of the dig, I'm sure. And he's an entertaining fellow. He lives in an area near the Loch of Harray, spelt "a-y" but pronounced "Harry", so he calls himself the Harray Potter.'

A remote, nearly uninhabited island somewhere north of nowhere didn't sound much like my idea of a pleasant spot for a vacation. And if there was no ferry, how were we to get there? Swim?

Shadowy visions of Helen made me keep my thoughts to myself. 'Why not?' I said brightly. 'Call him back and find out how we book that holiday cottage. For . . . a fortnight, maybe?'

Alan knows me very well. His mouth twitched, but he didn't quite laugh. 'You'll like it, love. I promise.'

I was happy to let him make arrangements for the journey. It's a long way from the south of England to the northern reaches of the United Kingdom. The Shetland Islands are farther north than Orkney, but Orkney's plenty far enough. A little research on the Internet told me the climate was 'temperate'. I've lived in England for quite a while, but I'm American by birth, and I know that 'temperate', to the Brits, doesn't mean quite what it does in America. I packed, for the week in mid-June, wool sweaters and fleece pants, with warm, waterproof jackets and hats and gloves. Alan worked out a circuitous route to Aberdeen, where we'd get a car ferry to Kirkwall, the larger of the two cities on 'the Mainland', as I found out the principal island was called. 'It would be simpler just to fly from London,' he said with a sigh.

'But then we couldn't take Watson,' I said firmly. I've been a cat person all my life, but our lovable mutt Watson had become so firmly entrenched as a part of our family that a holiday without him was unthinkable. We'd had to leave him behind on one or two occasions and none us had cared for the experience, the dog least of all.

So we asked Jane Langland, our indispensable next-door neighbour, to look after the two cats. Jane loves looking after animals, even cats, though she's a dog person. Samantha and Esmeralda would scarcely notice our absence, but of course they'd berate us when we returned, complaining that they'd been abandoned and left to starve. Cats are, I'm afraid, terrible liars.

After several years of living in the adopted country I love so much, I've learned that it doesn't really rain all the time in England, despite what I thought as an American tourist. There are periods of weather so perfect I think I'm living in Eden. Warm, sunny Mays with a hundred different varieties of flowers blooming in extravagant technicolor. Julys so hot, one can actually enjoy a visit to the seashore and welcome the cool breezes. Mellow Septembers rich with the scent of apples and the golds and rusts of the harvest. Halcyon days.

However. While all the above is true, it is also true that there often seems to be a particular malevolence that singles out Alan and me when we plan a holiday. Not always, mind you. We'd had a lovely time in Wales a while back, with brilliant sunshine nearly every day. But as if to pay us back, or perhaps to punish me for my slanderous meteorological prejudices of yore, the gods conjured up disgusting weather for our trip north. The roads, once we got past London, were unfamiliar even to Alan, and driving rain made it hard to see anything but the largest signs. And of course Watson required periodic stops. At least he enjoyed the rain as little as we did and took care of his business with admirable promptness.

We had decided to take it in slow, easy stages, so we spent the first night in York, one of my favourite cathedral cities in England. That leg was only a bit over 200 miles, but it took us all day in the rain, and we arrived far too tired to appreciate the charm of the medieval city. Indeed, Alan's normally equable temper was visibly fraying as he dealt with the traffic, the inevitable result of modern vehicles – many modern vehicles – crowding streets designed for horses and pedestrians. We reached our hotel at last, and paused only to shake our umbrellas, remove our dripping raincoats, and settle Watson, before heading straight to the bar.

'Two large Jack Daniels, please,' said Alan to the barman. 'And some nuts or crisps or whatever you have in the way of snacks.'

'Right you are, mate,' said the man in a voice straight from London. 'And would the lady like some ice?'

I've given up trying to figure out how I am still instantly recognizable as an American, before I even open my mouth. I've lived in England for years. I buy my clothes here. What little make-up I wear comes from Boots. I even wear hats. I sighed. 'No ice, thank you, just a very little water.'

The bourbon helped. The crisps didn't do much to allay our hunger, but the barman offered a plate of smoked salmon, which did take the edge off. Although it was scandalously early, we went on in to dinner and worked our way through a solid meal, satisfying if somewhat unimaginative. Then, without so much as an exchange of glances to confirm our decision, we went up to our room.

'Not the evening to explore York,' I said as I got into a flannel nightgown. It was still light outside, a wet, depressing sort of half-light glimpsed through the rain that coursed down the window panes.

'No,' Alan agreed. 'One of the benefits of old age is that one can go to bed in the daylight without apology to anyone.'

'Amen to that,' I said with a yawn. 'Watson, move over. I'm allowed some of the bed.' I yawned again. 'I don't think I'm even going to unpack my book. Good night.'

'Good night, love. A better day tomorrow.'

But it wasn't much better. The rain continued. We thought half-heartedly about a walk through the Shambles, the somewhat self-consciously quaint part of Old York, or a brief tour of the Minster. On a nice day both those things would have been high on my to-do list. In the rain, with another long drive ahead of us, not so much. An early start seemed the better idea. We were making today for Edinburgh, where, the TV weatherman said, the sun would be shining.

Weathermen lie as often as cats.

We did pass through some sunny patches of pretty country on our way north, rolling hills dotted with sheep in the delightful English manner. Watson, who apparently has some sheep dog in his eclectic mixture, wanted to chase them and sulked when we wouldn't let him. I began to think about 'England's green and pleasant land'. Except by then we were, I thought, in Scotland, whose residents would not have been happy about the quotation. We stopped for lunch at a pub where the accents confirmed my guess. The rain began again, harder than ever, just as we were heading back to the car where we'd left our brollies. Watson waited until we were safe in the car to shake himself dry.

At least the traffic abated as we ventured farther and farther north. It was bad around Edinburgh, of course, but once we found our hotel and settled in, we wouldn't have to drive any more until morning. The rain had slackened to a mere drizzle by the time we'd fed Watson and unpacked the necessities for a one-night stay.

'What do you say, Dorothy? Shall we venture out?'

'Definitely. I haven't seen Edinburgh in years, and besides, I'm tired of being cooped up. Two long days in a car without a walk have left my joints stiff as old leather.'

Watson heard the magic word 'walk' and was ecstatic. He was usually happy about whatever his humans wanted to do, but a walk was high on his list of favourites. He'd get wet, of course, but not drenched. We decided to take him along.

Our hotel, the Glass House, was a few streets away from the centre of town, but a short walk brought us to Princes Street, what I would, back in Indiana, have called 'the main drag'.

The street had changed since I'd seen it last, or maybe my memories had painted it in brighter colours. No city looks its best in the rain. But certainly there hadn't been huge holes in the street when I was there last, nor had the sound of pneumatic drills poisoned the air. 'What on earth?' I shouted to Alan above the din. He shrugged, but a passer-by answered me. 'New rail line to the airport,' he shouted. 'Bloody nuisance!'

Well, at the moment it was all of that. The construction added to the dirt I hadn't noticed in earlier visits, rubbish blowing about and gathering in corners. Traffic was crawling snail-like, spewing fumes into the already rain-saturated atmosphere. Even pedestrians were finding it hard going, with many of the side-walks (pavements, in Brit-speak) closed, and the streets slippery with mud.

But when the inevitable jostlings occurred, everyone was polite about it. And the Castle still loomed at the top of its amazing hill, protecting or threatening the city, depending on one's point of view.

'It's changed,' I said to Alan when we had moved away from Princes Street and I could make myself heard. 'But it's still a great city, isn't it?'

Alan smiled and squeezed my arm. I paused to try to wipe off Watson's muddy paws (which he didn't appreciate), and we sauntered on happily under our umbrellas.

When hunger began to be an issue, we looked around for a cab back to the hotel, but decided in the end that we'd get there just as quickly on foot. That was when our noses led us to a very nice Indian restaurant, where we had a leisurely meal (leaving poor Watson to languish outside) and then discovered, to our delight, that the theatre across the street was playing *Oliver*. So we established Watson back in the hotel room, spent a pleasant evening at the theatre, and then got a good night's sleep to prepare for what promised to be a long day.

The actual distance from Edinburgh to Aberdeen isn't that far as the crow flies, but the roads unfortunately cannot fly like the crow. Edinburgh sits on the southern coast of the Firth of Forth, at a point where it's very wide, so there are only two bridges, the old Forth Bridge for rail traffic only, and the sixties-vintage Forth Road Bridge, for vehicles. We had planned to take the road bridge to pick up the M90 near a place with the unlikely but delightful name of Inverkeithing, on to Perth, and thence to Aberdeen.

Although it was Sunday, we were unfamiliar with Edinburgh churches and eager to be on our way, especially since we were traveling unfamiliar roads, and the rain had strengthened again. We'd take the most direct road out of Perth, rather than the scenic one.

Humans plan, says the old adage, and God laughs. We packed quickly and went down to breakfast, and happened on the way to glimpse the television in the lounge.

A news programme showed a massive traffic jam. I thought at first they were showing the Golden Gate Bridge and wondered if there'd been an earthquake in San Francisco. I stopped to look.

Behind me, Alan muttered something.

I turned. 'What?'

'That's the Forth Road Bridge,' he said glumly.

'Not headed north, were you?' said one of the desk clerks cheerily. 'They reckon it'll be hours before that lot is cleared away.'

It seemed a lorry had overturned on the bridge, strewing its load of liquid detergent over all four lanes. In heavy fog and rain, a multiple-car accident had quickly ensued, with three people killed, several others hospitalized, and debris everywhere.

So much for Inverkeithing. Alan rummaged in one of the bags he had brought down, pulled out the road atlas, and took it in to breakfast. ⸙

There was another bridge about sixteen miles west of the Forth Road Bridge, across a much narrower part of the River Forth. The village on the other side, Kincardine, had a road leading to Perth, not motorway, and therefore slower, but possible. Or we could go along the river back to Inverkeithing and take up the route we had planned, but the traffic would probably be frightful, given the backup of people trying to get off the bridge. The waiter, asked for advice, was newly arrived from Pakistan via London and had no suggestions.

'We'd better be on our way,' said Alan with a sigh. 'The trip just became at least an hour longer, and we've the ferry to catch.' So we finished our meal hastily, stowed Watson and our bags in the car, and Alan got behind the wheel and turned the key.

Nothing. Not so much as the hint of a purr. Not even a click.

I kept still. The day was already going badly, and there are moments in married life when almost any comment is the wrong one. Alan, not a profane man, muttered something under his breath, made various adjustments to this and that, and tried again.

Nothing.

At home the car sits in a tiny garage, just big enough that Alan can explore under the bonnet in moderate comfort. Here we were in a large exposed car park and the rain was coming down like stair rods. He sighed, got out, and began to peer at the mysterious workings. I lowered my window a crack so I could hear Alan if he asked for help.

'Spot o' trouble, eh?'

The man appeared apparently out of nowhere, but really, I thought, from the little ticket-taker's shed. He held a huge umbrella and wore a rosily cheerful expression.

'The battery seems to have given up the ghost, but it shouldn't have done,' said Alan in what for him was almost a testy voice. 'New just months ago.'

'Ah.' The stranger reached in and did something I couldn't see. 'Connections all tight, right enough. Have ye far to go?'

'Aberdeen, and then the ferry to Orkney.'

'Ach, then ye'll need to get it put right. Ye'd not want to be stranded in Orkney!'

The man made it sound like the wilds of deepest Nowhere. I shivered. If even a Scot thought that of Orkney . . .

But he was continuing: 'There's a garage in the next street with an honest mechanic. If ye like, I can give him a ring and ask him to have a look.'

'We'd be most grateful,' said Alan immediately. 'Very kind of you.'

'But it's Sunday,' I said in a low voice.

Alan shrugged. 'Maybe he's Jewish. A lot of Jews in Scotland, you know. And let's not cavil, shall we?'

The next couple of hours went as most such times go. The man from the garage came, assessed the situation, and gave the opinion that the car would have to be towed in for a more thorough inspection. The result of the inspection was not encouraging. At least that was what I gathered from the gloomy expressions and head-shakings. I have difficulty following some Scottish accents, and when nearly all the words have to do with the innards of an automobile, I'm easily defeated. Time was when I knew a bit about the internal combustion engine, when there were carburettors and distributors and the like, but once everything became computerized I gave up.

Alan, who understands me, came to where I was sitting discon-solate in a corner. 'It's not so good,' he said. 'I don't think you'd understand what's wrong, and I'm not sure I do, but something's gone adrift in the electrical system, and the car's not going anywhere for several days.'

'Oh.' I pondered for a moment or two. 'A train for home, then?'

'That's one possibility. But there is another. We could continue our journey to Orkney.'

'A rental car? But would we be in time to catch the ferry at Aberdeen? It's getting later and later, and the weather doesn't seem to be improving.'

I suppose I sounded as depressed as I felt, because Alan took both my hands. 'You're cold, love. No, we probably couldn't catch the ferry now, but there's a better way. We can fly from here to Kirkwall and get there hours sooner than we would have done by ferry, and hire a car there.'

'But what about Watson? That little airline that flies to Kirkwall won't take him, remember?'

Watson, who had behaved admirably during the delay, looked up from the corner of the garage where he had gone to sleep, and whined. He knew quite well that he was being discussed, and he didn't altogether like my tone of voice.

'That's just it. Mr MacTavish here knows of a man with a private plane who would give us a lift, Watson and all.' Alan gestured toward the mechanic. 'His brother, in fact. He'll give him a ring if you agree to the plan.'

I was beginning to feel rather strongly that my determination to follow in Helen's footsteps was foolish. I would very much have preferred to board a nice, comfortable train back to my own hearth and home.

Alan, as usual, read my face. He's told me I must never try to play poker. 'It's quite warm in Kirkwall, and the sun is shining. Meant to carry on that way for several days.'

Alan's moods are not as easy to read as mine, but it was quite obvious that he was pining to get to Orkney. I suppressed a sigh. 'Well, then, let's head for the sunshine.'

Alan smiled and Watson wagged his tail. Or else Alan wagged his tail and Watson smiled. Either way, it was evident that I had pleased the males in my life.

Alan phoned Andrew to tell him we'd arrive a day sooner than expected. Mr MacTavish the mechanic made the arrangements with Mr MacTavish the pilot, who picked us up at the garage and drove us to the airport.

I was a little surprised by the Edinburgh airport. Edinburgh is, after all, a city of major importance in the United Kingdom, but the airport is small and almost homey. We didn't have to jump through all the usual hoops, of course, since we weren't boarding a commercial flight. No elaborate security scans, no tickets, no boarding area. Mr MacTavish parked his car near the tarmac, walked us out, helped us and our luggage (and Watson, of course) aboard, and we taxied out to the runway.

The plane was very small indeed. I'd never flown in anything smaller than the smallest commercial prop plane with about twenty seats. This one had two, in addition to the two up front in the cockpit. 'No co-pilot for a short hop like this,' said MacTavish cheerfully. 'No catering service, either, ye'll understand, but there are some crisps and a chocolate bar or two about somewhere. I've no got a crate for your wee beastie, so you'll want to keep him on the lead and close by your side, in case we run into any weather. We'd no want him to be tossed aboot.'

No, indeed. Nor did I want myself to be tossed aboot. I looked for one of those discreet little paper bags just in case, but there was no seat in front of me with a pocket to hold such an amenity.

Very well, Dorothy, I admonished myself. This is an adventure. Stop being a wimp and go with the flow. I sat down, strapped myself in, said a quick prayer, and prepared to be terrified.

Have you ever had a medical procedure that you dreaded so much you worked yourself into a real stew, only to have it turn out to be such a nothing that you felt like a fool for getting all worked up? Then you'll understand my reaction when the flight turned out to be so smooth and pleasant as to be almost boring. We flew at quite a low altitude, so we could see the terrain we were flying over. At least, it wasn't terrain for very long. I don't know what the word is for the watery expanses that soon formed our underpinnings. They weren't very interesting, once I stopped being convinced we were going to end up down there trying to avoid being drowned.

'There was no speech about emergency procedures,' I commented to Alan.

'No. I'm sure there are life jackets somewhere if we should need them.'

But it was apparent we weren't going to need them. The air was perfectly smooth, without so much as an alarming downdraft, and the sun, as Alan had promised, came out quite soon after we took off. The sea below us sparkled and I saw the occasional fishing boat. Not that I know a fishing boat from most other craft, but they weren't sailboats or ferries, so I made the assumption.

And then we were approaching land, and flying over a field full of sheep that paid not the slightest attention to this odd bird over their heads, and then with a couple of small bumps we were on the ground.

'Well.' It was almost anticlimactic. I hadn't realized how accustomed I was to the usual rituals of flight until they were missing. No speeches about seatbelts and tray tables. No tray tables, for that matter. No admonitions about staying in our seats until we'd arrived at the gate, no canned thanks for flying with them We landed. We got up, collected Watson and our belongings, and got out onto the tarmac.

Mr MacTavish accepted an embarrassingly small amount of money from Alan, waved us in the direction of the tiny terminal, and there we were in Orkney.

'Well,' I said again. Watson sat down, not quite sure of the next procedure. I wasn't sure, either.

'Why don't the two of you make yourselves comfortable while I find the car I've hired,' Alan suggested. So Watson and I trotted obediently to the terminal café, where I had a cup of coffee and Watson was kindly given a bowl of water, which he disposed of noisily.

It was all an airport should be, in miniature. Everything was contained in one fair-sized room, including a gift shop and coffee shop. There was one arrival and one departure gate, a tiny baggage-screening area, and a minute lounge. It was charming, and utterly without the impersonally intimidating aura of big airports.

I had only just finished my coffee when Alan returned. 'Ready, darling?'

'That was quick.'

He picked up our bags, I collected Watson, and we went to the car.

While we drove, Alan gave me a quick geography lesson. Orkney consists of some seventy islands, only seventeen or eighteen of them inhabited. We were on the principal island, called the Mainland, which has two towns. The bigger one, Kirkwall, boasts the airport, the cathedral, and – Alan added with a grin – the important Highland Park Distillery. The smaller Stromness, about twenty miles away, is noted principally for the ferry landing, with huge car ferries from Scrabster coming in several times a day. The population of the whole island group is only about 20,000, in an area of maybe 400 square miles.

After that dry selection of facts, I settled in to see for myself what Orkney had to offer. I could claim that I was enchanted with the place from that very first drive from Kirkwall to Stromness. It would make a better story that way, but it wouldn't be true. I was pleased with the bits of Kirkwall that we saw. The cathedral was impressive, and many of the houses were pretty. But when we got out into the rolling countryside I was aware of a vague uneasiness that I couldn't quite put my finger on.

The weather was perfect. The sky was that chill, pale blue of a northern country, with wisps of high cirrus clouds making a painter's dream. The pastures were nicely filled with sheep and cattle grazing together, something I'd never seen elsewhere. Small stone farmhouses dotted the landscape here and there, with their outbuildings sprawled in the manner of farm buildings everywhere in the world. Cottage gardens appeared in front of most of the houses, and neat kitchen gardens at the back. But . . .

'Alan, there are no trees!'

'No. The winds in winter can be rather fierce, I understand, so trees don't thrive. Wildflowers, on the other hand, grow in profusion, including a kind of wild orchid that's found nowhere else.'

'Hmm. I like trees. I *need* trees.'

'There's a nice little wood at the castle on Shapinsay, though I don't know if we'll go up there on this trip.'

'Castle?' My ears perked up. I'm a sucker for castles.

'Not a real one. Not medieval, that is. Victorian, or thereabouts. We'll have to find you a guidebook or two, and you can read all about it.'

We drove on. There was almost no traffic, which was a good

thing, because the road was quite narrow. The landscape was beautiful, no denying it. The sweep of hill and sky made me wish I were a painter. But it all seemed much of a muchness, the same pattern of fields, livestock, farm, road repeating around every—

'Alan! What's *that*?'

Alan slowed the car to a stop by the side of the road to let me gape to my heart's content.

Quite close to me, a piece of stone rose out of the ground. More than three times as tall as it was wide, and quite flat and thin, it looked like a piece of modern sculpture. The top slanted at a perfect forty-five degree angle. Nearby, three other stones thrust against the sky, one nearly a twin of the nearest one, another appearing to have been damaged, and the third more like a petrified tree trunk.

'What *is* it?' I repeated. I had edged a little closer to Alan. Something about those stones . . .

'It is what remains of an ancient stone circle, a henge, probably around five thousand years old.'

'Something like Stonehenge?'

'A bit, but much older.'

We sat in silence. Even Watson seemed struck dumb, until someone walked down the road with a dog in tow, and our dog barked, breaking the spell.

'I took us a bit out of our way to show you that,' said Alan as he turned the car around. 'It's far from the most impressive monument on the islands, but I wanted you to have a glimpse of Neolithic Orkney straight off.'

'It's . . . uncanny, somehow. I'm . . .' I couldn't finish my thought. I wasn't sure what I felt, or what I wanted to say. If I remembered what I thought I remembered of high school French, I was *bouleversée*.

If this was the effect of a few minutes at one of the less impressive sights, I wondered whether I'd have any wits left at the end of a week.

TWO

We found our holiday flat without the slightest difficulty. It would, indeed, be a little difficult to get lost in Stromness, which has only two principal streets, the one skirting the harbour, by which we entered town, and the one above it (above in the literal sense: the town is built on a hillside). Our modern flat faced the harbour, almost across the street from the ferry landing. It had an attached garage, which was an important consideration, since parking is always at a premium in old towns.

'Where will we get the key?' I asked as Alan pulled the car up in front of the garage door.

'Andrew said the door would be open. No one ever locks doors in Orkney.'

Sure enough, the door was unlocked. It opened on a minute entrance hall and thence directly into a lovely, well-equipped kitchen. There was a pot of flowers on the table.

'From Andrew,' I said, reading the card. 'How nice of him! Is that one of his own pots?'

'Probably.'

'It's beautiful! And look,' I said as I continued to explore the kitchen, 'he's given us some food, as well. Cereal, bread, butter, milk, tea, coffee . . . even a couple of bottles of wine!'

'He's a good chap. I've not seen him for years, but we've corresponded. I'm looking forward—'

There was a knock at the door, but before either of us could get there, it opened and a man walked in.

If he'd had a beard, he would have made a perfect Santa Claus. White hair, rosy cheeks, little wire-rimmed glasses, and the most delightful smile I think I've ever seen.

'Andrew! What a pleasure! It's been too long, my friend.' They shook hands heartily. 'Andrew, this is my wife, Dorothy Martin.'

I held my hand out, but Andrew enveloped me in a hug.

'And a bonny wife you are, indeed,' he said, kissing me on both cheeks before releasing me.

'Goodness! Thank you for that, and for all you've done to make us welcome.' I gestured around the kitchen. 'Flowers, food, even wine. I'll pour you a glass if there are any glasses.'

'Not just now, thanks, but I'll take a rain check. I just stopped in to welcome you to Orkney and invite you to dinner tonight. Sigrid can't come; she's at her weekly mah-jongg tournament, but I'd love to have your company. Alan, you remember the Royal Hotel up on The Street?'

'I can find it.'

'Splendid. I'll see you at seven, then.'

I spent a little time unpacking and getting acquainted with my home for the next week while Alan found the garage door opener and put the car away. Then we set out for a walk with Watson.

Alan hadn't been to Orkney for many years, but it's a part of the world where things don't change rapidly. The ferry terminal was new, built to accommodate the huge 'RORO' (roll on, roll off) car ferries from Scrabster. That had changed the appearance of the harbour a great deal, and not, I suspected, for the better. But with tourism an important source of income for the islands, it was plainly necessary to make their transportation convenient. We had, after all, planned to arrive at Kirkwall on just such a monstrosity, so it didn't behove us to throw any stones.

We moved away from the harbour street, though, up to the one that had several names on the map, but was locally called simply The Street. It was the oddest roadway I'd ever seen. For one thing, at its widest it barely allowed two small cars to pass, and the pedestrians who shared the same thoroughfare had to back into doorways whenever a car came along. At the narrowest point, where it curved a little and buildings jutted out on either side, even one car was hard put to get through. The driver had to exercise great care. I pointed out to Alan the scrapes on the walls where various drivers over the years hadn't been quite careful enough.

'They were, as I recall, talking about widening the street when I was here last,' said Alan.

'And that would have been . . .?'

'In the 1970s sometime.'

We both chuckled.

The street wasn't terribly busy, it being Sunday, so we were able to get a good, leisurely look at our surroundings. There were two hotels, a grocery-cum-bakery-cum-post office, several take-aways, two banks, a pharmacy, a bookstore, clothing stores, a church, gift shops, charity shops, all jammed cheek-by-jowl into the one street, mixed in with houses and B & Bs. Steep little lanes (for walkers; most had steps) led on up to houses at the top of the hill, or down to the harbour. We caught glimpses of tiny, riotous cottage gardens crammed under front windows.

We wandered, getting our bearings, and then decided to wander back to the apartment for a nap before dinner. We hadn't got very far, though, before Watson stopped dead in his tracks, braced all four feet, and began to growl, low in his throat.

Alan and I stared at each other. Watson never growled.

Then we saw the problem.

Around one of the corners, in the exact middle of the street, lay a large orange cat. The biggest cat, in fact, that I've ever seen. One ear was nicked; the tail was bushed. His white bib looked somehow aggressive. He simply lay there and looked at Watson, ignoring the pedestrian traffic, ignoring the car that was approaching, ignoring everything except this dog that had dared encroach upon his territory.

Now, Watson likes cats. He lives with two of them, and they all sleep together. He passes the time of day amiably with the neighbourhood cats in Sherebury.

But he didn't like this one, and he was making it plain.

I tugged on his leash. I might as well have tried to move the wall next to me.

'Watson!' said Alan sharply.

The dog ignored him. The cat began to growl, too. Its hackles rose. Its tail bushed.

The car, meanwhile, had come to a stop, unable to pass the cat. The few pedestrians stopped to watch. I was at a loss. Our sweet-tempered dog had never acted this way before.

Alan made a move to grab Watson's collar. He growled and snapped. The cat hissed and spat, and lifted a fully armed paw.

Behind us, a door opened with a bang. 'Don't get between

them.' The woman who had emerged spoke urgently, but quietly. 'Let me deal with this.'

She crouched and looked the cat in the eye, from a cautious distance. 'Bad cat! Stop it this instant!'

The cat looked at her with what I would have sworn was a sneer.

'Be off with you, then!' The woman took the water pistol out from behind her back and aimed a stream straight at the cat's face.

The cat unleashed a string of feline profanity that would have made a sailor blush, but it took off, disappearing into someone's garden.

Watson sat back with a silly grin, plainly feeling he had been the victor in the skirmish. He was still there, and unharmed. The cat was gone.

'Ninny!' I said. 'You didn't do a thing except make threats. And whatever made you act that way, anyhow?'

'Don't worry,' said the woman with the squirt gun, which she now tucked away in a pocket. 'It's not your dog's fault. That cat antagonizes everyone, and he can do a lot of damage if he wishes.'

'Is he yours, then?' asked Alan, with deceptive mildness. He didn't like to see animals left untrained.

'No, praise the Lord! He doesn't belong to anyone; he's the town menace.'

'Does he have a name?'

'He has several names,' said the woman grimly. 'Some of them are polite.'

We laughed at that, and the scene broke up. The patient driver steered her car past us, and we followed the woman back into the cat rescue shop she'd come from.

'You can come in for a moment if you like, but you'll have to leave your dog outside,' said the woman, pleasantly enough. 'We're not open. I came over to feed our strays, and most of them are afraid of dogs.'

'But . . . if the orange cat is still around . . .'

'He won't be. He'll be washing his face and plotting revenge somewhere.'

Alan took Watson back outside, and I gave the woman a

quizzical look. 'But you must like cats, or you wouldn't be working for a cat charity.'

'I love cats, but not Roadkill.'

'Roadkill!'

'That's one of his names. You saw him lying in the middle of the road. It's his favourite place. The sun warms the stones, you see.'

'And as the whole town belongs to him, he sees no reason why he should move. I understand. Well, he's a character.'

'He's all of that. But do be careful of him. For all he's adapted to living around humans, he's truly a feral cat, and can be truly dangerous. Keep your dog on a short lead, and don't let him out on his own. The cat knows him for an enemy now.'

I promised to keep Watson under control, put a donation in the jar by the cash register, and re-joined my husband and dog. 'The serpent in paradise?' I said.

'As you say.' Alan was rather silent on the way back to our apartment. I thought he'd taken the encounter more seriously than I had. But then he's an Englishman, and dogs are Very Important Persons to the English.

We had a cup of tea before settling down to a nap, and then showered and changed for our meal with Andrew.

Alan told me not to dress up. 'Orkney is very informal,' he assured me. So I put on clean slacks and a nice sweater, with a cardigan on top of that and, of course, a hat. This was a woolly one meant to keep my head warm, but bright orange with crocheted flowers and really quite decorative. I'd been right about the climate. Though the sun was shining brightly (still, at seven in the evening), the air was nippy with a brisk wind. I added wool gloves to the ensemble, and we headed up to The Street.

Our meal was delicious. Once on a trip to Iona I'd learned to eat haggis, and actually quite liked it. This time it was served as an appetizer, a 'starter' as the Brits call them. The haggis, which is basically a mixture of oats and meat and spices, had been rolled up into little balls, breaded, and fried. It was hot and crisp and tasty, and was served with a whisky sauce, since the trad-itional drink with haggis is whisky. Then we had local lamb and local vegetables, fresh and tender and wonderful, and finished up with sticky toffee pudding, the most decadent dessert ever created. By the time we were ready to leave, I felt they could have simply rolled me down the hill to the apartment.

But the real substance of the meal was archaeology. We had barely tucked into our haggis when Andrew began.

'So when are you going to visit our latest discoveries?'

'Can we actually visit? You made the site sound nearly inaccessible,' said Alan.

'Nearly is not quite. I can take us over in my launch. It'll have to be tomorrow, though, because I'm leaving for Spain the next day with a load of pots. And we should go in the morning, because I want you to have time to see everything, and there's a meeting of the Friends in the evening. You'll want to go to that, of course.'

'A Friends' meeting?' I echoed with a bit of a frown. 'I'm not sure—'

Andrew gave a shout of laughter. 'Not Quakers, love! The Friends of Ancient Orkney. And it could turn out to be quite interesting, because these days "friends" is perhaps not the most appropriate word.'

Alan tilted his head to one side in a quizzical look.

'This is an important site, you understand. Huge, or it could be when we've finished. Rich in artefacts. We could learn more about the Neolithic in this part of the world than . . . well, one can scarcely imagine the limits. So of course there are, shall we say, a few differences of opinion on various matters.'

'Such as?'

Andrew laughed again, but I thought it sounded a little hollow this time. 'It would be easier to list the non-controversies. The archaeologists are arguing over the extent of the dig, the farmer who owns the land is ready to do murder over his compensation, the museums are fighting over who gets the artefacts . . .'

'And I suppose there's the usual difficulty about funding.'

'Oh, there's difficulty, all right, but not in the usual way. The money's pouring in. We can scarcely spend it fast enough.'

'Then what's the problem?' I asked.

'The problem, really the biggest problem of them all, is the donor.'

'Donor, singular?'

'Oh, very singular indeed. He's American, and he's very, very rich.' Andrew didn't need to say more. His tone of voice said it all.

'You don't need to be diplomatic, Andrew,' I said with a grimace. 'I'm no fonder of the genus "Arrogant Wealthy American" than you are. I take it he's a pain in the neck?'

'I'd locate the pain a bit lower,' said Andrew. 'In fact, saving your presence, Dorothy, he's a right bastard. The project is getting terribly expensive and depends utterly upon his support, and he knows it. If he pulls out, the dig will have to close down, and God knows where we'd find funding to start up again. So he throws his weight about at every opportunity. And the worst of it is, the man fancies himself an archaeologist, so he's trying to force some vital decisions.'

He took a healthy swig of his wine and then a deep breath. 'Not the sort of conversation for a pleasant dinner, is it? Let's talk about something else. Dorothy, that's an astonishing hat you're wearing.'

THREE

Before we went home for the night, Andrew arranged to pick us up at seven in the morning. I wasn't terribly happy about the hour. I am not at any time a bright and shining morning person, and this was supposed to be a vacation. But it was going to take quite a time to get to the island with the odd name, so we needed to get on with it.

Watson is always excited about the prospect of a ride, no matter what the hour, so the three of us bundled into Andrew's car the next morning and he drove us north and east to the tiny village of Tingwall, where his launch was berthed. He indicated various points of interest along the way, but I was too sleepy to pay a lot of attention. The sun had been up for hours, but though my body was ambulatory, my brain was still curled up in bed.

I'd prudently taken a ginger capsule before we set out, since I'm a terrible sailor, and the rest of the trip was by sea. Andrew had cheerfully announced that the water 'could be a wee bit rough', which, as I know to my sorrow, is the seaman's way of describing anything up to gale-force winds and boat-swamping waves.

The launch was a pleasant little boat, and fortunately Watson seemed quite happy to climb aboard. Andrew had thoughtfully brought along coffee and buns. I thought I'd better avoid food, but I drank the coffee, strong and hot and wonderful, and began to wake up a little and even to enjoy the beauty around me. It was a gorgeous day, warm for these northern lands, with just enough of a breeze to make the air feel like a tonic.

'All right, love?' asked Alan, who knows my unfortunate reaction to water travel.

'I'm fine. Really. I think I might even have a bun with my coffee.'

He looked dubious, but I didn't see how one rather bland bun could do me any harm. Nor did it. I clapped my hat down firmly and left the shelter of the cabin to stand out on deck and watch the passing scene.

From the sea, the islands were remarkably similar. We passed close to the shore for much of the start of our journey, in a progression from one 'sound' to the next. Gairsay Sound, Eynhallow Sound, Wyre Sound: wonderful names. The exciting Neolithic sites weren't obvious from there, though I could see the odd standing stone here and there. But mostly there were fields, tiny villages, roads, and sky – limitless sky. Watson wasn't interested in the view, but he was fascinated by all the new and enticing scents. For a dog brought up in the Cotswolds and now living in a cathedral city far from the sea, this was an entrancing world.

We passed ferries on the way, small car ferries with one or two vehicles aboard. I popped back into the cabin to query Andrew. 'I thought you said there was no ferry service.'

'Not to where we're going, only to the principal islands. We could have gone most of the way by commercial ferry, but the launch is a lot quicker. We'll be heading out into open water soon. How are you doing?'

'Nary a qualm. You're an excellent driver.'

'Ah, yes, I always choose the flattest water when ladies are aboard.' And he turned his attention back to the wheel.

When we turned north into open water, the wind grew a bit stronger and the sea a little less like a lily pond, and I thought it prudent to take another ginger capsule and retire to the quietest part of the cabin with eyes firmly shut. I didn't want to tarnish a new friendship with Andrew by being sick all over his boat.

The trip seemed, after that, to take a long time, although Andrew told us later we had travelled less than twenty nautical miles. I think I actually dozed for part of the way, but I opened my eyes now and then, saw water and sky, and closed them again. Then Alan was touching my shoulder and saying, 'Re-entry time, darling. We're here.'

'Here' was a beautiful place, a little cove of sparkling white sand dotted with black rocks. I saw what looked like hundreds of birds, gulls and others I didn't know. And: 'Look, Alan! Seals, as I live and breathe!'

There were dozens of them, sunning sleekly on the rocks or surfacing briefly out of the water before diving again. 'I suppose they're fishing,' I said to Andrew, 'but they look like they're just playing.'

'P'raps they are playing,' said Andrew. 'P'raps they're selkies.' I had never heard of selkies, so Andrew had to explain to me, straight-faced, about the seals that could transform themselves into humans and back again. 'They like to play.'

Andrew had been taking the boat around a corner to a landing place where there was a rudimentary dock. 'There's better mooring on the other side of the island,' he said as he was making her fast to a post, 'but it's closer to the dig, so it's needed by the workers. She'll be safe here for a bit, till low tide. I'm sorry, but we'll have to leave Watson on board. Dogs aren't allowed at the dig. Can you climb a bit, Dorothy?'

We left our disconsolate dog behind, and with Alan's help I had no trouble scrambling up the gentle slope to the grassy plain above. There I stopped, struck motionless in sheer amazement.

As far as I could see, the surface of the island had been transformed into a series of excavations. The effect was of the top layer being scraped away to reveal what lay just below. And what lay below was astounding.

'It's a long way from being open to the public, you'll understand,' Andrew was saying. 'But they know me. It'll be all right so long as you mind how you go. Can't have you falling in a five-thousand-year-old pit, now can we?'

But I was paying little attention, caught up in the sheer wonder of it.

Once, back home in Indiana, I'd been doing some gardening and turned up an oddly shaped stone. I realized after a time that it had been shaped by a long-dead hand, notches cut out at one end to allow for fastening the thing to a stick or whatever, for use as a tool or weapon. I wasn't sure when the native peoples inhabited my part of the state, but I knew the Europeans had come in the late seventeenth century, so this stone had lain there under my chrysanthemum bed for many hundreds of years. I was thrilled.

Now I was looking at structures, houses or temples or workshops or whatever they might have been, that had been fashioned by human hands not just hundreds, but thousands of years ago. They were below ground level now, and perhaps they always had been. I didn't know enough even to guess. The roofs were long gone, so one could look directly down into them, and what a sight they were.

To my dazzled eye, there seemed to be dozens of them, separate structures, all of roughly the same size and shape. They were more or less rectangular, the corners somewhat rounded. The walls, butting up against the supporting earth, were of carefully worked stones, thinnish and flat, laid atop one another like bricks, but without mortar, at least so far as I could tell. Many of the structures were still being excavated, but the ones that were nearly completed showed one main room, with an entrance area and one or two small rooms. In the centre of the main room was what looked very much like a hearth, and there were box-like constructions along the side walls, with sides one stone thick and nearly perfect right angles. At one end, consistently, there was a construction that looked, astoundingly, rather like a bookshelf.

'Andrew,' I said when I could catch my breath, 'what *is* all this?'

He grinned. 'A village. Almost, in Neolithic terms, a city. The largest such find in history. So far they've found twenty houses, far more than there are modern ones on the Island, and five other structures, one very large.'

'So these are houses?' I gestured at the buildings closest to us. 'How do they know?'

'Well, for one thing, they've found the middens.' He looked at me doubtfully. 'You'll know what a midden is?'

I nodded. 'A rubbish heap. A garbage dump, in American terms.'

'Yes. And in the middens they've found bones, from birds and deer and cattle. They've found shards of pottery, broken tools, even broken needles, and combs, and toys – everything you'd expect as the detritus of several hundred years of ordinary house-hold living.'

'Several hundred! Good heavens, how long did people live here? And how long ago?'

'Ah, well, that's part of what we don't know yet. Carbon dating takes a bit of time, you'll understand. But so far as we know now, the settlement we're looking at now is a little younger than Skara Brae.' He turned to Alan. 'You've taken her to Skara Brae?'

'Not yet. We only just arrived yesterday afternoon. We did drive past the Stones of Stenness.'

Andrew waved away the Stones. 'Magic! Superstition! This –' he gestured broadly – 'this was real! Real people lived here. They had *potters*, man!'

'Well, that, of course, indicates they had reached the pinnacle of civilisation,' said Alan drily.

'Damn right,' said Andrew, the Harray Potter. 'Now.' He consulted his watch. 'We've not got too much time here, so let's go to the other end and look at the community centre.'

'For the workers, you mean?'

'No, for the village. High Sanday, they're calling it.'

I was still mystified, but Alan and I followed, carefully picking our way around working areas where dirt was being patiently sifted for artefacts. I kept being distracted by one thing after another – a section of wall made of stones that looked as if they'd been painted, a stack of pottery shards that showed rather elaborate decorations – until Andrew stopped somewhere near the middle of the dig and pointed.

'There!'

He proudly indicated an area that looked at first like a large gravel pit. Stones, large and small, were everywhere, scattered seemingly at random. Then my eyes adjusted, and I saw the patterns. I saw the thick outer walls enclosing an area roughly the size of two or three football fields. I saw the rough outlines, beginning to take shape, of thinner walls within the structure, rooms within rooms.

'What on earth is it? Was it?'

'We don't know. We *think* it might have been a temple of some sort, but that's little more than informed guesswork. We also think it might have had a very high roof, judging from the thickness of the outer walls. They could have supported quite a weight of slate. And we've found a great deal of slate in the ruins. It had to come from somewhere. Why not a roof?'

'Is slate native to the island?'

'Not now. But there are areas where slate could have been mined five thousand years ago, mined to the limit.'

'So you're saying the . . . the village, town – I don't know what to call it – the site is five thousand years old?'

'Ah.' He glanced at his watch again, and then up at the sky. 'I'm sorry to say it, but we'd best be getting back. We've not got a lot of time, and the weather's looking just a wee bit threatening.'

I didn't need to be asked twice. If I had to be in a boat in threatening weather, I wanted to get it over as soon as possible.

In the event, it wasn't too bad. The wind and the sea were running fast, but they were running our way. We got back to Tingwall a lot faster than we had come, and though I hadn't been happy, the ginger capsules did their job and I was fine once I set foot back on solid ground. Watson, too, was happy to be out of the boat, and demonstrated his approval by marking every post and flagpole he could find in Tingwall till we loaded him back into Andrew's car.

We stopped for an early tea/late lunch in a village on the way back to Stromness and then made arrangements to meet Andrew at the meeting that evening. He gave Alan careful instructions about how to get there. They were full of 'you can't miss it' assurances, which to my mind always mean that you can, and probably will. Andrew finally conceded that we might just have a little trouble and offered to pick us up, an offer we gladly accepted.

We were in good time for the meeting. Andrew staked out seats at the front for all of us, and then went to chat with friends. I'd had a nap and was feeling refreshed and ready to be interested, and when I learned that the speaker was to be the director of the High Sanday dig, I became impatient for the meeting to start. I should have remembered the old admonition to be careful what you wish for, because you might get it.

FOUR

O f course things didn't start out with a bang. This was the AGM, the Annual General Meeting, so there was the usual business to be transacted. The president of the FAO, one James Larsen, presided over elections of officers, speeches of thanks, and so on. The proceedings were all cut and dried and were kept to a decent length, and I took advantage of the boring part to slip out with Watson for a quick R & R session. He whined a bit, wanting the walk that had been denied him all day, but I promised him a good one tomorrow and chivvied him back inside just as the speaker was getting started.

I was enthralled, and so, judging by the rapt silence, was the rest of the room. The director of the dig (Robert Fairweather, Andrew told me in a whisper), was personable, obviously intelligent and knowledgeable. He was tall, with fairish hair, a pleasant face, and spoke with an English accent, not Scottish or the somewhat thicker Orcadian; I made a mental note to ask Andrew about his background. The man was plainly excited about the project at High Sanday. He had a slide show to illustrate his talk, and the pictures were splendid, showing in much greater detail what I'd been able only to glimpse earlier in the day. There were photos of some of the more exciting artefacts that had been found, including large pots, painstakingly pieced back together and revealing incredibly detailed decoration, geometrically incised. I wondered if the designs had any religious or ceremonial significance and made a mental note to ask Andrew about that, too.

The coloured stones I had noticed had, indeed, been painted, the earliest such decoration known in all of Britain. The excavators had even found a 'paint shop', a small building where the paints had evidently been prepared from ground stone (the mortars had been found) and some medium like animal fat. I thought about the paint in my living room back in Indiana, years ago, and how it had needed to be renewed every few years. And here was paint thousands of years old still adhering, albeit in flakes, and still bright!

Mr Fairweather made frequent references to Skara Brae, which I realized I needed to visit as soon as I possibly could. It was apparently a fully excavated Neolithic village on Mainland, but much smaller than High Sanday. No one, I gathered, knew how big High Sanday was going to be when it was all uncovered, a work of many years to come. The universal opinion, however, was that it was going to be huge, occupying most of the island of Papa Sanday.

When the formal presentation had ended, to hearty applause, the meeting became even more interesting. The speaker called for questions, and a burly, weather-beaten man stood up. An uneasy murmur rippled through the room.

'What I want to know is where me beasts are goin' to find gress when ye've turned the whole bluidy island into a pit!'

At least that's what I thought he said. His accent was strong and his dialect a bit hard to follow, but his import was clear. He was seething with rage and also, I thought, with alcohol. I edged a little closer to Alan. Watson, who dislikes human discord, whined from beneath my chair.

Mr Fairweather opened his mouth to reply, and perhaps to placate, but another man stood. 'This is neither the time nor the place to discuss your grievances, Andersen. We've been over and over this business. You'll be fairly treated, but we'll talk about it later.'

The tone was commanding, the accent pure American. The speaker, tall and well-dressed, remained standing and glaring at the farmer Andersen.

I queried Andrew with my eyebrows. 'Henry J. Carter,' he whispered. 'The American with the money.'

I studied Carter with new interest. So this was the arrogant American. He looked the part, I had to admit. He was dressed in slacks with a sharp crease, a white shirt I'd bet had cost more than anything in my wardrobe, and a blue sweater that looked so soft it had to be cashmere. His watch looked, from here, like a Rolex. In that casual assemblage he was as out of place as if he'd worn a three-piece suit. He certainly carried an air of the boardroom about him, almost as tangible as the expensive cologne whose scent wafted my way.

I wondered if it was accidental or deliberate that the farmer smelled, rather strongly in that small room, of sweat and manure.

He was also redolent of unmitigated fury. 'I want me rights! I'm warnin' ye, give me my due or ye'll be sorry for it!'

Carter moved toward the angry farmer, two men rising to go with him. I didn't see quite how they managed it, but somehow Andersen was escorted out of the room, quickly and quietly, and the meeting, including Watson, breathed a collective sigh of relief. Someone rose with a technical question about dating a certain section of the excavation, which didn't interest me all that much. I grinned at Andrew. 'Slick,' I whispered.

'Oh, he's all of that,' Andrew muttered.

The questions continued. Someone wanted to know how long it might take to finish the excavation.

'That's a very difficult question to answer,' replied Fairweather. 'As you have seen, we have already uncovered a far more extensive area of interest than had been anticipated when we first started. We have not yet discovered any definitive limits to the excavation. And as most of you know, archaeology is a heartbreakingly slow undertaking, even in a consistent climate. Here, where the winter must necessarily put a stop to our activities, the work may go on for years.'

'What about funding?' asked a woman with an English accent. 'Isn't money always a problem for archaeologists?'

Carter had returned, and now stood. 'I can answer that question. As long as this dig continues to uncover the important and the exciting, I will make sure that money is not a problem.'

Fairweather uttered so quiet a sigh that no one not sitting near the front could have heard him. 'Mr Carter has been extremely generous to us, and with so many other sources of funding drying up these days, I'm sure we're all grateful for his support.'

I was feeling undercurrents I couldn't quite understand, and Andrew was scowling at the floor, so I couldn't meet his eyes. But Carter wasn't through talking.

'Everybody here who's connected with the dig knows that I support it, and have from the very beginning. This is the most exciting thing to come down the archaeology pike since Schliemann discovered Troy. Who knows what we may find? Evidence of the kind of sacrifices that were practiced here, perhaps. Evidence, even, of the nature of their rituals. Treasures of all kinds, even the more tangible kind. And I intend to see to it that nothing interferes with High Sanday being just as thoroughly and completely excavated as was Troy.'

The woman with the English accent stood up again. I noticed now that she had a pad and pen in her hands. A journalist, perhaps? Or just someone with more than a passing interest in archaeology? 'If I remember my school books properly,' she said, 'Heinrich Schliemann used some practices in his excavations that would make modern archaeologists blanch. In particular, did he not destroy several structures closer to the surface in order to reach the ones he felt were the actual remains of Troy?'

'We know a good deal more about how to go about digging than he did, certainly,' said Fairweather, taking control of the meeting again. He glanced at his watch. 'I believe we're out of time – er, yes, Mr Norquist?'

A little man who looked remarkably like the legendary cartoon Casper Milquetoast stood and spoke in a thin, colourless voice. 'Charles Norquist, director of the Ancient Orkney Museum. I'd just like to point out that Schliemann was also responsible for removing artefacts from their native country, a practice modern archaeologists deplore. Please be assured that all artefacts belonging to Orkney will stay right here in Orkney.' He sat down to applause, but Carter was on his feet again.

'That's all very well, but some of the artefacts we'll find pretty soon are from Norway, Viking gold, left here centuries ago. Are we going to send those things back there, since they came from there? Over my dead body! I'd sell them before I'd let that happen, and a pretty price they'd bring, I can tell you.'

That brought a rumble of obvious anger. Someone said, 'Shame!' Fairweather brandished his watch again. 'Right. We'll stop here, and I invite you all to share in the refreshments. Thank you.'

I was eager to ask Fairweather more questions, but Andrew took me firmly by the elbow and steered me out of the room before I could even snatch a cookie and a glass of wine. Alan, bemused, followed us.

'What is it, old man?' my spouse asked when we were in the car roaring out of the car park.

'The man's an ass!' Andrew pounded the steering wheel; the car veered dangerously near the edge of the road, beyond which was a steep drop to a loch. I suppressed a yelp, and Watson whined. 'Sorry,' said Andrew in a more moderate tone, 'but he is, you know.'

'The reference to Schliemann,' said Alan. It wasn't quite a question.

'Of course!' Andrew pounded the steering wheel again, but less vehemently. The car stayed where it belonged. 'Everyone in that room knows more about archaeology than Henry bloody Carter.'

'Maybe everyone but me, Andrew,' I said meekly. 'I'm really ignorant. I know Schliemann dug up what he thought was Troy, in the 1800s sometime, wasn't it? And I think I've read that there's been a lot of controversy over the years about what he really found, and his sloppy techniques. But I'm probably all wet.'

'No, the only bit you've got wrong is the controversy part. Modern archaeologists are in absolute agreement that Schliemann destroyed at least one city that might have been the Troy of the *Iliad*, if the *Iliad* was ever anything but a myth, and that the city he claimed was Troy, near the bottom layer, was centuries too old, probably about 2500 BC, whereas the Trojan War supposedly took place sometime in the twelfth century BC. Furthermore, Schliemann blasted his way through the early layers – blasted, mind you, with dynamite – stole artefacts left and right, falsified data, et cetera, et cetera. And that's the kind of dig Carter is determined we're going to run here!'

'Andrew, are you saying there are layered structures here, as at Schliemann's site?' Alan asked.

'There is at least one level of building below the top one. We don't know yet how many others there might be. We don't know how long people lived at this site, nor how long ago the first ones began building. Now, I don't suppose Carter would actually advocate blasting, but he's hell-bent on going down as far as there's anything to find, and furthermore, he claims he's certain there's Viking gold buried somewhere at the site, which is idiotic! The Vikings came in the eighth century AD, and the most recent structures at High Sanday are at least three thousand years older than that, but you heard what he said. Everyone's tried to tell him – me, Fairweather, Norquist, Larsen, even the media people.

You heard that woman tonight. She's no archaeologist, but she's a conscientious reporter, and she's done her homework. He won't listen to anyone. I tell you, the man is a slick, plausible bastard, and an absolute ass.'

'Oh, dear, it does sound like it,' I said, shaking my head. 'And he's the man with the chequebook.'

Andrew's reply to that sounded very much like a growl.

We invited him in for a drink when he delivered us back to our temporary home, but he declined. 'Sigrid and I are off early tomorrow, and I've a load of pots to pack up before then. I'm sorry I won't get a chance to show you around properly, but I'll ask Fairweather to call in on you and tell you what's what. Good night.'

'Well,' I said when we had closed the door behind him, 'I need a drink, after that. I don't know that I've ever attended a more uncomfortable meeting.'

'There were cross-currents, certainly. And I don't think I understood all of them, either. Why don't we take Watson for a walk before we settle down to our libations? It's still quite light, and a lovely evening.'

The clock on the big electronic sign board outside the ferry building read 22:47, but it was indeed still light. I clipped the lead on our eager dog, and we set out. There weren't a lot of people about at that hour, and the harbour was very quiet. We walked down to the edge of the jetty and listened to the waves lapping gently against the wall.

'Do you know,' I said after we'd stood in companionable silence for a few minutes, 'one of the things I was hoping to do up here was some star gazing. There are so many lights around the Cathedral, we can't really see them at home. I thought on a remote island there'd be lots of stars to see. It never occurred to me that it wouldn't get dark enough to make even the moon very bright.'

'We're very near the top of the world here, and this is the longest day, remember? I suppose it'll be twilight for a few hours, but no darker than that. Sorry, love. We'll have to come back in winter. It'll surely be dark enough for you then.'

I shivered at the thought. 'No, thank you. It's quite cold enough in the middle of summer. Oh, it's nice just now, but I'm wearing two sweaters and a jacket. And in fact, I'd like to get moving. It's chilly standing still.'

We walked toward the end of the harbour road and on up into the town. 'I hope Roadkill is safely asleep somewhere,' I commented. 'I've had enough conflict for one day.'

'That really was an extraordinary display of discord,' Alan said, and I knew he wasn't talking about Watson's run-in with the cat.

'Yes, and I'd have said Andrew was the last person to lose his temper, but he was really upset with that man Carter.'

'You're developing an almost English talent for understatement, my dear. Andrew was not upset. He was in a blazing rage, and you're quite right. That isn't at all like him. He's normally the mildest of men. It comes of being a potter, perhaps. He can take out all his aggression on the clay. But I do think if even half what he says about Carter is true, he may be justified. The man sounds like someone both stupid and stubborn. It's a dangerous combination.'

'And don't forget to add in, wealthy and therefore powerful. That can be a lethal combination.'

'As some recent politicians have demonstrated. But after all, it's nothing to do with us. We're here on holiday, to soak up some lovely peace. Just listen.' He put a hand on my arm. We stopped. Watson sat obediently at my side.

We had climbed up to The Street, a street now devoid of traffic, human, animal, or mechanical. Somewhere in a cottage on up the hill a radio or television was playing soft music. That was the only sound to be heard.

I sighed happily. 'Peace. Let's enjoy it while we can.'

One of the Fates was listening then. In the quiet surrounding us, we ought to have heard her mocking laughter.

FIVE

'**D**orothy.'

Alan's voice was quiet, but there was a quality in it that brought me instantly out of my pleasant dream. 'Um. What time is it?' The sun was streaming in brightly through our east-facing window, but then it had been doing that for hours. Sunrise happened on an entirely different schedule than the one I was used to back in southern England.

'Just past six. I'm sorry to wake you so early, but Andrew called. There's been a terrible accident.' He handed me a cup of coffee, but I didn't really need the caffeine to bring me to full wakefulness. A 'terrible accident' that called for a six a.m. phone call could mean only one thing. At least it wasn't one of our family. That kind of horrible news would have come straight to us, not through Andrew.

'Tell me.'

'Henry Carter was found at the dig this morning, half-buried under a wall that had caved in. Apparently he went there late last night or early this morning and missed his footing.'

I sipped my coffee, my brain working at double time. Alan stood watching me, saying nothing.

I put my coffee down. 'You're thinking the same thing I am, aren't you?'

Alan grimaced. 'It could be a nasty accident, pure and simple.'

'And that was a pig I just saw flying by the window. Alan, everybody who was at that meeting last night hates the man. Hated. Are you trying to tell me his death, his very convenient death, wasn't engineered?'

'I'm not trying to tell you anything. I'm stating the facts. I quite agree, they are open to any number of interpretations. And now that you're thoroughly awake, how would you like to take Watson for a walk while I see what I can do about breakfast?'

'And then we'll go over to the dig.'

'Of course.' He spread his hands. 'We'd have wanted to do

that anyway, but as it happens, Andrew has persuaded Fairweather that I might be of some help. I gather Andrew told him I was, or had been, a policeman, and . . .' He shrugged, and I smiled to myself.

I kept Watson's walk short, and stayed on the harbour road, nervous about a possible encounter with Roadkill. It was, I thought, a terrible name for the poor beast, however apt it might be. Or maybe, given his manners – or lack of them – it was a matter of wishful thinking. At any rate, though I adore cats, I sincerely hoped we wouldn't run into this one.

Alan made good use of his time. When Watson and I returned to the flat, not only had my wonderful husband whipped together a terrific breakfast, he had, he informed me as we sat down, made arrangements to hire a launch to take us to Papa Sanday.

'Can you – er – drive a boat? If that's the right word.' I conveyed a forkful of bacon to my mouth and slipped Watson a small piece.

'Pilot. If you don't stop feeding that dog table scraps he's going to weigh fifty pounds. You forget, darling, that I was brought up in Newlyn. I've been messing about in boats since I could walk.'

Newlyn is a fishing community in Cornwall, a stone's throw from Penzance. We had visited some years before, and I'd heard about Alan's childhood there. 'I keep on learning new things about you. And can you find the island?'

'The boat is equipped with GPS. But I have a second string to my bow. I phoned Andrew back and got the phone number of the museum director, Norquist. He's coming with us. And that's probably him at the door now.'

In keeping with standard Orcadian practice, we had not locked the door, but Mr Norquist tapped politely. Alan opened the door, and Norquist sidled in. 'Do be careful,' he quavered. 'That horrible cat is out there, and you don't want him to come in.'

'No, we certainly don't. At least, if it's the cat I think it is, he and Watson don't get along at all.'

'I dislike cats.' The man was visibly distressed. In fact, he was almost wringing his hands, and he looked ill.

'I'm sure it's all right . . .' I began, but Norquist shook his head violently.

'It doesn't matter about the cat. This is a terrible thing, a terrible thing! I don't know what will happen now, I don't indeed. A terrible loss, an irreparable loss.' He was almost weeping.

Alan and I exchanged glances. I was the one who ventured to speak. 'I hadn't realized you were – um – fond of Mr Carter.'

'Fond of him! Fond of him!' Norquist's voice rose to a squeak. 'I detested the man! He was a charlatan, a poseur, the worst sort of American. I'm sorry, Mrs Nesbitt, but I have to speak the truth.'

Now was perhaps not the time to correct him about my name. I frowned. 'But, in that case, Mr Norquist . . . that is, you seem very upset . . .'

'My dear woman, the dig! How will it go on without the money? Excavations are quite dreadfully expensive. Where will the funding come from now, Mrs Nesbitt?'

'Actually, sir, my wife uses her own name, Dorothy Martin.' Alan sounded rather crisp, and I realized he was annoyed. I, too, was a bit revolted by Norquist's attitude.

He was quick to sense the frost in the atmosphere, 'I beg your pardon, Mrs Martin. I didn't know, did I? And I can see that you're not happy about my attitude.' He pulled himself up to his full height. 'I'm sorry if I offend you, but I can't pretend to a grief I don't feel. I will not mourn for Mr Henry J. Carter, but the loss of his funding is a blow, perhaps a mortal blow, to a monumental scheme, one that is dear to my heart. I am English by birth, as you can probably hear from my speech, but my father was born here in Stromness and I have lived here for many years. I consider myself a true Orcadian. I love these islands. A blow for Orkney is a kick in the teeth for me.'

Well, I still didn't think Mr Norquist was ever going to be my favourite person. But I had to admit there was a dignity to the little man, and I've always disliked hypocrisy. I nodded. 'You certainly have a point. Now, may we offer you some tea or coffee before we set out? Or something to eat?'

'Thank you, but I'm not feeling at all well. I've a dreadful headache. And the weather may be changing, so perhaps . . .'

'Yes,' said Alan. 'After you, Dorothy.'

I was pleased when Norquist accepted Watson's company in the back seat without a murmur, and even more pleased when Watson, after sniffing him thoroughly, made an absurd little noise of acceptance and settled down in the man's lap for a nap. I know, in theory, that there's no truth to the belief that animals can discern the character of humans. Alan has known any number of criminals who had devoted pets, and Hitler was reputed to be a dog lover. But I do feel better about anyone Watson likes.

'Just shove him off if he's a nuisance,' I said, to test the man. 'He sheds dreadfully.'

'Certainly not!' Norquist sounded shocked, and I was satisfied.

The trip from Tingwall to Papa Sanday seemed shorter this time, though the sea was a good deal rougher. I had forgotten to take my ginger capsules and was grateful that Alan had remembered to bring some along. Nevertheless, I retired to the cabin for almost the whole trip, and so did Norquist. The air was quite brisk, and I thought I might have a cold coming on, and he was presumably nursing his headache. So my first intimation of what the day was going to be like was an odd buzz of sound as Alan throttled back the motor to drift in to the dock.

A swarm of bees? Surely not. I poked my head out of the hatch.

No, a swarm of boats. Boats of all descriptions, from sleek launches to fishing boats to row boats to, I noted in disbelief, a jet ski. A police launch was darting about, trying to control the traffic. One of the men aboard turned his megaphone toward us. 'Turn back! No landing!'

Norquist shouted back, 'I am the director of the Ancient Orkney Museum! I have a reserved berth here!'

I doubted he was heard over the cacophony, but apparently someone on shore recognized him, because frantic signals were exchanged between the police boat and the quay, while Norquist fumed and shouted imprecations which were, I hoped, inaudible. At last the police boat came nearer to ours.

'Follow us, sir,' said the policeman with the megaphone, and we sidled around to a narrow inlet where there was, barely, room for us to pull in and approach the pier.

Norquist staggered out, one hand to his head, but when Watson and I attempted to follow, a uniformed constable stopped us. 'I'm sorry, madam, but this area is restricted.'

Norquist turned around. 'Don't be a fool, man. These people are with me.'

The constable stood his ground. 'That may be so, sir, but this is a crime scene, and I can permit only authorized personnel. I have orders to admit you, Mr Norquist, but no one else.'

I looked at Alan. He had no official weight to throw around, of course, but he had, after all, been asked to come. I could see his internal debate: produce his old identification, or not? He was saved the decision. Robert Fairweather appeared at the constable's elbow, looking exhausted and distraught, but in command.

'This man is here at my invitation, Watts. He is an experienced investigator and, not so incidentally, the retired chief constable of Belleshire. My apologies, Mr Nesbitt. I forgot to tell the authorities you were coming.' He offered his hand first to Alan and then to me, to help us disembark. Watson needed no help or encouragement. He scrambled up and stood at my side, obediently waiting, but panting eagerly for something exciting to happen.

'Nice dog,' said Fairweather, patting his head. Watson's tail wagged even more energetically.

I clipped on his lead. 'He is, but I know he isn't allowed at the dig, and I imagine you want to talk to Alan privately. Is there some out-of-the-way place where I could let Watson run off some energy?'

'Anywhere away from the dig, actually.' He waved a vague hand. 'So long as he leaves the sheep alone, he can have a good run in any of the pastures.'

'I'll keep him away from the sheep. Alan, I'll see you later.'

Of course I wanted to stick around, to see and hear everything to be seen and heard, but I have some sense of responsibility, and an active dog, with a crowd of people to excite him further, wasn't going to help anyone. He was as reluctant as I to leave the scene, but we both knew our duty. We headed away from the noise and activity toward the other side of the island, where a few farms still clung tenaciously to the hills.

Sadly, they didn't look very prosperous. A few cattle grazed in one field, a few sheep in another, but they were rather too lean to look happy and healthy. The farm buildings, too, were in need of attention. Peeling paint on window and door frames spoke of a shortage of both money and time. Roofs had been repaired;

fences were in order. Those were matters of necessity. Appearances had to take a back seat to the essentials of life.

When we'd got far enough away from the dig that we could no longer hear voices, I let Watson off the lead, and he gambolled happily, chasing here a seagull, there a rabbit, sometimes his imagination. He didn't catch anything, but he fondly imagined how wonderful it would be when he did.

I ambled down the road, shivering a little. The wind had picked up, and although the sun still shone, the high overcast was thickening perceptibly. We would have rain, and sooner rather than later, if I knew anything about weather. The darkening sky made the landscape even bleaker than before. No trees. Just hills and sky with a few disheartened houses.

I whistled for Watson. I was ready to turn back. He looked up and barked, but he was busy digging up something and refused to leave it.

I sighed. Watson is a good dog and usually quite obedient, but when he's found a treasure he insists on showing it to me. It can be anything from a long-dead bird or small mammal, to a bone, to some object whose interest for a dog defies human discernment. I whistled again, without much hope. He barked again, more urgently.

I eyed the single strand of barbed wire, no doubt electrified, that kept the cattle confined. Watson had run under it with ease. I looked for a gate.

Before I reached it, the rain began, gently at first, then with more force. I was soaked through and chilled to the bone by the time I reached my dog, and furious with him.

'Watson, you are a bad dog! You must come when I call you!'

He whined apologetically, but stood his ground, pawing at his find and barking sharply. Plainly he was going to stay there until I acknowledged his discovery, if we both drowned. I leaned down, trying without success to keep the rain from pouring down my neck.

He barked again and once more pawed at the ground, and through the grass and the mud (I hoped it was just mud), I saw the glint of gold.

For just one moment I was transfixed. Carter had been right after all! Gold! Viking gold! This could be the find of the century, and my dog would get the credit. And wasn't there a law about treasure trove? It belonged to the Crown, but the finder was paid its value. Untold wealth! Better than winning the lottery!

I forgot about being cold and wet and about what might be mixed with the mud, and reached eagerly into the mess.

And came up with – a Rolex watch.

The disappointment was so sharp I failed for a second to consider the implication. Then I dropped the watch as if it were on fire, and clipped Watson's lead back on. 'You're a fine dog, Watson.' I patted his head. 'I'm sorry I scolded you. But we have to get back to Daddy as soon as we can. And we have to leave this right here where we found it. No, Watson, leave it!'

That was a command he knew. Sadly, slowly, he followed me, dragging his heels and looking back longingly at his treasure, but accepting the inevitable. Humans had a very strange set of values, but one had been taught to obey.

SIX

My teeth were chattering before I got back to the dig, and then I couldn't find Alan. Or much of anybody else. The rain had apparently driven away most of the press and virtually all of the merely curious, for there were only a few people near the piers. Policemen, I thought, poor miserable functionaries who had to remain there keeping at bay hordes that were no longer there.

I found the one who had reluctantly allowed us ashore. 'Constable, I'm trying to find my husband and Mr Fairweather. Do you know where they will have gone?'

'I believe they took shelter in the big tent, madam. It serves as headquarters for the dig. The excavation crew stayed on Mainland today, what with the weather and a dead body and all.' He tried to keep the resentment out of his voice, but failed. A policeman's lot is not a happy one, I thought, but aloud I only thanked him. Watson and I plodded on.

The dog was at least as wet as I, so it shouldn't have come as a big surprise when his first act upon entering the tent was to shake himself vigorously. The resulting shower of rain and mud and manure didn't add to the level of cheer.

The level wasn't high to begin with, or so I thought from a glance at the faces. Along with Alan and Fairweather were Norquist, another man who looked vaguely familiar but whom I couldn't place, and one very official looking man wearing a dark suit and a formidable frown. 'The incident must be investigated,' he said now, in the tone of one who had been saying the same thing for some time. Obviously the policeman in charge of said investigation, I realized.

'But the man died in an *accident*!' Norquist was almost weeping. 'There's no point in making such heavy weather of it. He missed his footing, slipped, and fell into an unstable wall. It collapsed on him. There's no mystery about it!'

'I agree completely,' said the man I didn't know. 'The only

question is the man's reason for being at the dig in the middle of the night, but we have to accept the fact that he was eccentric, and very much a law unto himself. Doubtless he wanted to check something for himself.'

'Or steal something!' That, of course, was Norquist again. 'He admired Schliemann, don't forget. He's probably been looting the dig all this time, and—'

'Now, Charles.' Fairweather spoke in soothing tones. 'There's no reason to believe—'

'There's every reason—'

'This is no time for unsubstantiated—'

'Quiet!' The policeman spoke just loudly enough to make himself heard over the uproar. 'This is an unexpected death and must be investigated. Without question. There are certain anomalies—'

'What do you mean, anomalies?' Norquist would not be silenced. 'It's perfectly plain—'

'I would be obliged, sir, if you would let me speak. I cannot reveal at this point what we have so far discovered, but rest assured that there are questions I need to have answered. And I will find the answers. Now, before we disperse, I need to take statements from each of you individually. Mr Nesbitt, I'd be obliged if you would stay, sir. If your lady wife wishes to return home, it would be perfectly in order. I'm sure,' he said, 'you must be quite uncomfortable.' He said it with a smile, which sat oddly on his lined and dour face.

'Thank you, but I'll stay. The fact is, I have . . . there is something I need to tell you.' Alan looked at me with a query on his face, but I ignored it. 'If I might speak to you alone?' I went on.

Now it was the policeman who was taken aback, but I was due certain courtesies as the wife of an important police officer, albeit English and retired. He nodded to the other men in the tent. 'Gentlemen, if you will retire to another tent, I'll send for you shortly.'

'Who's the other one?' I whispered to Alan as they filed out in varying degrees of disgruntlement.

'Larsen. President of FAO.'

Oh, yes. That was why he'd looked familiar.

'Now, Mrs Martin. What was it you needed to tell me?' The

police officer sounded indulgent. 'That is, I beg your pardon. I haven't introduced myself. My name's Baikie, and I'm looking into this wee matter.'

I proffered my hand. 'You know who I am, of course, and I'm sure I'm very sorry to interrupt, but I thought you needed to know about this right away. I've found – that is, my dog has found – a watch, half buried in a cow pasture out there. I believe it to be Mr Carter's.'

'I see . . .' Mr Baikie paused. 'And what are your reasons,' he went on slowly, 'for thinking that?'

'Actually, I'm almost certain. I saw him wearing the watch, or a very similar one, last night at the FAO meeting. And I can't imagine that there are a lot of men in this part of Orkney who sport extravagant gold Rolexes.'

'Probably not.' He paused again. 'Well, we'll have to go take a look, won't we? Mr Nesbitt, would you mind accompanying your wife to the – er – location? I need to stay here and speak further with these men. Mrs Martin, I hate to ask you to go out again in the rain, but perhaps you'd like to borrow my waterproof. I don't know how warm it is, but at least you'll be dry.'

I was quite certain I'd never be warm or dry again, but I accepted his offer. It meant getting out of that charged atmosphere, and besides, I wanted to talk to Alan.

'My dear,' he said when we'd got out of earshot of the tents, 'you've put the cat among the pigeons with a vengeance.'

'Wh-what do you mean?' I said through chattering teeth. The wind had strengthened still more, and Mr Baikie's coat was, as feared, not very warm. 'Surely this is the evidence they need.'

'That depends which "they" you're talking about. The authorities, Chief Inspector Baikie *et al.*, yes. Sort of. The others, Fairweather and Norquist and Larsen, have made up their mind that Carter's death was an accident. You must have noticed.'

'I wasn't up to n-noticing very much.'

Alan put his arm around my shoulders and pulled me close. 'We'll talk about it when we get you warm and dry. Meanwhile, how much farther do we have to go in this ungodly weather?'

Pointing was easier than talking. Watson was straining at the leash, so I freed him, and he dashed straight under the barbed wire to his discovery. Alan followed more slowly, using the gate, as I had. I sought the shelter of a standing stone near the road. It was too narrow and slender to deflect the wind much, and no matter which side I stood on, the wind seemed to shift around to direct itself at my face.

Alan was taking forever. I huddled miserably, my face buried in my coat collar, not knowing what he and Watson were doing, and not much caring. I was startled, therefore, when the wind dropped for a moment or two and I heard a man's voice raised in anger, close by.

'And what the bluidy hell d'ye think ye're doin' on my land?'

I looked up in alarm, but the anger was being directed not at me, but at Alan. The speaker was Andersen, the farmer who'd been so upset at last night's meeting. He was approaching Alan at a rapid clip, and he had a lethal-looking pitchfork in his hand.

I screamed. Pure reflex, because there was no help in sight. But the scream was apparently all Watson needed. If he'd been uncertain about the situation for a moment, now he knew what he needed to do. With a full-throated growl, that mildest of dogs sprang for the farmer.

I screamed again, for my dog, this time. That pitchfork . . . But Watson's aim was sure. He caught the farmer's arm just below the elbow. The pitchfork went flying as Andersen, howling with rage and pain, fell to the ground. Alan managed somehow to catch hold of Watson's collar and haul him off the farmer in time to prevent serious injury.

I ran as fast as I could, Watson's lead in my trembling hand. Alan took it from me and clipped it to the dog's collar, and helped Andersen to his feet.

The farmer wasn't badly hurt, as far I could see. He was, fortunately, wearing a heavy work jacket, and no blood was visible on the sleeve. He was jibbering with rage, though, and that, too, was fortunate, because before he could get out any articulate statement Alan took over.

'You asked, sir, what I am doing on your land. I am Chief Constable Alan Nesbitt, and I am collecting important evidence in a murder case. Had you been successful in attacking me, I would have charged you with assaulting a police officer. Luckily, my dog is trained to protect me. Now, what have you to say for yourself?'

At least one word of that speech got through to Duncan Andersen. 'Murder? Are ye accusin' me of murder? By God, I'll—'

'I have made no accusation as yet. I will have some questions for you later, however. Meanwhile I must caution you not to leave this island. And I suggest, sir, that you endeavour to keep your temper in better check, or you'll find yourself in serious trouble. Good day.'

The three of us left him standing in the field, wet, muddy, furious, and with what was doubtless a very sore arm.

'That was,' I said, after I'd recovered a little, 'the stuffiest speech I've ever heard from you.'

'Also probably the biggest string of lies,' said Alan. 'Your teeth aren't chattering anymore.'

'No, I'm not cold anymore. Adrenaline, I suppose. Lies?'

'I'm no longer a chief constable. This is not yet officially a murder case. I was, in fact, trespassing on Mr Andersen's land, and I have no power to charge anyone. In fact, he would have every reason to charge me with both trespass and assault, not to mention impersonating a police officer.'

'He won't, will he? Try to have you arrested?'

'I doubt it. I think he'll go back and think about a murder charge and keep mum.'

'What I think he'll do is go back and get roaring drunk. Anyway, did you get the watch?'

'I did. I also took a good many pictures of it, *in situ*. Of course, you and Watson had disturbed it somewhat, but I couldn't help that. I wish I'd known before I started that it was Andersen's farm. I'd have sent you for backup. But it worked out well enough, thanks to our friend, here.' He bent down to pat Watson, who was trotting along with a satisfied smirk on his face. 'You're a good dog, and you're going to have a nice chunk of steak as soon as I can find you one.'

'He's a silly dog. I can't figure out why he was interested in a watch, of all things.'

'Oh, that's an easy one.' Alan plodded on.

I stopped dead. 'Well, are you going to tell me?'

'I thought I'd wait until we got back to the good Baikie. But if you insist . . .' He reached into his pocket and pulled out a plastic bag. Inside, covered in mud and looking rather humiliated, was the watch. 'If you'll look closely, my dear . . .'

I peered at it, trying not to tip rain from my hair onto the bag. 'I don't see anything unusual. For a Rolex, I mean. Gold all over the place.'

'Perhaps the conditions aren't the best.' He put the repellent object back in his pocket. 'But when I dug it up, I was reasonably sure that there was, mixed in with the mud, a fair amount of blood.'

SEVEN

I looked at him sharply. 'Should you have dug it up, then?'

'No. I should have left it to be examined properly by a forensics expert. In an ideal world. But I'm not a miracle worker, woman, just a plodding ex-policeman trying to do the best I can in less than ideal circumstances. The rain is pelting down and has already washed away who knows what evidence. Then there's Watson, here, and doubtless other animals around who might take an interest. Sheep are odd animals and can be very curious.'

'And there's Duncan Andersen, panting to dig up the whole area in search of Viking gold. He caught a glimpse of that watch, I'm sure, at least enough to see the colour. All right, I take your point. If we had all of Scotland Yard here we – that is, you – could conduct a proper investigation. As it is, shall we get back to the tents? I'm freezing again.'

The rain had settled down to the sort of steady drizzle that can go on for days. Even Watson had lost his enthusiasm for a walk and splashed along as disconsolate as the rest of us. When we got to the tents, I ducked into one that was unoccupied, so Watson could shake himself without getting yet more rain and mud on the group in the big tent. I should have been interested in what was being said, in the reaction to Watson's find. At the moment I was interested in nothing but getting warm and dry. I sat on a miserably uncomfortable camp stool and shivered, trying to wipe my streaming nose with a sodden tissue from my pocket. Watson sat on my feet and shivered, whining now and then in sympathetic distress. Once or twice I sneezed.

When Alan came to find me, he took one look at the pair of us and held out his hand. 'Mr Norquist will stay here for a bit, but I've organized transport back to the boat landing for us,' he said. 'Not deluxe, but it'll keep you from getting much wetter.'

'I couldn't get any wetter if you threw me in the sea,' I croaked. 'I thought you said we were supposed to have good weather all week.'

'The weather chaps lied. And you're coming down with a cold. Come along, wench. There's a thermos of coffee in the boat, and Baikie insisted I take his flask of whisky. I know you prefer bourbon, but for medicinal purposes one form of alcohol is as good as another.'

'Any Scotsman would boil you in oil for classifying good single-malt as medicine, but I'll take a dose with pleasure.' He handed me the flask, which I put in my back pocket as I followed Alan to the vehicle he'd found somewhere, a sort of golf-cart thing with a canvas awning over the top. It afforded little protection against the rain and none at all against the wind, but at least it kept our feet out of the mud. Watson sat on the seat next to me, seized with occasional spasms of hard shivering. We were both feeling exceedingly sorry for ourselves.

The boat wasn't much warmer, but at least the cabin was out of the wind. I dried myself and Watson as best I could with a rough blanket I found in one of the bench seats. Neither of us was very dry when I'd finished, and the blanket was a whole lot muddier. We'd have to buy a replacement.

'You said something about coffee?' I called up to Alan at the helm. The boat was bobbing about a good deal, but I was too cold and achy to worry about seasickness.

'In one of the cupboards in the galley,' he called back. 'There are only plastic cups, sorry, but there are sugar packets somewhere.'

'I'll pour you a cup, too, shall I?'

'Too windy up here to drink it. I'll be fine until we get to dry land.'

He didn't sound fine. He sounded tired and cross, but there was nothing I could do about it. I poured myself a half-cup of coffee, laced it with plenty of sugar and the Scotch, and took a cautious sip of the pseudo hot toddy.

It wasn't actually too bad. The smoky taste of the whisky went rather oddly with the sweetened coffee, but it was hot, and my sense of taste was diminishing as my sinuses filled. I don't really like Scotch, much preferring good old American corn likker, but any port in a storm . . .

And speaking of ports, I wondered where we were, but I felt too sluggish to go up and look, and had the sense not to call

up and ask. 'Are we there yet?' is an extremely annoying utter-
ance, even when it comes from an adult, and it's virtually
impossible to keep the whine out of one's voice when uttering
it. I curled up on the deck, my back against the bench and
Watson planted firmly at my stomach to keep me from rolling,
and tried to nap.

But the coffee, or my aching sinuses, or something, kept me
from settling. It didn't help when Watson resettled himself with
his tail in my face. And the boards of the deck weren't designed
as a mattress. I gave up, shoved Watson away, and managed to
get up off the floor (not my best act, ever since my knee surgery)
and back to the bench.

I tried to think, though my head seemed to be stuffed full of
cotton, hay and rags, as 'Enry 'Iggins claimed was the case with
all women.

What had Alan and the others talked about, there in the tent?
How had they reacted to the discovery of Carter's watch?

If it *was* Carter's watch. I had seen it for only a brief second
last night at the meeting. Was it only last night? It felt like a
week ago.

But if it was his, what was the significance? Well, it proved
he'd been on the island. But his dead body proved that beyond
any need of verification. The watch didn't prove, necessarily, that
he'd been in Duncan Andersen's pasture. A watch is readily
removable, and might not even be missed by the owner for a
while. Although a big, heavy Rolex, not only weighty but very
expensive, and a status symbol, moreover . . .

I gave it up. When we got back to Stromness, Alan and I
would talk it over. And I hoped that would be soon, because the
motion of the boat was becoming increasingly erratic, and my
stomach was beginning to vie with my stuffy nose and achy
muscles for attention.

'Dorothy!' Alan's call was loud and urgent. 'Wake up and put
on your life jacket!'

'Alan! Are we in trouble?' I tried to stave off panic.

'Not yet, but it's rough out here, and this is an unfamiliar craft.
Find a life jacket and put it on, and then bring me one.'

I was absurdly reminded of the routine safety announcement
on an airplane. 'Put your own oxygen mask on first and then

assist others.' Inappropriate humour, I told myself firmly, is the beginning of hysteria.

I looked around frantically, having no idea where to find a life jacket. It was no more than a few seconds, I suppose, before I saw the prominent sign. Life jackets, flares, life preservers, a raft, a boat hook, all were neatly together at one end of the cabin. I put on a jacket, with some difficulty, and then staggered up with Alan's, nearly falling on the wet steps.

'Here,' said Alan. 'Take the wheel a minute while I get into this thing.'

'I don't know a thing about steering a boat! And I can't see through the wind and rain!'

'Just keep it steady. We're all right for a few seconds.'

Almost as soon as he had taken his hands off the wheel, he had his jacket on and was prying my hands off. 'No need for the death-like grip, darling,' he said with the hint of a smile. 'But do you think you could bear to stay up here for a few minutes? We're quite close to Tingwall, but as you say, the visibility's a bit tricky, and I could use a second pair of eyes.'

Well, that terrified me almost as much as taking the wheel, but I took a firm grip of the rail, made sure my lifejacket was securely fastened, and tried to see my way through the driving rain.

Oh, how I wished I had a hat, one of those lovely broad-brimmed rain hats. Of all the days for a dedicated hat-wearer to go out without one! But I put my hand to my brow as a visor and peered.

Alan had cut the engine back to dead slow, which left us pretty well at the mercy of the wind and waves. On the other hand, any faster would have been extremely risky in the limited visibility. Everything looked grey to me, but some of it began to seem thicker, somehow, more solid.

'Alan, there's a boat ahead, just on the left. Port, I mean!'

'I see it. Can you see any lights anywhere?'

'No-o – yes! A green light! The green light at the end of the pier!' I was getting light-headed and irrelevant again.

'Thank you, F. Scott. Where, exactly? I don't see it.'

I sobered. 'Just ahead and slightly to the right – starboard. At about not quite one o'clock. I can't tell how far away.'

'All right. I see it. You can relax, love. We're here.'

I could barely stagger out of the boat, and for a few awful moments I was sure I was going to be sick right there on the pier, but Alan took my elbow in a firm grip and said, 'There now, you're going to be fine,' and somehow I was, not fine exactly, but functional. Watson seemed relieved to be back on land, too.

'You might want to leave your life jacket in the boat,' he said gently. 'All the gear belongs to the hire firm.'

'Oh, I suppose we should stow them back where they belong,' I said feebly. 'And there's a blanket – it's all muddy—'

'Tomorrow will do for that. I'll ring them up. Right now we both need some hot soup and a hot bath as soon as we can get them.' Alan returned my life jacket to the boat while I watched Watson, and then we all climbed into the car, which was going to need a thorough cleaning before we turned it in.

The drive back to Stromness was a nightmare, but after several eternities we arrived, had our baths, and sat down at the table in our jammies and robes in front of bowls of steaming chicken noodle soup, courtesy of Campbell.

'Good Scots name, that,' said Alan, pointing at the familiar red and white can.

'Mm,' I agreed wordlessly. My throat was getting sorer by the moment, and anyway I was busy absorbing the soup.

'You're feeling dreadful, aren't you?'

I nodded and put down my spoon. 'I think,' I croaked, 'that I'll have some tea and go to bed.' Not that I have anything against chicken soup, but the universal remedy in my childhood had always been sweet, milky tea.

'I'll make the tea.' He got up to suit the action to the word. 'Where did I see the pot . . . oh, there. Nothing like an unfamiliar kitchen to sharpen one's powers of observation. Do you want to know what Baikie and the rest said about the watch?'

'As long as I don't have to talk,' I whispered.

Alan put the kettle on to heat and found the tea bags. 'The reaction was mixed. Larsen and Fairweather agreed that the watch was almost certainly Carter's. Norquist said it was too dirty to draw any conclusion about it, and was all for cleaning it up then and there, which of course Baikie wouldn't allow. He, Baikie, did tell me privately that there was no watch found on Carter's body.' He assembled milk, sugar and cups on a tray and rummaged in the cupboards for biscuits. 'The varied conclusions drawn, though, were most interesting. Baikie, who is somewhat inclined to treat Carter's death as a murder case, thought his watch – if it is his watch – being found so far from the body strengthened that view. He didn't say so, but I was a policeman too long not to see it in his manner.'

The kettle whistled. Alan filled the pot and brought the tray to the table. 'The others could see it, too, and they united in opposition. It was a bit funny, actually. They expressed themselves differently, of course. Larsen and Fairweather were trying diplomatically to suggest that the project would suffer greatly from any adverse publicity, in addition to the financial blow of their principal donor's death. Norquist, predictably, fulminated. I'm having a very hard time trying to like that man.' He poured the tea, with plenty of milk and sugar in mine.

I sipped gratefully, cleared my throat, and essayed a question. 'What's Baikie going to do?'

'He didn't confide in me. In his place the first thing I'd do would be to confine Andersen to quarters. He's the obvious suspect, though there are a good many questions about the whole situation. But he hated Carter, he has a filthy temper and considerable strength, and he was presumably here last night.'

'Do we know that?'

'No,' Alan admitted. 'But where else would he be? He doesn't seem the gad-about type. Besides, he has livestock to tend.'

'I don't know. Getting himself polluted in a pub somewhere, maybe. Alan, I can't think. My head's booming like a drum. I'm going to bed.'

I found a couple of elderly cold tablets in my traveling bag, swallowed them, and drifted off into deep if somewhat uncomfortable sleep for the best part of the next twenty-four hours.

EIGHT

My method for dealing with a minor respiratory illness has been the same for at least forty years. At the first sign of a sore throat or stuffy nose, I take myself to bed. The theory is that, given rest and fluids, the body will heal itself. I have to admit that it doesn't always work, but this time it did. When I woke on Wednesday afternoon, I was hungry, able to breathe, and more or less in my right mind. I got out of bed and wandered into the sitting room.

'Ah,' said Alan, who was sitting with newspapers on his lap and a cup at his elbow. 'It's the Sleeping Beauty.'

I looked down at my crumpled nightgown and ran a hand through my unkempt hair and over my unwashed face. 'Sarcasm is the tool of the devil. Is there anything to eat?'

'You're feeling better.'

'Much. And I'm starving.'

'How's the throat?'

'Better. I'm not quite ready to address Parliament or sing *Madame Butterfly*, but I think I'm up to some comfort food.'

'Good. If you want to get cleaned up a bit, I'll have some scrambled eggs ready when you are.'

Dear man! He didn't quite wrinkle up his nose, but I was aware that I badly needed a shower.

I felt nearly normal when I had showered. I poked my head out of the bathroom. 'What's the weather like? Sunshine, I can see, but what about the temperature?'

'Probably a little chilly for a pampered American,' he called back from the kitchen. 'I suggest layers. And hurry up. The eggs are almost done.'

I hurried. Cold eggs are an abomination unto the Lord.

One of Alan's many virtues is that he can cook. He was a widower for many years and learned to fend for himself. It's true that scrambled eggs aren't terribly taxing, but they can be awful if badly made. These were soft and creamy, perfect for a touchy throat, and he'd served them with a bit of smoked salmon that melted in the mouth.

'Wherever did you find this? I wouldn't have thought the co-op would run to this standard of luxury fare.' Stromness boasts two grocery stores, one (called a co-op for reasons I could not discern) a mini-supermarket with a good selection of most necessities, the other the glorified convenience store. Neither seemed a likely source.

'Andrew gave me a brochure when he took us out to dinner. He smokes the stuff himself. May catch it himself, for all I know. Yesterday when you were dead to the world I decided to visit his shop in the village. You'd like it, by the way. It's tiny, but full of mirrors that make it look a lot bigger. The window sign giving hours of operation reads: "9.48 to 5.53 weekdays, Sundays 1.53 to 5.57".'

I chuckled as Alan went on. 'So I bought some of the salmon. I also bought . . .' He performed a bit of legerdemain and brought from behind his back the most beautiful wine goblet I'd ever seen. It was made of pottery, beautifully shaped with a pattern incised in the clay, and finished in a lustrous black glaze. It was breath-taking.

'My word! It looks like a chalice! Andrew made this?'

'And a whole set like it. I bought eight. I hope you don't mind, but I couldn't resist.'

'Mind! They're gorgeous. I had no idea he did this sort of thing. One thinks of pottery as rather more . . . I don't know . . . earthy, I guess.'

'My dear, he does every sort of thing. You cannot imagine. The man's not only a genius, he's an incredibly prolific genius. You must come with me, and I think you'd like to visit the pottery, as well. The woman in charge of the shop says there's a far greater variety out there.'

I polished off every bite of my meal, drank every drop from the big pot of tea Alan provided, and sat back, replete. 'You, my dear, are the answer to a maiden's prayer. Also a superannuated matron's. Now, tell me what's been going on in the world of crime while I did my Rip Van Winkle routine.'

Alan had been tidying the kitchen, clearing away dirty dishes, putting things in their places. Now he sat down at the table and sighed. 'I'm not sure you want to know. For a start, they've arrested Duncan Andersen for the murder of Henry Carter.'

I considered his words and his attitude. 'And you don't think he did it.' It was not a question.

'The evidence is there, Dorothy. He was seen at the meeting to utter threats. He fetched up at a pub in Kirkwall after he was hustled away, and drank enough to fell an ox, if reports are accurate, growing more and more bellicose. His last words before the landlord threw him out were: "I'll kill the wee bastard before I'll see him take another foot of my land!".'

'Baikie and Co. have been busy. How did Andersen get to the pub? Kirkwall's a good long way from the meeting hall.'

'An FAO member drove him. He'd brought him to the meeting from the harbour in Kirkwall, and was taking him back there when Andersen decided he needed some refreshment. The driver tried to talk him out of it, but not too strenuously, one gathers. Anderson was in a fury, and not quite safe to argue with.'

'Indeed. What did Andersen do after he left the pub?'

'They haven't been able to trace his exact movements. He had come to the meeting in his own boat, and presumably he took it back home. It was a dark night; it's a miracle he made it safely.'

'God is said to watch over fools and drunkards. But they don't know when he got home?'

'Dorothy, you've seen the place. He has no near neighbours, and even if he did, he's such a surly fellow, I'd think everyone on the island would keep clear of him.'

'And there aren't all that many people living there, are there? I didn't see any sign of a village or anything like that. Although it's true I didn't do much looking around.'

'The only village is the tent village for the excavation people, and even they aren't there all the time, as you discovered yesterday. I gather they hole up in rooms here and there when the weather is intimidating. The permanent population of the island is about twenty, I gather, and diminishing all the time.'

'Sad. The era of the small farmer is gone for good, isn't it? But anyway, just what is the evidence against Andersen? Beyond the fact that he was breathing fire and destruction at the meeting.'

'The watch is one of the most damaging bits. It was Carter's, for certain, and the blood found on and around it was almost certainly his blood. There hasn't been time for sophisticated tests, but the experts say it's extremely likely, and Carter had abrasions on his wrist, which indicated the watch might have been removed by force. Well, anyone might have done that. It's a valuable little piece of property, with the diamonds and all.'

'*Diamonds?*'

'Diamonds. Instead of numerals, the thing is set with twelve diamonds. A flashy sort of man, Carter.' Alan, who dresses very conservatively, made a little grimace of distaste. 'But the truly damning bit came to light only this morning. They got a warrant to search Anderson's house and outbuildings, and found blood in the pigsty.'

'Carter's?'

'Human, for certain, and possibly Carter's. It was on the edge of a stone trough, and was just about the right size and shape to have caused one of Carter's injuries. So they took Andersen in and charged him.'

'But you still don't think he did it. Why?'

Alan ran a hand down the back of his neck in a familiar gesture of frustration. 'I have no sensible answer for that. It just smells wrong. Of all the people who hated Carter, Andersen is the most obvious, and the least appealing as a person. It pleases everyone to think that he might be a murderer, given the others in the field. A museum director? The director of the dig? The president of Friends of Ancient Orkney? Respectable men, all of them, and responsible in some degree for bringing new lustre to Orkney. Pit them against one churlish, smelly, drunken farmer, and what are the odds?'

'Trial by public opinion. You're right. It smells as bad as Andersen. Do you think Baikie is incompetent?'

'I don't know. He's the highest ranking officer in Orkney, but I don't know enough about the policing structure up here to gauge what that means. Politics rears its ugly head everywhere, you know.'

I sipped my tea thoughtfully before asking, 'What are we going to do about it?'

Bless the man. Really, I often wonder how I managed to get so lucky with both my husbands. Frank was a perfect dear whose only real flaw was dying too young, and now Alan was just as much on my wavelength as Frank had been. He could have said,

'Why do we have to do anything about it?' Or some variant of Tonto's 'Who's we, white man?' He said neither of those things, but got up to make more tea, and said, 'I'm not sure. Do you have any suggestions, or is your head still full of nothing but sinus congestion?'

'It's clearing, in more senses than one. I can't suggest anything concrete at the moment. We don't know enough. But surely we can both do what we do best. That means that I go around talking to people in my artless, wide-eyed American way, and you go around sniffing out the situation like a policeman. You've had a lot of experience by now in doing that unofficially, without stepping on too many toes.'

'Oh, I don't know about that. Seems to me there are a good few squashed toes throughout the UK, and even on the other side of the Atlantic.'

Alan was remembering the murder case back in my home town in Indiana, where his unofficial status had been a source of considerable frustration to both of us. 'But you saw justice done in all those cases. What are a few trampled egos to that?'

He raised the teapot in salute. 'Thank you, madam. I would amend that to say that *we* saw justice done. So, are you ready to venture out in search of some justice?'

'As soon as I've had another cup of tea and made a list, I am.'

I am never without a little notebook, which I use for all sorts of things, grocery lists, phone numbers (usually with no name attached, so I have to call them to find out whose they are), lists of books I want to read, and my ubiquitous to-do lists. I've always found that making a list gives me a spurious feeling of having accomplished something. Once in a blue moon I actually check off most of the items and feel industrious indeed.

'So,' I said, clicking open my pen. 'People for one of us to talk to. Norquist, obviously, though I admit I don't look forward to it. Fairweather. Larsen. I wonder, by the way, where Mr Fairweather is from. That's a very English-sounding name, and he speaks like an Englishman, too.'

'That's one of the things you might ask him. Why don't you tackle him, at least to begin with. You might have a hard time tracking him down, though. With the weather so fine today—'

'Fair weather,' I put in.

Alan ignored me. '—he's probably at the dig.'

'Do you think so? Wouldn't the police still have it sealed off? And anyway, if the funding's in question, with Carter's death . . .'

I left the sentence unfinished, and Alan gave me a peculiar smile. 'Oh, I didn't tell you, did I? That's the other thing I found out this morning. It's all unofficial at this stage, of course, but Baikie's been in touch with Carter's lawyers, and apparently the man left most of his very considerable fortune to the FAO. The dig's future is assured.'

'Oh, no! And so all those highly respectable men move way up on the suspect list.'

'Unless one of them killed Carter. Don't forget that a murderer is not allowed to profit by his crime.'

'And that makes a good reason for all of them, collectively, to make good and sure Andersen's convicted. Alan, I'm liking the smell of this less and less.'

'Yes, it does reek, doesn't it? All the more reason for us to help find out what really happened. What else goes on the list?'

'Well, so far there isn't much. You're going to talk to Norquist, and I'm going to talk to Fairweather, if I can find him. I'll need somehow to get to where he is, don't forget. And if it's the dig—'

'But you've convinced me that he's probably not there, for one reason or another. And why do you have to go to him? Why couldn't you simply ring him up and invite him for tea, or supper, or a drink, or whatever sounds – er – inviting? He involved us in the investigation, after all. He'll hardly turn you down.'

'Alan, that's brilliant! Does he have a wife, do you know?'

'I've no idea. But I do have his phone number. Somewhere.' He rummaged in his pockets and handed me a crumpled piece of paper. 'I don't know if that's his home, or a hotel, or his mobile, but it ought to reach him somehow.'

It reached him on the first ring. He answered as though he'd been waiting for a call. It certainly wasn't mine, but I pretended I didn't know that. 'Mr Fairweather? I'm so glad I caught you. You must be frantically busy just now. This is Dorothy Martin. How are you coping with all this?'

'Oh, Mrs Martin. Er – how nice to hear from you.'

'I hope you're managing, with all that's happened.'

'Yes, it's a bit – I'm a bit – but of course I can't work at the dig just now, so I'm actually . . .'

He ran down, and I jumped into the breach. 'I called, really, to see if you'd like to relax for a while over drinks this evening, and perhaps supper to follow if you have the time. I'd like to meet your wife – if you have one, that is – and I've so many questions about the dig that I never got the chance to ask.' I winked at Alan, who made a face back.

'That sounds . . . well, my wife is back at home in Surrey. I was expecting a call from her, actually. But if I'm welcome by myself . . .?'

'You're most welcome. About six, then, if that's convenient? And do stay for supper, if you don't have other plans. It won't be anything fancy, just a simple supper.'

He made appropriate noises, and I told him where to find us and punched the phone off. 'There, that's my good deed for the day. I'll need to do some shopping and some cooking for the rest of the afternoon, and I'll need you to help me carry the doings. Once we have them back here, you can go off and beard Norquist in his den.'

Not knowing what Mr Fairweather preferred in the way of drink, we laid in a varied supply, from sherry to Highland Park Whisky, Orkney's own liquid gold. Then, assuming that an Englishman would enjoy curry, we found lamb and various other ingredients at the co-op and lugged it all home, where I settled down to some cooking while Alan set off for the museum and the acerbic Mr Norquist.

NINE

The problem in conducting an investigation as a detective without portfolio is always how to begin. A policeman can approach a suspect, or a witness, and say, 'I'd like to ask you a few questions about XYZ.' Then even the first reaction of the person being questioned is instructive. He or she may refuse to answer, may answer so prolifically that it might be a smokescreen, may be glib with obvious lies, may be nervous or combative, and all these responses tell the investigator almost as much as the words he hears. But someone like me, having no conceivable excuse for asking questions at all, must be a good deal more devious about the task.

I thought about that as I chopped onions and browned chunks of lamb, discovered I didn't have several of the spices I needed and made a quick run to the co-op for them. Watson was delighted to come with me. He was getting distinctly bored with his regime, which involved a good deal less freedom than he enjoyed at home. He was well enough trained to stay close to the flat if I let him out, but I was nervous about Roadkill. I'd never before met a cat that frightened me, but this one did. So I kept Watson on a short leash during our little errand, much to his disappointment.

The flat had a little patio area, securely walled in. When we got back I surveyed the height of the walls, decided that any cat able to scale them would belong in a circus, and let Watson go out. At least he could breathe fresh air out there, even if it wasn't real freedom.

I resumed my curry preparations, musing about fear. Fear for Watson's safety was causing me to take actions he didn't like. For his own good, I reasoned. I was the responsible party in this relationship. I was the human, able and indeed obliged to make decisions for my dog's welfare. But he didn't look at it that way. He saw my decisions as arbitrary, and although he obeyed my dictates like the good dog he was, he made sure I knew he didn't like them. He didn't understand the fear that motivated me, nor did he realize that the fear was in turn motivated by love.

Motivations. Motives. How often, I wondered, is fear a motive for crime? Fear for another person, fear of reprisal, fear of loss. Well, all the fears were of loss, ultimately, weren't they? Loss of something or someone I hold dear, or need, or desperately want. I don't want to lose Watson, so I keep him close to me. Duncan Andersen doesn't want to lose his land, so he . . . what?

I tasted the curry, decided that with some simmering time it would do, and Alan walked in. 'Something smells good,' he said, sniffing appreciatively.

'It isn't quite what I'd produce in my own kitchen, but I think it'll be all right. Alan, what are you afraid of? Anything?'

'Heavens! What brought that on?'

'Too long a train of thought to explain. But it's a serious question.'

'Hmm. I'll have to think about it. Failure, I suppose. Losing someone I love. The usual physical things: stroke, heart attack, dementia, problems with my sight or hearing.' He looked at me quizzically.

'The same things most people fear, in short. And it all boils down to the fear of loss.'

'I suppose it does. Do you mind telling me what this is about?'

'It started with Watson, thinking about him and that terrifying cat.' I outlined my thoughts. 'And then I started wondering. What did someone fear so much that it made them kill Carter?'

'That's rather astute of you, Dorothy, boiling down all the motives to fear. Because I can tell you what our Mr Norquist is afraid of.'

'That someone will discover he's an ineffectual idiot?'

Alan shook his head. 'I think that's too well known to represent a threat. In fact, even he knows it, poor man. Do you know, Dorothy, I feel positively sorry for him. He knows his inadequacies, and that's why his overpowering fear is—'

'That he'll lose his job?'

'Worse. He'll lose his treasure.'

'You lost me. Treasure? You're surely not talking about the mythical Viking gold!'

'No. His treasure is very real, and far older than the time of the Vikings.' When I still looked blank, Alan said, 'The artefacts, my dear. The glory of Ancient Orkney. Pots, axes, building stones, the lot.'

'But that's . . . oh. He thinks of it as his.'

'And cherishes it to his bosom. You should have seen him, Dorothy. He was crooning over a rather ordinary pot like a mother over her firstborn. Truly, it was more than a bit odd, almost as if the thing were alive. I wonder if he's quite all there, to tell you the truth. But one thing I know for certain. If he'd believed Carter even thought about selling any of the artefacts from High Sanday, he would have fought to protect them.'

I took a deep breath. 'And where was he last night?'

'Unfortunately, just as I had worked up to that question some people came into the museum needing his attention. It's virtually a one-man operation, except for some volunteers, and none of them were about. I could hardly press him further.'

'Of course. It's frustrating to have no authority, isn't it? But speaking of authority, who has it in Norquist's case? I mean, he's afraid he'll be fired. Who would do the firing?'

'That I did manage to find out. The museum is run by a board of trustees, but the chairman of the board is also the president of Friends of Ancient Orkney.'

'Larsen. The third person who benefits from Carter's will, at least in a way. This is getting to be a neat little circle. And what do you want to bet all three of them will protect each other, thereby protecting themselves.'

'We don't know them well enough to make that kind of judgement, Dorothy.'

I glanced out the window. 'Well, we're about to get to know one of them better. Fairweather's just outside the door, looking for a parking place. Quick, you go out and tell him he can park in front of our garage door, while I set out the nuts and biscuits.'

Parking is at a premium along our part of the harbour road. There's a huge car park for the ferry, and it hadn't seemed to be very full most of the time, since we'd been there, anyway, but it's reserved for ferry patrons and I didn't want a guest of ours, and an Englishman at that, to risk a clamped wheel. Besides, I hoped our friendly offer of a space for his car would soften him up.

Alan kept him talking outside for a minute or two, long enough for me to let Watson in and get at least minimally organized, and they were laughing amiably when they came in, which seemed a good sign.

'Mr Fairweather, welcome!' I said after Watson had expressed his greetings, volubly and with much tail wagging. 'I'm so glad you could come. There are nibbles in the sitting room upstairs; what would you like to drink?'

When we'd dealt with that, and I'd poured some very nice sherry into three juice glasses, Alan carried the tray upstairs for me, and we settled down in the squashy furniture for what might prove to be some rather awkward conversation.

I never was much good at small talk. As a teenager I used to suffer agonies at parties, unable to chatter with people I didn't know, and it didn't get much better when I grew up. When I'm with friends, the trouble is getting me to shut up, but I'm not at my best with strangers.

So I raised my glass in a silent toast and started my bright, merry remarks with an apology. 'I'm sorry about the glasses. It was pretty much a choice between these and water tumblers that hold about a pint.'

Fairweather, to my relief, smiled. 'Ah, the joys of the holiday accommodation. My wife and I stayed once in a lovely little cottage in Cornwall. We were impressed with how spotless the electric cooker was, until we discovered that there were no cooking utensils to be found, positively not a single pot or pan in the place. We survived for a week on Chinese and Indian take-away and soup heated in the microwave. There were lovely sherry glasses, though!'

Well, of course we all laughed at that, and the ice was broken. 'Speaking of pots,' I said in what I hope wasn't too obvious a transition, 'I couldn't believe the beauty of the ones you've found up at High Sanday. Some of them were almost intact, and that's incredible after – what – four thousand years?'

'Something like that, perhaps closer to five. We're a long way from being able to assign accurate dates even to the structures, much less the artefacts. But it seems apparent that no one lived at the site after about 1500 BC, which was roughly the beginning of the Bronze Age, so four thousand years, give or take, is a reasonable guess.'

I was caught up in the awe again. 'Four thousand years! Think of it! Hundreds of generations ago families lived right here, in houses, and cooked in pots and slept in beds and tended their animals and probably drank something fermented, just like us. I was never much interested in archaeology until I came to Orkney, but now it's got a grip on me. I can understand how someone like you can spend his whole life literally digging into the past.'

'It's a pity,' said Alan, topping up Fairweather's glass, 'that you'll have to shut down the dig for a while.'

'We'd not have been able to get much done in yesterday's rain in any case,' Fairweather said with a sigh. 'Today would have been a good day to work, but alas! With Andersen safely in the nick, though, we're hoping we can get started again soon. Summer doesn't last forever, and even aside from weather considerations, most of our crew are students, and once university takes up again, they'll be gone.'

'You think Mr Andersen did it?' I asked oh, so casually.

But not casually enough. Fairweather stiffened and put his glass down. 'That seems to be the general opinion.'

'How do you think it happened, then?' asked Alan. 'I can't imagine what would have taken Carter to the island in the middle of the night. It's not the easiest journey, and there'd have been nothing to see in the dark.'

'None of us have been able to work that out,' Fairweather admitted. 'He was a strong-willed man, and when he took a notion to do something, he'd do it, no matter who or what stood in the way. But he was also a man who liked his comforts. I'd have expected him to go straight back to his expensive room at the Ayre Hotel after the meeting broke up.'

'Ah, yes, when did the meeting end? Dorothy and I left rather early.'

'Andrew pulled you away, didn't he?' Fairweather unbent a trifle and picked up his sherry again. 'Not a great fan of Carter's, our Andrew.' He took a sip.

'We gathered that,' I said primly. 'In fact, was anyone a great friend of Carter's? No one seemed to have a good word to say for him, except on the score of his generosity.'

Fairweather sighed. 'He was no worse, and no better, than any other very rich man. He knew what he wanted and he had the money to get it, whether it was things or influence. It's no secret that not everyone approved of his goals for High Sanday.'

'Would he really have insisted that you dig down as far as you could find anything interesting, no matter how much you destroyed on the way?'

'It's a vexed question, Mrs Martin.'

'Dorothy, please.'

Fairweather nodded in acknowledgement. 'The best archaeologists in the world can't agree on proper procedure in a case like this, which is not as rare as one might think. When a site is a good place for building a city, or even a village, it's easy to understand how successive generations might go on building there, especially when early settlements are destroyed by earthquake or fire or storm or warfare or simply the passage of time. Hence the Troy phenomenon. It's natural to want to know what's at the very bottom of the heap. It's also natural to want to preserve what's on top. There's no good way to do both, except by a kind of terraced dig, and that's possible only when a site is very large.'

'Like High Sanday.'

'Exactly. But there, little matters like the water table create other complications. How far down can we, in fact, dig before hitting water?'

'But surely, if people lived there—' I began, at the same time that Alan said, 'I suppose sea levels have changed over the millennia.'

'Exactly. We think it has risen a good deal, in fact. Studies haven't been completed, but we're reasonably certain that there were far fewer but bigger islands in the Neolithic period, before the sea rose and covered most of the lower land. So there may well be villages, indeed whole civilisations buried far under water.'

'Atlantis!' I said, going all dreamy again. 'Do you suppose there are drowned bells—'

'Since these villages would have existed millennia before there were Christian churches with bells, it's doubtful.' Alan's chill voice of reason shattered my sentimental vision. 'Getting back to Carter and his dreams of glory, how far would he have gone? Would he have pulled his money out of the project if you and the others overruled him?'

'He threatened to do just that after the meeting, when nearly everyone had left. Norquist and Larsen and I were tidying up, putting away our gear and so on, and Carter delivered a harangue to the effect that as he was paying the piper, he intended to call the tune, and if we wouldn't dance to that tune, he'd pull out. Then he stormed out, and . . . and that was the last time any of us saw him.'

'I wish I could be sure of that,' said Alan, and his voice was hard.

'Now, look here!' Fairweather put his glass down with a thump and heaved himself free of the grip of the sofa. 'I'm not sure I like your tone.'

'Oh, for heaven's sake, sit down and finish your drink,' said Alan. 'You agreed with Andrew that I could be of help with this mess, Fairweather. That gives me the right, indeed the responsibility, to speculate and to ask questions. Let's stop the pussyfooting. The police may be satisfied that Duncan Andersen killed Carter. I am not. I can think of no reason why Carter would have been out on that dig in the small hours of the morning. I think he was killed elsewhere and taken to High Sanday in the hopes that his murder would be viewed as an accident, or, failing that, would be laid at Andersen's door. It's perfectly obvious that the Ancient Orkney triumvirate would have had powerful reasons to see the man dead. So I'd like to know all of your movements on Monday night.'

'You're forgetting one thing, Mr Nesbitt.' Fairweather was still standing, looming over us. 'The triumvirate, as you are pleased to call us, stood to lose everything, rather than to gain by Carter's death. Without his funding the dig could not have continued.'

'And with his funding,' Alan said grimly, 'the dig could have continued only under his terms. So the important question at the moment is, who knew the terms of his will?'

There was a long pause. Fairweather sat back down, or rather collapsed into the sofa. 'Well,' he said at last, 'I did.'

TEN

Alan simply waited. As for me, I couldn't have said a word at that moment.

When Fairweather went on, he looked and sounded defeated. 'You see, my solicitor knows Carter's. Carter's is American, of course, a member of a big New York firm, and mine's in London, but they met at some conference or something. I don't remember the details. At any rate, Thompson, that's my man, found out the gist of the matter one night when they were drinking, and he told me, oh, weeks later. We were having a few, and I'd been complaining about Carter, and he hinted that I'd better be more discreet about what I said. So of course I asked why, and he told me why I'd . . . I'd be the prime suspect if the wretched man died suddenly.'

That was when I took myself off to start the rice cooking. I'd had too much information thrown at me, and I needed to process it.

So Carter, such a difficult, demanding patron, had been worth more to High Sanday dead than alive, and the director of the dig knew it. That was a serious lapse of confidentiality on the part of two lawyers who should have known better, but alcohol had probably lubricated both the unwise conversations. At any rate, Fairweather had known.

And who else? Whom had he told? On the night of the meeting, when everyone was thoroughly fed up with Carter, had Fairweather told the others he was tempted to bash the man on the head? Or said he hoped his car ended up in a loch? Or something of the kind?

It would have been a natural enough kind of thing to say. We've all uttered, or thought, such sentiments about people we couldn't stand. Reprehensible, no doubt, but there it is. Not one in a thousand of us, in ten thousand, would dream of acting on our thoughts. But what if . . .?

Alan was probably asking him that very thing right now. Who

else knew? If he was smart, he'd say that lots of people knew, the triumvirate and others. That would share the suspicion and perhaps divert it from him. On the other hand, if the people he named then denied that they had known any such thing . . .

I gave up and set the table, using Andrew's lovely wine goblets to make up for the utilitarian china. I had started the ball rolling with this probably ill-fated invitation. Let Alan take it from here. I wished I had chosen a less incendiary entrée than curry.

By the time the rice was done, however, and I called the men to the table, Alan had somehow managed to bring the conversation back to a normal level of civility. He gave me a look, as we all sat down, which I interpreted to mean 'leave it alone for now'. I was quite ready to do that in any case, so our table talk centred on the weather, always a safe topic in the unpredictable British Isles, and everyone's health, particularly mine. Henry Higgins would have been delighted.

I was hoping that Fairweather would take himself off when we had finished our meal. I was tired and longing for my bed and besides I wanted to hear what Alan had gleaned after I left the room. But Alan brandished the bottle of Highland Park and suggested after-dinner drinks. That suggested that civility did indeed reign, and also that Alan wanted to get rid of me. He knows I don't care for Scotch, and didn't offer me the bourbon. I can take a hint. I waved them upstairs. 'I'm going to finish up here and then go and deal with my cold. You two carry on.'

So it was morning before I got a chance to find out what Alan had learned. We ate our breakfast quietly, neither being chatty first thing in the morning, but when we reached our second cups of coffee, Alan tented his fingers in his familiar lecturing style and began.

'Fairweather claims he told no one about the will.'

'That's surprising! I was sure he'd say lots of people knew.'

'The fact that he didn't makes it the more likely that he's telling the truth. Of course Carter's attorney was grossly at fault for letting the cat out of the bag, but for whatever reason, he did it. It could be he didn't care any more for his client than anyone else did. However it happened, Fairweather at least was able to be discreet about it.'

'Maybe he was thinking ahead. If he *did* one day decide to

murder his impossible patron, he could then claim he knew nothing about the bequest. Or no, his lawyer would spill the beans.'

'Unless *he* decided to keep mum for the sake of his own professional reputation. For whatever reason, Fairweather says he didn't tell Larsen or Norquist. Particularly not Norquist, he says.'

'Why so particularly him?'

'My dear, you answered that question yourself when we talked about Norquist yesterday. The man is neither competent nor reliable. He is in fact a babbling brook. He's right, incidentally, about losing his job, poor chap. Fairweather let that slip last night.'

'Oh, dear. Well, at least he probably won't be convicted of murder. He's virtually dropped out of the running if he didn't know about the will, hasn't he?'

'Probably. Motive, as you know, is the least important factor in any investigation. He had the opportunity, as they all did.'

'Oh, yes, you were finding out what they all did after the meeting. Could I have some more coffee?'

Alan poured some for both of us and sat back down. 'Trying to find out, is more like it. No one can actually be accounted for definitively, but they do have alibis of a sort. When Carter had had his say and stormed out, Fairweather took Norquist to a pub for a drink. Norquist confirms that, incidentally.'

'Why would he have done a thing like that? I thought he didn't like Norquist.'

'He doesn't, particularly. He doesn't particularly dislike him, though. He said the man was extremely upset about Carter's pronouncements, and he felt sorry for him. Fairweather felt sorry for Norquist, that is. He said he bought him a drink or two, hoping to calm him down, but that Norquist had no head for drink and became maudlin instead.'

'Aha!' I said. 'That would explain Norquist's headache the next day.'

'Indeed. Fairweather thought the man had best not drive home, so he drove him home about midnight and put him to bed, then went home himself. Part of that can be checked, of course, with the publican. There's not much hope of checking when each of them reached home. Fairweather's temporary digs are in a cottage near Tingwall harbour, with no near neighbours.'

'And Norquist? I'll bet he lives with his ancient mother.'

Alan's chuckle was a bit rueful. 'You're close. He did in fact live with her until a year or two ago when she had to go into a care facility. Now he lives in a flat not far from the museum.'

'Alone.'

'Got it in one.'

'And of course either of them could have left again at any time during the night. What about Larsen?'

'Well, of course I haven't talked to him yet, but Fairweather assumes he went straight home after the meeting. He lives in Kirkwall near the college. He's a lecturer in archaeology and ancient history when he isn't busy running the Friends. And before you ask, he's divorced and lives alone.'

'You know,' I said, finishing my coffee, 'these things were easier in the Golden Age when everyone lived in big houses with relatives all over the place and servants so thick on the ground one tripped over them. Alibis meant something back then.'

'If you lived in an Agatha Christie novel, at least. Her view of the world was distinctly from the upper class side. But we're stuck here in modern-day Britain, and the sober fact is that none of those chaps has a really solid alibi.'

'So disappointing. It's always the one with the perfect alibi who ends up being the killer. What about means? If we discount – what was it, Andersen's pigsty?'

'Feeding trough therein. The theory is that there was a fight, and Carter fell against the trough. The trough hasn't yet been definitely identified as the murder weapon, but the general shape's about right. And if that is what killed him, it pretty well lets out anyone except Anderson, but it lets in the possibility of accident. If it isn't, then they're looking for something with a sharpish square edge, like a poker, only it would have to be fatter than they usually are. Something like a brick would do, although it wouldn't be easy to wield that edgewise.'

'A plank. An unabridged dictionary.'

'If a plank is long it's unwieldy. If it's short it's not heavy enough. As for a dictionary, same objection as the brick. Easy to throw, or drop on the head. Hard to get the leverage to strike with the edge.'

'Our killer might have got lucky with the throw. Let's see.' I looked around the room for inspiration. 'I know! Any of those things, squareish, heavy, inside a carry bag! You could swing it. The handles would give you the leverage.'

'Or one could use a suitcase, or a briefcase filled with papers. Does anyone carry a briefcase anymore?'

'They don't need them,' I said with a sigh of regret. 'And they used to be so elegant. I had a lovely leather one once, for carrying papers back and forth to school. Nowadays everything's either in a canvas carryall, or stored electronically on a gadget the size of a paperback novel. And those aren't heavy enough to damage anything much bigger than a mosquito. Even Fairweather wasn't carrying a briefcase the night of the meeting, as I recall, just a laptop for his presentation – and those aren't very heavy these days, either. Do you suppose the police are looking for any of those possible weapons?'

'No, because they have the ideal suspect in hand. They'll be waiting for the analysis of that blood on the trough. If it turns out not to be Carter's, then they'll start looking.'

'But by then it'll be too late! Our murderer will have cleaned the weapon, or thrown it into the sea, or buried it . . . Alan!'

He looked at me, his head on one side.

'Why are we inventing all sorts of ingenious murder weapons when the very best one is at hand, all over the place?'

Alan raised his eyebrows.

'The stones! Those flat building stones the Stone Age people used! Square edged, thin but not too thin, heavy enough to do the job, and available everywhere you turn. There must be thousands of them at High Sanday. Which, furthermore, is where Carter was found. Someone lured him there, killed him with one of the stones, and then arranged for a little wall to collapse and hide everything.'

'They're terribly heavy, Dorothy. Far too heavy for one person to lift.'

'The big ones are, but there are shards. I saw them myself, About the size of sheets of paper, except of course a lot thicker. Someone could pick up one of those with one hand, and in the dark . . .' I shivered.

'It's possible,' said Alan slowly. 'It's more than possible, actually. And it leaves all three of our favourite suspects with arguable opportunity and probable means, and one of them with a strong motive.'

'But the other two, unless they knew about the will, had strong – what you might call anti-motives. Is that a word? Anyway, it hardly matters at this stage, because we have no proof of anything. What do we do next?'

'I think what I have to do next is go and talk to Baikie, though I don't know how welcome I'll be. I know how much I appreciated it when police from other jurisdictions tried to interfere in one of my investigations.'

'And suppose I invite Mr Larsen over for a little talk. We learned a lot from Fairweather's visit. What's Fairweather's first name, by the way?'

'Robert. He made me free of it last night.'

'How jolly. When do you think you might be home? I don't think I want to entertain a possible murderer alone.'

'I'll be back by lunchtime, I expect. Why don't you see if he can come to tea? I can stop by that bakery and pick up some goodies so you don't have to fuss.'

'Good. I love to bake in my own kitchen, but not in somebody else's. I can manage scones, though, I think. I'll take Watson for a walk and pick up some jam and clotted cream, if they have it.'

'I can feel my arteries hardening at the very thought. Be careful of that cat!'

I didn't have to be told. After I'd phoned Mr Larsen and cajoled him into coming to tea, Watson and I took the long way to the co-op, taking the harbour road down to where it joined The Street and then backtracking. I had seen Roadkill only at the other end of the village, and hoped we'd be safe.

I tied Watson's leash to a bike rack outside the store, not without some trepidation, and told him to behave. I'd only be a few minutes, I told myself. He'd be fine for such a short time.

I found the clotted cream, somewhat to my surprise, and some very expensive strawberry jam. At that price it'd better be good. I also got a small chunk of stewing beef for Watson. He'd been so good I wanted to reward him.

That was a mistake. There was a hole in the plastic covering the package of meat, so of course Watson smelled it the moment

I got outside the store. So did a couple of other dogs, and one cat.

Roadkill.

I kept a tight hold of Watson's leash and backed into a doorway. He was growling low in his throat, and the cat was snarling and moving ever closer. I didn't know what to do. The meat was at the bottom of my bag. If I tried to get it out and throw it to the cat, Watson would probably lunge after it. If I didn't . . .

I backed more firmly up against the door, and nearly fell inside when it opened.

'Come in, quick, and bring your dog!'

I didn't need a second invitation, nor did Watson. He was trembling, though whether with fear or rage I didn't know. 'Thank you! If you hadn't opened that door I don't know what I'd have done. Really, that cat is a menace.' I stooped to pet Watson and reassure him. 'That is – I hope he isn't your cat?'

'I feed him. So does half the town, if it comes to that. He can be quite sweet, actually, but he's never been neutered, and other animals send him into a frenzy. There's a female in season living just across the street, and she's driving poor Sandy to distraction because they won't let her out. The next thing, if anyone can catch him, is a trip to the vet. I think that'll settle him down.'

I was still back at 'Sandy'. 'Is that his name?' I asked doubtfully. 'I've heard him called . . . other things.'

'I'm sure. He's not very popular up on The Street. Sandy's what I call him. Look, I'll give him some food, and that'll keep him busy long enough for you to get away. You'd better leave by the back way and go through the garden down to the road. I'll feed him at the front door.'

It worked well enough, but I was nervous all the way back to the flat, setting a pace that surprised me as much as it did Watson. Those titanium knees had a better turn of speed than I'd thought.

I told Alan about the encounter when he came home. 'Even animals operate out of fear,' I mused. 'Watson was afraid he was going to lose his treat; Roadkill was afraid he wasn't going to get it; everyone, including me, was afraid they were going to get hurt. It's a powerful stimulus.' I got out the materials for a salad. 'What did you learn from Baikie? Or did he clam up?'

'I didn't talk to him.' Alan sighed. 'A sizable spanner has been thrown into the works, love. There's been a terrorist threat to the oil terminal on Flotta, and it's all hands to the pump. I'm afraid no one has much time to spare for a possibly accidental death of one American.'

ELEVEN

I sat down, stunned. 'Where's Flotta?' I asked finally.

'South of Kirkwall, more or less in the middle of Scapa Flow.'

I shook my head. I didn't have the geography well enough in my head for that to mean much. 'How far from here?'

'I'd have to look it up, but probably not more than fifteen miles or so.'

'Oh, dear.' As inadequate remarks went, that was a prize-winner, but I was still trying to process the unwelcome news. 'Um . . . what might happen if . . .?'

'I gather there are bomb threats. If a bomb were to go off at a place where a great deal of oil is stored, it could be quite serious.'

I giggled nervously. 'Yes, I'd say so. Are there many people on the island?'

'I don't know, love, but I did read a while ago that a new facility of some sort is being built. That presumably means a fair number of construction workers on site, as well as the regular employees.'

'Well, then. How serious . . . do they think . . . what are the odds of something terrible happening?'

'I've no idea. But they have to take this sort of thing very seriously indeed.'

'Of course they do.' I pulled myself together. 'There aren't a lot of policemen – er – police personnel in Orkney anyway, are there?'

'Enough, in ordinary circumstances. But no, not a great many.'

'So. But they won't just forget about Carter's death, will they?'

Alan smiled. 'We never "forget about" a major crime. But investigation sometimes has to be deferred, and this is one of those times. Add the current crisis to the possibility that we might be dealing with an accidental death rather than murder, and you see the situation. However –' he held up a hand to forestall my comment – 'Baikie has, in effect, given me permission to do what I can – what we can – on our own. He left this note for me.' He handed me a piece of paper with a hasty scrawl on it.

I handed it back. 'Read it to me. I have a hard enough time deciphering the handwriting in this part of the world when it's done carefully.'

'"Must rush off. Blood on trough not Carter's. Andersen released. Follow up if you wish. Will try to stay in touch." And it's signed with something that might be a B, if one uses one's imagination.'

'Well, I call that a handsome offer! And we were right. He didn't do it.'

'Well, he's not quite in the clear. There's still the watch to hold against him. But in his favour, the publican where he did his drinking on the night in question says he was barely able to walk when he left the pub, and it was a miracle he ever got home. And you needn't sound so jubilant about it. If he didn't kill Carter, it almost certainly means someone we like a lot better did.'

'Yes, I hadn't forgotten that. I wish you could have talked to him about Fairweather's motive.'

'I left him a note. I think he'll like it, once he has a moment to consider the matter. Money is a good solid incentive to murder, much better, one might think, than the fear of losing one's property, especially such rundown and unproductive property as Andersen's. And Fairweather is English. Yes, he's respectable, and yes, he's brought business and tourists to Orkney, but he's a foreigner. That makes him almost as desirable a villain as poor old Andersen.'

'Well, it's a pity, either way. I didn't care for Carter, at least the brief glimpse I had of him, but murder is the ultimate crime, the ultimate failure of civilisation. Murder of even the most despicable person is unspeakable, and Carter wasn't that, by a long shot. That miserable Roadkill is more of a menace to society than Carter, and I don't wish even him dead.'

Alan looked startled for a moment and then smiled. 'Sorry, love, I didn't hear the upper-case R at first. I agree about the menace, but I'm not sure the triumvirate would rank the cat lower on the scale than the capitalist. And speaking of the triumvirate, I hope Larsen is coming to tea, because now that I more or less have free rein, I'm eager to speak with him. Not to mention the fact that I bought enough carbohydrates to send us into sugar shock if we eat them all ourselves.'

'He is. I had a bit of trouble convincing him, because he's busy with some project at the university, but he succumbed to my famous charm. And I'm making scones and a few sandwiches to contribute to the feast. That's why we're having a salad for lunch.'

Alan took Watson for his afternoon walk, feeling a bit more capable than I of dealing with Roadkill, if necessary, while I fretted over what to say to Larsen. He wasn't nearly as good a suspect as Fairweather, but I still wasn't sure how to approach any questions about the murder. Ah, well, I had a good many questions about the dig, and archaeology in general, and doubtless Alan would help with the rest.

The scones turned out better than I'd dared hope, and Larsen arrived punctually at four, looking far more like a professor than a working archaeologist. He was both clean and tidy, and had gone so far as to put on a tie.

'This is very kind of you, Mrs Nesbitt.'

'Martin,' I correctly automatically. 'I kept my own name when Alan and I married. But I wish you'd call me Dorothy. Surnames are awfully formal. And we're having our tea comfortably at the table, even if the sitting room is more proper. I hate balancing plates on my lap and dropping things on the floor.'

'And Watson doesn't need the goodies that he'd snap up before they even hit the floor,' said Alan. He extended his hand. 'It's a pleasure to see you under less stressful circumstances, and conditions, than the last time.'

'This is certainly more pleasant, in every sense. The dig is a marvellous place to be when the weather is good. When it isn't, the wind and rain can scour off one's skin. And of course . . . but we shouldn't talk of the recent tragic events, I suppose.'

'Not until we've had our tea, at any rate.' I hoisted the teapot. 'Milk, Mr Larsen? Sugar?'

'Neither, thank you, and it's Jim. I prefer informality, too.'

'Good. Then please help yourself to anything you like, and

then tell me about High Sanday. How was it discovered, for a start?'

In between bites of sandwiches and scones and little pastries, Larsen complied. 'It was found in the usual way. Nothing dramatic like the storm that uncovered Skara Brae. A farmer was ploughing a field, and the plough ran into something so unyielding that it broke the ploughshare. The farmer wasn't best pleased, of course, and when he got down to examine the damage, he saw the stones just under the surface.'

'I've been wondering how often that happens, and the farmer ignores the whole thing and goes on about his business. Surely no one wants his land overrun by archaeologists. Look at Mr Andersen.'

Larsen uttered what would have been a guffaw if he hadn't been so polite. 'Andersen doesn't really give a fig about his land. He's bone lazy. He's let that farm ruin itself for lack of mainten-ance. He's just interested in screwing as much cash out of the Friends as he possibly can. That's why it surprised us so much when he was arrested for killing Carter. One, he was too drunk that night to kill a fly, and two, with Carter gone he didn't have a prayer of getting any money at all.'

'But now he does,' said Alan quietly.

'I grant you that.' Larsen finished spreading jam and clotted cream on a scone and took a bite. 'These are heaven, Mrs – Dorothy. Yes, Alan, Carter will get his due now. No more than that. Or perhaps a bit more, just because he's such a nuisance. But he couldn't have known that before Carter died. No one had the least idea the man was going to leave us all that money.'

I swallowed the last of a smoked salmon sandwich and was careful not to look at Alan, who took up the questioning. 'So you don't think Andersen is our killer?'

'The police thought so, to begin with, didn't they? But now I hear they've let him go, so they must have doubts. Sensible of them. The man's a lout, but I think he's more bark than bite.'

'Do you have any ideas about what happened, then?'

'It certainly looked like an accident, didn't it? Carter took a fall in the dark, hit a wall, it caved in on him. But there are problems with that scenario, too. What was he doing there at dead of night?'

'I'd wondered that, too,' I put in. 'Surely he couldn't have expected to see or do anything in the pitch dark.'

'Well, of course it was never quite pitch dark, was it? That was the night of the solstice, and it was a lovely clear night. There were a few hours of twilight, that's all.'

'Oh, yes. Remember, Alan? We took Watson out when it was nearly eleven, and we could see perfectly well.'

'Ye-es.' Alan sounded doubtful. 'But they think Carter died around two. That would be the darkest part of the night, surely. Was there a moon?'

'Not much of one,' I said eagerly. 'I remember seeing that it was just a sliver.'

'Well then, I still maintain it would have been too dark to see anything meaningful at High Sanday, and I don't understand what the man was doing there.' Alan ran a hand down the back of his neck.

'He had a boat, didn't he?' I asked.

'Oh, lord, yes. A huge, luxurious cabin cruiser with a galley and bar and God knows what. Named *Vanderbilt*, after the American tycoon. Carter used to boast that she could sleep six. "Eight, if they're good friends," he'd add. Nudge, nudge, wink, wink.' Larsen finished his tea. 'I'm sorry, but he was an odious man. I can't feel much grief at his passing.'

'But back to the boat, Jim. Oh, yes, I'll have some too, love.' Alan handed me his cup as I refilled Larsen's. 'I don't remember seeing anything that big when we all converged on the island after Carter's death.'

'No. She wasn't there. I told that police inspector, and I suppose they're looking for her. She isn't berthed at Kirkwall, either, because I looked. You can't miss her, really.'

'Goodness! That's important! I hope the police find it – her. There might be some important evidence on board. Did he have a driver – er, pilot?'

'No, he fancied himself as a boatman and carried no crew. Of course, when he gave a party he'd hire someone to cater, while he swaggered about in a yachting cap and blazer.'

'But no pilot who could have taken the boat away,' Alan mused. 'So how did he get to Papa Sanday?'

'Obviously someone else took him there,' I said. 'Someone

who owns a boat. At least, I wouldn't want to hire a boat if I were planning to kill someone, would you?'

'Never having planned to kill someone, I couldn't say.' Larsen was looking at me rather oddly. 'You must be – er – a reader of crime novels.'

'I am,' I admitted. 'The Golden Age, mostly. I do love Miss Marple and Lord Peter and the rest.' I shut my mouth firmly and smiled. Let Alan tell him there was a little more to my interest in crime. Or his, for that matter.

'And I,' Alan said with a grin, 'am a retired policeman. I thought I might as well tell you, since you'd probably find out anyway. You're good at digging, aren't you?'

'Passably. Also fairly good at a synthesis. Am I to conclude that you are investigating Carter's murder, and view me as a possible murderer?' He gestured at the tea things. 'Was this not quite the friendly, innocent invitation you would have had me believe?'

I chose to answer that. 'You're right, in part. We are investigating the crime, originally at Mr Fairweather's behest. He felt that a man with Alan's experience might have a few more ideas than the local police. My husband is too modest to tell you that he was a chief constable for some years. I don't know exactly what that's equivalent to in the Scottish ranks, but—'

'Never mind. I get the idea. But you said "we" are investigating?'

'I've assisted Alan from time to time, in a purely amateur capacity, so yes, it's "we". And as for the invitation, we wanted to get to know you better, and I for one have lots of questions about the dig. So do you think we could leave the subject of murder for a while? I'll brew another pot of tea, and we'll finish all these sinful things and just talk.'

The kitchen and dining area were really one, so I went on talking as I put the kettle on. 'The first thing I want to know is, how in the world do you determine the age of an artefact, or even its use? I mean, a piece of stone could be an axe head or a tool for working leather, or even just an oddly shaped stone. How do you know?'

'We don't, of course. Well, the age part is fairly easy, given carbon dating. Where in the dig something is found is also an indispensable indicator, it being a reasonable assumption that in most cases, the deeper we go, the earlier we go. So dating is more-or-less straightforward.

'The usage questions are much harder. We can't get back there into the heads of the people who made that tool, or, as you surmise, even be absolutely sure it was a tool at all. All we can do is make an educated guess. If we can see that the stone has certainly been worked, shaped by a human hand, then it's reasonable to assume that it had a use. Again, we can't go back there and ask, but when the only tool you have to work a stone is a harder piece of stone, you probably don't go to the trouble just to make it pretty. So that part's fairly easy. As for use, we make guesses the same way you would if you went into a shop and saw a tool you didn't know, with a head, two flat planes on that head, and a longish handle. You'd conclude it was a hammer or mallet of some sort, right?'

'And the label that said "Sledgehammer, four pounds ninety" would help, too.'

Both the men laughed at that. 'Well, your identification task would be a little easier than ours, I agree. Thank you,' added Larsen, as I poured his tea.

'I do take your point, though. Once my first husband and I – oh, years ago now – we walked into a hardware store that carried a lot of other stuff, kitchen gadgets and the like. I picked up something and asked him what he thought it was. Neither of us could imagine, and neither could two of the clerks we asked. Finally someone told us it was a ravioli cutter. Now, never having made ravioli in my life, I couldn't possibly have guessed. And I'll bet you have some of the same difficulties. As you say, you didn't live then. Surely many of their chores were quite different from ours. So how do you work out the puzzle when you come across something that would have no modern use?'

'That's where the education part comes in. We rely a lot on research done by other archaeologists. Of course their conclusions are based on educated guesses, too, so . . .' He spread his hands and we laughed. 'In all seriousness, though, it's a fascinating job, this business of identification, and I'm sure we don't always get it right. But . . .'

He trailed off. I cocked my head.

'I'm sure you'll think this next bit is pure make-believe, a children's fantasy,' he went on diffidently, 'but it's actually quite true, and any archaeologist will tell you, that sometimes we just . . . know. I'll pick up a tool and . . . oh, no, it sounds too absurd.'

'Not to me,' I said. 'You hold it in your hand, and you do go back. For a moment you're the man, or woman, who used that tool thousands of years ago. And you *know*.'

'It isn't something I often admit to a layman,' he said drily. 'And if you ask me about it in public I'll deny I ever said such a thing. How did you know what I was going to say?'

'Because I've felt it, too. Here in these islands one isn't quite living in the twenty-first century. The people who lived at Skara Brae and the ones who put up the standing stones, they're all still here, somehow. Not ghosts, I don't mean that exactly. I guess I don't know what I do mean, but I've felt the living presence of antiquity ever since I came here.' I looked around the very modern kitchen, with its electric stove and dishwasher and fridge, its spotless white cabinets and the sleek modern chairs we were sitting on. 'And if that doesn't make any sense, and I admit it doesn't, then at least I'm glad I'm in good company.'

'My wife,' said Alan blandly, 'is acutely tuned in to the universe.'

'Oh, for Pete's sake, Alan, that makes me sound like some New Age type, instead of a plain ordinary Anglican. Speaking of which, I don't suppose there's an Anglican church around here, is there, Jim? I think I remember that almost everyone in this neck of the woods is Presbyterian, am I right?'

'We call it Church of Scotland, but yes, most of us are what you Americans call Presbyterian or Calvinist. But there are at least two Episcopal churches – that's what it's known as here – one in Stromness and one in Kirkwall, though I don't suppose you'd want to go that far.' He gave us directions, and then stood. 'This has been delightful, but duty calls. I have to go and mark papers from one of my classes of dunderheads. Thank you for inviting me. If you're staying in Orkney for a few days, I'd like to show you over the dig, when the police let us have it back.'

We made vague promises to the vague invitation, Jim slipped Watson the last sandwich, and we closed the door behind him.

TWELVE

'Well,' said Alan. 'Productive? Or not?'

'We didn't learn a lot about Carter's murder, did we?'

'Except the bit about the boat. That's very interesting. It's almost certain that Baikie knows about her, but of course he's not going to be able to do anything about a search, at least for the present. I noticed you didn't mention that we're the principal investigators for the nonce.'

'No. They'll probably figure it out soon enough, but meanwhile it's useful to be a little less visible. Unfortunately we don't have the resources to go scouring the islands for the *Vanderbilt*.'

'No, and even if we did, there are such a lot of islands, and some of them have sea caves where a boat could be hidden with ease. And of course the easiest way to hide a boat—'

'—is to scuttle it,' I finished, nodding. 'But I can't work out why someone would hide this one. Seems like it would be less conspicuous just to leave her wherever Carter usually berthed her.'

'But if Carter's murderer went to Papa Sanday in the *Vanderbilt*, with Carter, and then came back after he'd done the deed, he might be afraid he'd left damning evidence behind. In fact, he probably would have. Hair, fibres from his clothing, even fingerprints if he was really careless. My guess is that they won't find the boat, because by now she's at the bottom of the sea.'

'But Alan! It's not that easy to scuttle a boat, not out in deep water, unless you have some way to get away safely. And I don't know about you, but I wouldn't want to try to swim in these waters. They're deep and they're bitterly cold, and I'll bet there are currents.'

'The *Vanderbilt* probably had a dinghy. Anyone who knew how to pilot a boat that size would know how to launch a dinghy.'

'Maybe, but I'm still not convinced. I think as soon as they have time to search, they'll find the *Vanderbilt* someplace, and when they do, they'll be able to nab the murderer.'

'If this fine theory I've spun will hold water.' Alan began to clear the table. 'I hope you haven't planned anything for dinner. I couldn't eat a thing.'

'There's leftover curry, if you change your mind. We may not have learned a lot about the murder, though I do think the boat business is important, but we learned a lot about Larsen, don't you think?'

'For a stolid Calvinist, he certainly has a turn of fancy. Was that bit about your feelings of . . . er . . . empathy with the ancients genuine, or were you just trying to get his reactions?'

'Oh, no, it's entirely genuine. I hadn't mentioned it to you because I knew you'd think I'd gone off my rocker, but it's real. You know I've always believed in atmosphere, and been sensitive to it, and there's an atmosphere in Orkney that's almost tangible. It isn't spooky, or at least I don't find it so. For me, it's just the conviction that those ancient people never really left, that they're still here somehow. I can't get closer to it than that, but I have to admit I can sympathize with poor old Norquist in his love for the antiquities. To hold in one's hand a pitcher that a woman used for water four or five thousand years ago is to confirm a connection with her and her way of life. It will be really sad if he loses his job and they hire someone efficient who treats the artefacts like numbers in a catalogue. Here, you dry.'

We ended up finishing the curry for supper, after all, and turned on the gas logs in the sitting room fireplace while we sat and read and talked. It had turned very chilly indeed, and the warmth was welcome, although the fire itself was a poor substitute for a real wood fire. Tidier, yes. Safer, undoubtedly. But I wanted the scent, and the crackle, of wood, and the lovely glowing embers as the fire died. 'I like real things,' I commented, and Alan nodded with full understanding.

We went to bed early. I still had the remnants of my cold and thought rest was a good idea. Once I was settled, though, nice and warm and cosy, next to Alan's comforting presence, I couldn't seem to get to sleep.

What *was* the source of the feelings of awe I'd experienced ever since I saw the first standing stones? Was awe even the right word? Was there a word in the language to describe those sensations?

I think of myself as a sensible, down-to-earth woman, not prone to hearing things going bump in the night. My religion is middle-of-the-road Christianity. I'm not a mystic, but neither do I pooh-pooh the Biblical miracles. Not all events have a practical, scientific explanation. I have a tendency to believe in ghosts, at least in the medieval churches and homes of England. But I think spiritualism is a gigantic scam, and I've never gone in for astrology or palmistry or the Tarot. In fact, psychically speaking, I'm dead boring.

And yet here I was mooning on about atmospheres and other-worldly, or at least other-timely, presences. Was I going off my nut? Alan thought Norquist was at least part-way round the bend. Was it catching?

I turned over and scrunched myself deeper into the pillow to try to shut out the voice that was saying, quite firmly, *But they're real, those feelings. There truly is something uncanny about this place.*

I liked real things, I'd told Alan, and it was true. Real fires and real flowers and good, honest, real food, not something out of packages with twenty unpronounceable additives. The sky here was real. The sea was undeniably real, and sometimes dangerous. The sheep and cattle were real. Duncan Andersen was certainly all too real. You could smell him coming.

But, the standing stones were real, too. They had really stood there for millennia. The other monuments I hadn't seen yet were real, like the Ring of Brodgar. Alan had told me about that and I'd seen pictures. A henge far bigger than Stonehenge, and far older, it had been built by those people who lived in Skara Brae, or High Sanday, or the other ancient dwellings dotted all over Orkney. For what purpose? Why had those people gone to great trouble to shape those huge, thin stones and stand them up so securely that many of them stood to this day? An astronomical calendar? A place for religious celebrations? A place, possibly, for sacrifices? Even human ones?

Probably not. Probably not. I thought I remembered reading that the idea of human sacrifices at Stonehenge had been pretty well discounted by the experts. Sacrifice possibly, but of birds or other animals, most likely.

But suppose the experts were wrong? Could it be that the

spirits of men and women who had died in agony were crying out for pity, or for revenge? Was that what I was feeling?

The door to the bedroom creaked a little, and my heart was in my mouth before I realized that Watson had found it insecurely latched, and had decided our bed would be the best place to sleep. He gave a joyous spring and landed squarely on my stomach.

So much for thoughts of hobgoblins. Watson was unmistakably real, and very solid. I gave him an ineffectual shove, sighed, and moved into the small space left to me.

I slept.

In the morning I remembered enough of my late-night musings to ask Alan, 'Could we go see the Ring of Brodgar today? And maybe Skara Brae? I'd like to take a breather from murder, maybe clear my head.'

'Why not? It's a fine day, even warm. And the two sites are quite close together. How are you feeling?'

'I think I'm well. And what do you mean by warm?' I've learned that weather terms have entirely different meanings to the Brits.

'Warm. Ten, at least.'

'*Ten!*' I yelped. 'Oh, Celsius. Right. That's about fifty Fahrenheit. Fifty, my dearly beloved Englishman, is not warm for late June.'

'It is for Orkney, my pampered Yank. Put on your snowsuit, and we'll be off.'

It was, in fact, quite nice in the sun. I thought I might be almost too warm later, but I had no intention of saying so.

The hills were beautiful in the sunshine, and the grazing animals looked sleek and contented. 'Quite a contrast to Papa Sanday,' I commented.

'Yes, this is rich land and supports the livestock generously. Orkney is famous for its beef. There are fields of barley, too.'

'Which goes straight to the distillery, right?'

'Right. Now, just coming up round this next bend, if I remember correctly . . . there!'

I despair at even trying to describe the Ring. Don't think Stonehenge. Those stones are massive, and rough, either because they were terribly hard to shape or because the weather hasn't been kind to them over the years. Many of them have lintels, making pairs of stones into doorways. Stonehenge is undeniably impressive – but this!

There are no lintels at the Ring. The stone, I learned later from the guidebook, fractures naturally into slender slabs with parallel sides and a consistent angle at the ends, so it would have been possible to flatten them for lintels only with incredible effort. The ancient builders chose not to do that, but left them in their natural state, pointing, it seems, to the sky.

Twenty-seven stones stand alone, aloof, in a circle over three hundred feet in diameter. They are widely spaced, so the sky forms as much a part of the Ring as the stones. Thirty or so more used to be there, so the circle would have been more complete when it was new, but it's hard to imagine that it could have had more dignity, more sheer impact.

There it stands on its hill, silhouetted against the sky, a monument to . . . to what?

'It was a temple,' I said in a whisper. Somehow I felt compelled to whisper.

'That's one theory, at least.' Alan was speaking quietly, too. So were the other tourists.

'It's more than a theory. It *was* a temple. It still is.'

'You "just know"?'

'Yes.' I made no attempt to explain, or defend myself. I did know, beyond doubt. This had been a place of worship, and the spirits, or the gods, or the echoes of the worship, were still here.

At some point we had left the car. I didn't remember getting out, but there we were, standing on the hill, the wind soughing through the Ring. I took Alan's arm.

'All right, love?'

'Just a little lightheaded. Who wouldn't be?'

He looked at me with concern.

'Alan, I'm fine,' I said with some impatience. 'Just overwhelmed by this place. You didn't *tell* me it was like this!'

'It's a bit like what you always say about the Grand Canyon, love. One can't describe it in any meaningful way. Even pictures don't convey the magnificence. A person must experience it to understand.'

I nodded. I didn't want to talk. I wanted to walk, and look, and listen to the wind moaning among the stones, and let the centuries seep into me.

We walked around together, Alan now and then consulting the guide book he'd bought somewhere and quoting something from it. I wished he wouldn't. I love my husband dearly, but I wanted him to shut up and let me just be. After a while, and another worried glance or two, he saw that I wasn't paying attention and was silent.

Suddenly, though, I wanted information. 'Alan,' I said urgently, 'did they ever make sacrifices here?'

'I don't think so.' He leafed through the booklet. 'It says quite definitely that there was never human sacrifice, but it doesn't mention animal sacrifices, either yea or nay. The gist of it is, I suppose, that they don't really know. It's like so much else. They have to rely on educated guesswork. Why? You aren't . . . er . . . getting any strange vibes, are you?'

'No terrifying ones, at any rate. But sacrifices to the gods are such an important part of most ancient religions, I wondered. Even the ancient Hebrews. Abraham thought he was going to have to sacrifice his son.'

'But it didn't turn out that way.'

'No. There was the ram in the thicket. But the ram died, didn't he? Oh, I *wish* we could know what these people believed, what rites they practised! I'd like to be able to imagine this place in use as it was meant to be used. It would be strange, even perhaps repugnant, but I'd like to know.'

'I think it's a good thing that tomorrow is Sunday. We can go practice our own rites, and exorcise the demons.'

A crowd of tourists arrived, with some noisy children who seemed not to feel the atmosphere of the place. The spell was broken. I smiled at Alan. 'Let's go see Skara Brae.'

The ancient village is just a few miles down the road from the Ring. We had to enter through a visitors' centre and pay for tickets, which seemed a little odd until I considered how much it must cost to keep these places in repair. Medieval cathedrals cost hundreds of thousands of pounds every year to keep up. How much more so a set of structures dating from around 3000 BC?

Walking up to the village, I was captivated by a series of stone markers comprising a timeline. 'Look at this, Alan! "Skara Brae, 3100 BC. Pyramids of Giza, 2500 BC. Stonehenge 2100 BC." This place is a thousand years older than Stonehenge!'

Behind me, a dry, petulant voice interrupted. 'They're wrong about that date, you know.'

I turned around to see the last man I expected, or wanted, just then. I smiled, of course, and nodded. 'Mr Norquist. How nice.'

'They've got that date wrong,' he persisted. 'I've told them and told them, but they won't change it. They're at least a hundred years off.'

I feigned interest. 'Is that right? Well, I don't suppose it makes a lot of difference when you're dealing with thousands of years.'

Norquist bristled. 'It makes a difference to *Them*!' He pointed in the direction of the village ahead. 'Five or six generations! Would you want your family history distorted that badly?'

'Well, no, I guess I wouldn't.' I exchanged glances with Alan, whose raised eyebrows and rolled eyes conveyed: *See what I mean? Humour the man.* 'But you see, it must have cost a lot to have these stones carved. I imagine they can't afford to change them.'

'They can afford it now! The Friends could pay for it. I intend to keep on making myself heard until they do something about it. We mustn't offend *Them*. Excuse me.'

He bustled off, back toward the visitors' centre.

Alan and I looked at each other. 'He really is just a little—' I said.

'More than a little, I'd say. Dorothy, I hope . . .'

I laughed. 'Don't worry, love! I don't believe they're still here, or not that way. Their influence, yes. But I don't see them hovering in wrath and casting a spell on us because we got a date wrong. And how does he think he knows, anyway? A hundred years is nothing in archaeological time!'

Alan shrugged. 'The man's a fanatic. He would probably say one of *Them* told him.' Alan pronounced it with a definite capital letter. 'Come on, let's see the village.'

The vibes, as Alan called them, were much different here. This had been a place of everyday life. I was enchanted with the houses. They had been built mostly below ground, their stone walls acting as retaining walls for the earth on the outside. The roofs were all gone; they had probably been shored up by scarce timbers that had rotted away centuries before. But we could look down into the dwellings and see the box beds the occupants had built out of the thin stones. There were structures that looked very much like the 'dressers', as they call them on this side of the pond, the hutches in one's kitchen that hold tableware. And, reading the guidebook, I found to my delight that the ancient people apparently used them for just that purpose, for potsherds had been found with them.

There were eight houses in the village. Most had a central hearth; probably each roof had had a hole for the smoke. And some had tiny rooms off the main room, little rooms with, improbably, drains.

'Alan!' I said, in great amusement. 'They had indoor plumbing!'

'Not so stupid, those old folks,' murmured Alan.

I read further in the book. 'And they were farmers. They raised cattle and sheep, or maybe goats, and barley and maybe wheat.' I skipped over the details of how the archaeologists knew, or surmised, all that. 'I can see them, Alan. I can just see the women bringing their pitchers, and their children, to the well, if there was one, and gossiping with the other women, while the men were tending the livestock. Ordinary people, going quietly about their everyday lives. Maybe that's why I can feel their presence so strongly. They were just like us!'

We saw no more of Norquist, for which I was grateful. I had some sympathy with the little man when he wasn't around. When he was, I found him almost unbearably irritating. Still . . . 'Alan, I wonder what he's doing here at this time of day. Shouldn't he be at the museum guarding his treasures?'

'I wondered, too. Saturday is surely a busy day for visitors, and a beautiful summer Saturday . . . You don't suppose he's already been sacked?'

'Surely he wouldn't be going around acting so self-important if he had been. At any rate, I want to see the museum. Shall we go this afternoon, or would you rather not, since you've already been there?'

'But I spent most of my time talking to Norquist. I'm happy to go again. But lunch first. All this time-travel has given me a powerful appetite. And thirst. Let's find a pub.'

THIRTEEN

We hurried through our pub lunch, because we'd left Watson back at the flat, and he'd be feeling bereft, and more than ready to go out. I hoped we hadn't left it too long. Someone else's house . . . But he'd been good; he was frantic, though, so Alan slipped on his leash. 'I'll walk up to the museum, just to make sure it's open in Norquist's absence.'

He was back before I had a chance to rest my aching back. 'No luck, I'm afraid. It's locked up tight. Saturday hours are supposed to be ten to five, and there's no note on the door, nothing. Just a securely locked door and no lights on.'

'Then he has been fired, after all.'

'But you'd think someone would have posted a notice.'

'You would, wouldn't you? Alan, I think we have to check this out. It's probably of no importance, but it's a peculiar thing, and with a recent murder, peculiar things take on a certain significance.'

'Agreed. I'll phone Fairweather. Perhaps we could take a drive in to Kirkwall.'

We weren't thinking clearly, either of us. I listened to Alan's end of the conversation.

'Ah, yes, Alan Nesbitt here. My wife and I were thinking of driving to Kirkwall a little later, and hoped we could buy you a drink. Ah. Oh, yes, of course. That's good news, isn't it? Would we be frightfully in the way if . . .? Good. We may see you later, then.'

'He's back on the dig,' I surmised. 'We should have known.'

'And pleased as a dog with two tails, by the sound of his voice. Are you up for the trip over there? It'll take most of the rest of the day.'

I looked out the window. The sea, at least in our harbour, looked like a millpond. 'Sure. But you know, once they get the site fully excavated, someone's going to have to organize a regular

ferry service from Kirkwall or somewhere. They can expect lots
of tourists, but only if it's easy to get to.'

'They won't need to worry about that for some years yet, I
expect. Bring something warm, darling. You know how quickly
the weather can change.'

I also took a ginger capsule and tucked the packet into my
handbag. Alan phoned the boat rental place and was pleased to
get the same boat we'd used before. The drive to Tingwall seemed
shorter than before, and this time I had much more of an eye for
the landscape. 'It does have an austere beauty all its own, doesn't
it? But I still need trees.'

'We'll have to go over to Shapinsay one day, and you can
wander in the castle's wood. That should help.'

The sea was still calm for the trip to Papa Sanday, and when
we got there the landing place was calm, too, unlike the last
time. Watson wanted to come with us when we berthed.

'Surely he'd be all right on the lead,' I pleaded on his behalf.
'He hasn't been getting nearly enough exercise lately. We can
always tie him up somewhere if he gets to be a nuisance.'

So he scrambled with us to the top of the plateau, and I was
once again struck by the sheer extent of the excavations. 'Alan,
this is going to be five or six times the size of Skara Brae when
they've finished. It's mind-boggling.'

'It's all of that. Have you got a good hold on Watson? Then
let's go and find Fairweather.'

Workers were out in force on this glorious day. The rain of a
few days before had created mud everywhere, so everyone looked
alike: mud-coloured from head to foot. Alan spoke to the nearest
mud-person.

'The boss? Over there, I think, at structure fifteen. That's the
big one, down at the far end.' The creature, whose sex was inde-
terminate, was by accent American. It pointed vaguely with a
trowel, grinned, and went back to work. We slogged over to 'the
far end', trying without much success to stick to grassy areas.
'I'm going to have to throw these shoes away when we get back,'
I complained. 'And Watson will need a major bath.'

The dog looked at me, alarmed by the hated word, but decided
I didn't mean it and lolloped along happily.

It took us a little while to find Fairweather, mostly because

he looked exactly like all the other mud-people. Eventually we
identified him by his English accent as he called excitedly to the
other workers.

They came slipping over the muddy, uneven paths, and we joined
them.

'Fairweather, is that you behind the mud pack?'

'Nesbitt? I'll be gorgeous when it comes off, if the cosmetology
propaganda has any truth to it. But just have a look at this!'

He held up an object as covered in mud as everything else,
and the workers crowed over it. Some of them did, anyway. Some
of them seemed as mystified as I.

'Oh, I forgot how ignorant some of you lot are. It's a bone
knife, and I've never seen anything quite like it. When this is
cleaned up, you'll see it's decorated. See the striations here, and
here? If those are natural grain, I'll eat this thing, mud and all.
And the decorations make it a . . .' He paused and looked up at
the workers.

'A ceremonial knife!' a couple of them shouted.

'I'm betting on it! And that makes this site—'

'A temple!'

Fairweather roared with laughter. 'You're as easy to fool as I
am! One knife does not a temple make, and we won't really
know about the striations until we get it clean. But if I'm right,
this is a major find, chaps.'

'Hey!' said one of the workers.

'And chapesses. Sorry, Frieda. So –' turning to us – 'you
showed up at an auspicious moment. It isn't every day we find
something really splendid. Most of archaeology is hard, slogging
work for damn little reward. But when you come across something like that – wow!'

'Congratulations!' I said, and meant it. 'But, Mr . . . I mean,
Robert, you hinted that a ceremonial knife meant this was a
temple. I know you were joking, but why would it mean that?
And I'm actually not at all sure I want to know the answer, come
to think of it.'

'I think you already know the answer. Yes, there were
sacrifices.'

I swallowed hard. 'And what were the sacrificial victims?'

'Oh, infants, the odd vestal virgin.' He was watching my face.

'You don't believe me, do you? And you're quite right. It's the old guesswork problem again, but from what's been found, in Orkney and other places, sacrifices were either of small mammals like rabbits, or were purely symbolic with sheaves of wheat burned at whatever stood in for an altar. It was probably all very dramatic, with special rituals and all, but not particularly gruesome.'

'Whew! I was imagining something straight out of a B movie.'

'Well, I won't keep you. You'll want to look around. Watch how you go. The mud's made everything twice as treacherous.'

'Actually, we wanted to talk to you for a moment,' said Alan.

'Of course, if we can talk here. As you see, I'm literally knee-deep in work.'

'Oh, this isn't especially private. It's just that we wanted to see the Ancient Orkney Museum this afternoon, but it's closed. Have the hours been changed?'

Fairweather sat back on his heels, looking furious. 'Not to my knowledge, and certainly not with my permission. I suppose the wretched man is ill or something. He might have let one know. This is the busy season for the museum, and there's only the one volunteer with a key and I think she's off-island just now. None of the others can get in if it's locked up. We're going to lose money, having it closed on a Saturday, of all days. Thanks for telling me, Alan. I'll see the idiot gets what's coming to him!'

'Oh, don't be too hard on him, Robert,' I pleaded. 'It's been a difficult week for him.'

'It's been a difficult week for us all, but the rest of us have gone back to work, haven't we? And in fact . . .' He looked covetously at the knife in his hand.

'Yes, of course. We'll let you get on with it. Good hunting.' Alan took my arm and led me away.

'You didn't tell him Norquist was perfectly well and kicking. Especially kicking,' I said when we were out of earshot.

'No. Fairweather was angry enough without that. And he had a knife in his hands.'

I laughed. 'He might be ready to do violence, but probably not to you, and certainly not with his precious find. I have to say it takes a lot of imagination to recognize that lump of mud as a knife.'

'Imagination and experience, and he has a lot of both,

presumably.' Alan sighed. 'Now that we're here, we might as well take a tour of the dig and increase our knowledge. We're not making progress on any other front.'

'At least Fairweather dispelled my disturbing images of human sacrifice. I count that as a plus.'

The dig was, in fact, extremely interesting. The workers were happy enough to stand up, stretch their muscles, and explain what they were doing, pointing out interesting bits. We were shown the 'paint shop' where they thought the paints for the stones had been prepared. The mortars and lumps of pigment had been removed to the museum, but the place still fascinated me.

'They went to all that trouble,' I marvelled, 'to make something beautiful. Martha Stewart, alive and well in 3000 BC.'

'You should not joke here.' That same high, pedantic voice came from behind us. '*They* would not like it.'

Watson whined and I took Alan's arm. 'But this isn't a temple, or any sacred place,' I said, as gently as I could. 'It's the paint shop.'

'The paints were made for the rituals. All places were sacred to *Them*. You must be reverent.'

A shout of laughter came from a distant area of the dig. Norquist frowned. 'They should be careful. There are punishments for those who blaspheme.'

He stalked off.

'Alan, let's get out of here. I'll swear that man isn't quite safe. I don't feel sorry for him anymore. I'm just plain scared.'

'I imagine Fairweather will deal with him, but I agree. Something's snapped in the last few days. He's a fool to come around here. He must know Fairweather would be out for his blood over his dereliction of duty.'

I remembered the knife, if it really was one. 'Poor figure of speech, Alan. Let's *go*.'

Watson, who clearly didn't care for Norquist now, led the way back to the boat.

FOURTEEN

The next day brought two bombshells in rapid succession. The first was before breakfast. Alan brought me the news with my morning coffee.

'Dorothy, it looks as though we may not have to worry about Roadkill anymore.'

'Why? Has that woman caught him and taken him to be neutered?'

'I'm afraid not. I've had a phone call from Fairweather, who went out to the dig early this morning. The cat's been found at High Sanday. I don't know how to say this to make it any less frightful. His throat's been cut.'

My hand began to shake. Alan took away my coffee cup. 'Easy, darling. He wasn't our cat. He wasn't even an especially nice cat.'

'That woman said he could be sweet. Oh, Alan! No, I didn't like him, but no animal deserves to be treated like that!'

'You're quite right. Wouldn't it be worse, though, if he was someone's beloved pet?'

'I suppose.' I sniffled and reached for a tissue. 'The woman who rescued Watson and me – I wish I knew her name – she liked him. She'll miss him. It was a horrible thing for someone to do! And Alan, I'll bet I know who did it.'

Alan sighed and nodded. 'He hates cats. He said so, remember? And the way he was carrying on yesterday, he might have done almost anything. Perhaps we're fortunate it was a cat and not . . .'

He left the sentence unfinished. I nodded and mopped my cheeks. 'A ritual sacrifice. I take back anything nice I ever said about him. He's a nasty little man, and I hope they throw the book at him.'

The awful news had left me with no appetite for breakfast, so I decided to take Watson for a walk before church. We went to the end of the harbour road and were coming back along The

Street when a door opened. The woman we had met earlier stood in her doorway, arms crossed in front of her.

'Now you can walk your dog safely, can't you? I suppose you're delighted.'

'No,' I said. 'I'm appalled. I was afraid of the cat, and Watson was terrified, but it's an awful thing for someone to do. I know you were fond of him. I'm sorry.'

'Yes, well, sorry won't bring him back, will it? He was a fine wee cat. You Americans think you can march into a town and do anything you want, even kill our cats.'

'But . . . but, madam – I'm sorry, I don't know your name . . .'

'And I don't want to know yours!' She slammed the door before I could protest further.

Watson whined questioningly. He was thoroughly confused. This woman had been so nice before, and now she was treating us badly. He tugged on his leash.

'Yes, you're right. Home is the place for us.'

People were abroad this Sunday morning, and I smiled and nodded to those I passed. Nobody smiled or nodded back. In fact, they ignored us.

I've lived in England long enough to know that in the small towns, everyone knows everything about everyone else. So it didn't surprise me a great deal that everyone in Stromness seemed to know who I was. The universal hostility did surprise me, though. I'd never met with that attitude before, anywhere in Britain, and I didn't care for it one bit.

By the time we got back to the flat, Watson's tail was between his legs, and if I'd had one it would have been in the same position. 'We're not very popular in Stromness just now,' I told Alan. 'They seem to think we, or one of us, killed the cat.'

'I was afraid that might happen. Norquist may not be terribly popular around town, but he's one of their own. We're outlanders. After church I'm going to go tell Norquist a thing or two.'

I was actually reluctant to go to church, but fear of being glared at was not, I decided, sufficient excuse to skip it. So I gave Watson an extra good breakfast to make up for earlier unpleasantness, put him out on the patio, and Alan and I walked up the hill.

I was glad I went. I'd been spending a good deal of time lately on an uneasy footing between the present and the distant past, and the past had wrapped me in frightening speculations about primitive religions. The soothing ritual of the Anglican Eucharist was the perfect antidote. The psalm for the day read in part, 'Had you desired it, I would have offered sacrifice, but you take no delight in burnt offerings. The sacrifice of God is a troubled spirit; a broken and contrite heart, O God, you will not despise.' The Eucharistic prayer echoed it with, 'And here we offer and present unto thee, O Lord, ourselves, our souls and bodies, to be a reasonable, holy, and living sacrifice . . .' This was our sacrificial mode now, to try to give everything we had, all of ourselves, to God, but in life, not in bloody death. It was all balm to my spirit, and when we left the church, my smiles were genuine, even when they were met with cold stares.

The cat charity shop was open when we passed it, surprisingly on a Sunday, so I asked Alan to wait, and boldly went in. The woman at the counter said, 'We're not actually open. I just needed . . .' Then she turned around. 'Oh. It's you.'

'It is, and I came in to say I'm sorry about the cat, and I had nothing to do with his death. It was a despicable thing to do.'

The woman gave me a hard look, and finally nodded. 'I told them I didn't see how it could possibly be you. How would you have got over there in the middle of the night? And why? And you're not the sort to kill a cat, not that way, at any rate.'

'No, I'm not. I have cats of my own, very spoiled, and very precious to me. I won't pretend I liked this one very much. I wouldn't have been sorry to hear that he'd stowed away on the ferry and gone to England, or preferably Timbuktu. But I didn't wish him dead. I just wanted you to know.'

'I believe you. And if you'll excuse me . . .' She nodded and turned back to her work.

Alan queried me with his eyebrows when I came out of the shop.

'Not what you'd call a cordial welcome, but I told her I didn't kill the cat, and she says she believes me. Now, what are we going to do for the rest of the day?'

'We're going to find a thumping good Sunday lunch somewhere, and then I don't know about you, but I'm going to go looking for Norquist to give him a piece of my mind.'

'Good idea. He certainly needs a piece of sensible mind, since his has gone missing. But you'll be careful, won't you, Alan? I do think he's gone completely off his rocker, and he's definitely dangerous.'

We saw to Watson's needs and then drove to Kirkwall for our meal, an excellent one, roast lamb with all the trimmings. Then we strolled around Kirkwall for a bit. I hadn't seen the cathedral, which is magnificent, though not a cathedral anymore, strictly speaking. A cathedral is the seat of a bishop, and St Magnus' belongs now to the Church of Scotland, which doesn't have bishops. Never mind, it's an impressive building. The ruins of the Earl's Palace, adjacent to the cathedral, were also interesting.

'We'll never have anything like this in America,' I said sadly. 'We tear everything down the moment it shows some signs of decrepitude. They tore down my elementary school when it was fifty or sixty years old, and still a perfectly sound – and attractive – building. And then Americans come over here and ooh and aah over the lovely old churches, and the ruins. It's madness!'

Alan made the appropriate responses. He's heard that particular rant before. We didn't linger long after that. Alan was eager to confront Norquist, or at least eager to get it over.

When we got back to the flat, Alan phoned Norquist's number and got no reply. Frustrated, he tried the numbers he had for Fairweather and Larsen, with the same result. 'The man must be somewhere! And someone must know where. I'm tempted to get in the car and scour all the Neolithic sites until I find him.'

'Look, dear, that's a lot of territory to cover. And Norquist might be almost anywhere. Why don't you call the police and see if they know anything about him? Even with all the madness in Flotta, they might be keeping an eye on Norquist.'

The office seemed to be short-staffed, as might have been expected. No one there knew anything about Norquist. Would Mr Nesbitt care to leave a message, in case anyone learned anything?

Alan punched the phone off. 'No, I do not care to leave a message!' he grumbled to the unhearing phone. 'I want to find Norquist, and all events are conspiring against me.' He told me what he had been told.

'Go over to the police station, then. Your chances of finding someone who knows something are better if you're on the spot. And if not, you can always wait and fret there instead of here.'

'Are you trying to get rid of me?'

'Yes. You're making me just as antsy as you are. I love you dearly, but I want to try to stop thinking about all this for a while.'

So Alan drove off. I took Watson for his afternoon walk, letting him off the lead for a while, to his delight, and then put my head down for the nap that I indulge in a lot more often than I used to.

I couldn't sleep, though. I kept seeing a large orange cat lying complacently, defiantly, in the middle of The Street, or confronting Watson, hackles raised, tail bushed. And then a pathetic little corpse, covered in blood, his spirit and defiance, his beauty and life and vitality, all gone. I punched my pillow savagely, wishing I could punch Norquist, or if not him, whoever was responsible for the atrocity.

When I finally dropped off, my dreams were filled with vague images, morphing from one to another in the way of dreams, but all of them somehow terrifying. There was blood, and then just sky and stone, and then I was being pursued, I knew not why or where, but I knew something horrible awaited me if I didn't get away, and I couldn't run.

I was able then to wrench myself free of the dream. Watson rose from the rug where he had been sleeping and came to lick my hand.

'Was I whimpering or something? Did I scare you, poor old boy?'

He woofed happily and tugged gently at my hand. Surely a dog as fine as he deserved a treat, yes?

'You're too fat as it is, dog,' I said in a severe tone that didn't fool him for a moment. 'So am I. Let's see what we can find in the kitchen.'

Another happy woof. 'Kitchen' is a word he loves almost as much as he hates 'bath'.

Alan came in as we were rooting in the fridge for something good. 'That was quick,' I said. 'Or did I sleep a lot longer than I thought?'

Alan sat down heavily and delivered the second bombshell of the day. 'Larsen and Fairweather turned up at the police station, also looking for Norquist, and Baikie called in while we were all there. No one has seen him. No one has the least idea where he is. He seems to have disappeared off the face of the earth.'

FIFTEEN

That was a stunner. While Watson gnawed at a bone Alan had brought him, and we humans munched on rather hard scones, Alan told me about it.

'Baikie's no fool, you know, Dorothy. If I've been inclined to underestimate him, I've changed my mind. He's come to all the same conclusions about Norquist that we have, and thought it was time to bring him in for some serious questioning. So he put a man on it yesterday, before returning all his attention to the terrorist business. The chap went first, of course, to the museum. When Norquist wasn't there the constable started looking at the ancient sites, which was where the man might be expected to be. Of course there are a lot of sites, spread out over quite a few islands. Apparently he kept missing Norquist. Odd, if you think about it, that we kept finding him. Or he'd kept finding us. Really, it did seem almost as if the man was following us. If I'd known the police were trying to find the man . . . but I didn't.

'In any case, when Fairweather found the cat this morning, he thought it was serious enough to call the police. There was little they could do, with almost all the police delegated to Flotta, but informal feelers went out. No one's seen the man. He didn't go to church, though he's a regular at the kirk here in Stromness. In fact, he was booked to be a sidesman or something this morning, and they were surprised when he didn't turn up.

'He isn't at his flat. His car is where he always leaves it. His neighbours haven't seen him. The constable even went, personally, to talk to the aged mother.'

'I'll bet he enjoyed that!'

'Not a lot. It seems the old lady's housed in something more akin to a mental institution than a normal care facility. She's at least as peculiar as her son, and probably has dementia as well. He got almost nothing out of her, but the staff told him they

hadn't seen Norquist in several days, which is unusual. He visits
her at least briefly almost every day.'

'So he's vanished without a trace. Like Carter's boat.'

'Exactly.'

'Baikie'd like to get some inquiries going, but his staff is fully
occupied with matters that, for now, are more important, so he
asked if I – if we – would mind making a few phone calls in his
stead. There are, plainly, only two ways to leave Orkney, by boat
or by plane. We'll need to go to the airport to check flight mani-
fests, and to the ferry offices as well. Careful records are kept,
because of customs and immigration laws.'

'But there are always private planes and private boats.'

'And therein lies the rub. They're subject to the same laws,
of course, and the airport authorities and the harbour masters
are supposed to keep close tabs on arrivals and departures, but
if someone decides to sneak out at dead of night, what can
they do?'

'Except, as you pointed out, night never gets all that dead up
here in the middle of summer.'

'It doesn't get all that dark, but there's not much going on at
two a.m. Someone would notice activity at the harbour here or
in Kirkwall, or the airport, but there are lashings of private boat
landings, and a few private airstrips as well. It could be done.'

'But can Norquist pilot a boat or fly a plane?'

'I asked that, too, and no one seems to know. He must be able
to pilot a boat, or how would he have got to Papa Sanday
yesterday? But no one thinks he owns one, and no one can
imagine he knows how to fly.' Alan ran his hand down the back
of his head. 'We're left with just no leads at all.'

'Of course,' I said after a pause, 'he could be . . .'

'He certainly could, and that's why Baikie is frustrated about
not being able to follow up properly. If Norquist is dead, Baikie's
dealing with a crime, a certainty, not a probability.'

'Unless Norquist killed himself.'

'Suicide is a crime,' Alan reminded me. 'But what he fears,
of course, is murder, and two murders in less than a week are
unheard of in these parts. He's a worried man, Dorothy, and so
am I.'

'You think he's been murdered, too.'

'I'm afraid I do.'

'"These are deep waters, Watson,"' I quoted, and our dog looked up, puzzled. 'So what's next? Check with the airports and harbours?'

'It's all we can do for now. Shall we split them up?'

'No, you'd better do them. You can wave your old warrant card in front of them and say you have Baikie's authorization. They wouldn't talk to me. No, I said a while back that I was good at talking to people, but what we've been doing so far, and what you need to do now, is more formal. Interrogation, almost, instead of just chatting. Let's use another approach. While you check with points of departure, and keep your good policeman's nose to the ground, I'll go around to the shops and the churches and whatever and talk to people. I may turn up nothing at all, but one never knows.'

'Or you may not get anyone to talk to you. Those were pretty cold shoulders you were being offered this morning after church.'

'I know. "See how these Christians love one another." That's why I stopped to talk to the cat charity lady. I think she'll spread the word, and the shoulders may begin to thaw. One can only hope. But for now, while you trot hither and yon, I think I'm going to try for a real nap. Otherwise I'll just sit here and snack and gain ten pounds.'

I had a lovely nap and woke feeling refreshed, which was just as well, because Alan came home somewhat disheartened and in need of some cosseting. He reported that the airport and harbour authorities had been pleasant and cooperative, but could say quite definitely that Norquist had not left Mainland by any commercial carrier, or by any of the private planes and boats that had followed procedures. 'So that's the easy bit done,' he said, accepting a glass of Highland Park without protest. 'Now there are all the private boats and planes, here and on all the other islands. That would take an army of men to check.'

'Yes, dear. So we'll just have to think of other avenues to explore.' I lifted my glass of bourbon. '*Skoal.*'

In Scotland, and even in Orkney (whose residents view it as almost another country), very few businesses are open on a

Sunday, so I couldn't begin my planned gossip tour until the morning. But I set out bright and early, Watson in tow, alert for any signs of a softening in local attitude toward me.

There was no outright cordiality. But no one was actively unpleasant, either, and one or two stopped to pat Watson. Encouraged, I made for the bakery. Telling Watson to sit by the door, and stay – an order he usually obeys – I went inside and smiled at everyone I saw.

'Good morning!' I said cheerily. 'Lovely morning!'

There were murmurs of acknowledgement. 'I'm needing some good bread for our morning toast,' I went on. 'You bake your own, don't you?'

'Yes. There's white, and wholemeal, and oat bread.'

'Oh, the oat bread, please. A friend told me it makes wonderful toast. Is it sliced?' I could see that it was not. While they sliced it for me I chose some pastries we didn't need, and as they were wrapping all my purchases, I asked, 'Do any of you happen to know when the museum will be open? It wasn't on Saturday, and I wondered . . .'

'Have you not heard that Mr Norquist's gone away?'

'Yes, I did know that, actually.' Better admit that; they probably knew already that my husband had been asking for him all over the place. 'But I thought they might have found someone else to run the museum while he's gone.'

'Not that I've heard,' said the oldest of the three women, who was apparently the proprietor.

'They say,' said a younger woman (a daughter?), lowering her voice, 'that he's no coming back at all. That maybe he's done away wi' himsel'.'

'Kirsty!' said the older woman, glaring, but the other young woman took up the tale.

'I heard that maybe he's stolen what's in the museum and made off wi' it!'

'That's enough, girls! You're speaking rumour and scandal, and I'll not have it repeated to a visitor.' The mother – I was sure by now she was their mother – was too polite to call me a 'foreigner', but that was plainly what she meant. 'It's true enough, though, that no one's seen him since the day before yesterday.'

'My husband and I saw him on Saturday, twice actually.' They probably knew that, too. 'We wondered then why he wasn't at the museum.' I hesitated artistically before adding, 'We thought his manner was a little odd, to say the least.'

'The man's gone daft!' said the mother. 'And before you turn my own words against me, me girls, that's not rumour, that's fact. He's been acting more and more peculiar ever since he took over the museum.'

'And it's no to be wondered at, is it, with his mither the way she is. And Mum, that's no rumour, neither, you know where they've had to put her, and no before her time, either. I used to be that scared of her, the wild way she'd talk, and wavin' that cane around like a battleaxe.'

I was eager to hear more, but several customers had come in, and the 'girls' (who looked to be in their forties) had to serve them, under Mum's eagle eye. I was tempted to wait around, but the shop was small, and several other people came in needing to do post office business, so I waved a cheery goodbye that I don't think the girls saw and edged my way past the displays to the door. One of the women waiting at the post office counter turned to me and spoke to me. 'If it's Mrs Norquist ye're wantin' to know aboot, the shop across the way is the place to try.' She pointed. 'They know her there.'

I thanked her and managed to get out the door without dropping my packages.

Watson was getting bored, so I thought I'd better take him home before I went to another shop he couldn't enter. The place in question sold yarns and clothing, and I couldn't imagine that he'd be welcome there. He's well-mannered, but he has an exuberant tail, and the yarn I could see from the window was displayed on low tables. Besides, we hadn't had our breakfast yet, and the oat bread smelled really good.

I woke Alan, who for once had slept in, scrambled some eggs, and had just popped the bread in the toaster when he came down.

'Any luck?' he asked, pouring us coffee.

'Some. Ouch!' I licked my fingers. 'That toast is hot!'

'Well, if you will insist on putting bread in close proximity to a heating coil . . .'

'Hand me a plate, dear, and stop being sententious! And butter mine while it's hot, will you? I went to the bakery, and got us this stuff, and gossiped a bit about Mrs Norquist, the mother, you know?'

Alan nodded and took the toast to the table.

'It turns out that she's been pretty crazy for a long time, and the women in the shop think her son takes after her. They also think he's either killed himself or robbed the museum and run away with the loot.' I sat down with the plates of eggs, and we dug in.

'He hasn't done that, at least. That was one of the first things the police checked when they couldn't find him. Not that it was very likely. Those antiquities are priceless in terms of scholarly interest, but very few of them would bring much on the open market.'

'Not to mention the fact that Norquist would probably rather lie down in front of a bulldozer than sell the least of them. Anyway, as soon as we've had breakfast I'm going back up to The Street and visit that shop opposite the bakery, the one with the gorgeous yarn and sweaters and things. And I think I'd better leave the d-o-g here.'

Said d-o-g learned how to spell that particular word long ago, but he'd fallen asleep under the table and only twitched an ear.

'Then I'll take him with me. He'll love a ride in the car. I'm going over to Kirkwall, for want of any better idea, and see if I can unearth anything interesting.'

The word *ride* penetrated Watson's consciousness. He yawned, stretched, scratched one ear, and went to Alan's side smiling his endearing doggy smile.

'Patience, mutt! I'm going to finish my breakfast first. And no, you are *not* going to get a bite.'

He did, of course. If there's any man who can resist the pleading of a pair of liquid brown eyes, I don't think I want to know him. Alan gave him the last few morsels of egg on his plate, and then we finished clearing up quickly, and I set off for the yarn shop while Alan and Watson made for Kirkwall.

As I half expected, my reputation had preceded me. I walked in the shop and the shopkeeper said, 'And where's your dog, then?' She was a comfortable-looking woman of about fifty, her grey hair a little flyaway.

I gestured at the tables full of luscious yarns. 'I thought it was safer to leave him behind. He's quite happy; my husband's taking him for a drive to Kirkwall.'

'Oh, well, then, he's a lucky dog, isn't he? Is there anything I can show you, or did you just want to ask me about Lillian Norquist?'

'I love most of this yarn, but it'd be wasted on me. I'm the world's worst knitter. I might buy some for a friend who's really good, though. She's our next-door neighbour, and she's cat-sitting for us while we're here in Orkney, though she's really a dog person. Bulldogs,' I added. 'Lots of them.'

'Now there's a sensible breed,' said the woman approvingly, as she straightened a pile of sweaters.

'And Jane's a sensible person, much like her dogs. In fact she looks a lot like a particularly nice bulldog. Sort of round and jowly, you know?'

The woman turned around and stared at me. 'Where did you say you live?'

'In Sherebury. Belleshire, you know, not far from—'

'Fancy! I thought you were American.'

'I am, but I've lived in Sherebury for quite a long time now. Why?'

'Is your neighbour Jane Langland?'

It was my turn to stare. 'You know Jane?'

'She's my godmother. I was born in Sherebury and went to school there. Miss Langland was my favourite teacher, and when I was baptized – I was a teenager – she stood godmother to me. My own parents were gone by that time, and she rather took me under her wing.'

I nodded. 'That's her specialty. I used to think it was a pity she never had any children, until I realized she'd had far more than any biological mother.'

'Well, well, fancy meeting a friend of dear old Jane's. We lost touch when I moved up here back of beyond, but I knew who you were talking about the minute you described her! My name's Ruth, by the way, Ruth Menzies. Ruth Bingham back then.'

'Dorothy Martin.' I held out my hand. 'It's a real pleasure to meet you.'

'I never did believe what they were saying,' Ruth said. 'I'd seen you with your dog, and I said you weren't the sort of person who'd murder an animal.'

'You're right. I'm not. Especially not a cat. I adore cats. Though I have to admit that this one wasn't my favourite. You know, I simply cannot call him by his usual name. It seems wrong to be rude about him, now that the poor thing's dead.'

'Call him Sandy. That's what Celia Freebody named him. She was the only one in town who had a kind word for him. She's a goodhearted soul, even if she did start that story about you.' She perched on the edge of a counter. 'Now, sit down and tell me why you want to know about Lilly the Loop.'

'About who?'

'Lillian Norquist. Loopy.' She made the classic circular gesture at her temple. 'That's what a lot of us call her.'

'It's not so much Lillian who interests me as her son. My husband is a retired policeman, and Mr Baikie's asked him to see if he can pick up any hints about Mr Norquist's whereabouts.' I knew she either knew that already, or soon would. Might as well be frank about it.

'Ooh! Did he really steal from the museum, then?'

'I'm not sure about that,' I lied, 'but I believe the police are a little concerned about his mental state, and are eager to find him.' That at least was the truth, if not quite the whole truth. 'And of course you know that they've got their hands full at the moment with the Flotta situation. So I thought, if I could find out a little about his mother, it might give us a clue as to where he is. And you know, sometimes women will pick up on little things that it would never occur to a policeman to think about, much less talk about.'

'That's true enough, though I think you're wasting your time. The man's dead, I'm sure.'

'Why do you think so?'

'He'd become as barmy as his mother, and she went round the twist years ago. If you've talked to the man at all, you know he has – had – all sorts of crazy ideas about the old religions. People around here didn't like it. I'm C of E myself, though I don't go to church as often as I ought. But a lot of the people here are stout Church of Scotland, with strong ideas about pagan practices. It's all very well to dig up the old houses and temples and that. It's interesting, and it brings tourists. But when it comes to talk about worship and sacrifice and all, well, that's too much for the good folk of Stromness.'

'And he was talking about worship and sacrifice?'

'He was. And I'll tell you what I think. I'm quite certain he was the one who killed—'

SIXTEEN

'**G**ossiping again, Mrs Menzies?' The man who walked in was rather thin, slightly stooped, and dressed in clerical grey. I recognized him as the rector of St Mary's, the Episcopal Church in town. And I fervently wished he hadn't interrupted just then.

My new friend got to her feet. 'Just passing the time of day with a friend of a friend. You've met Mrs Martin, have you, Mr Tredgold?'

He gave me his hand. 'We haven't met, formally, but you were in church yesterday, were you not? I'd no idea you had connections here in Stromness.'

'I didn't either, but it turns out that Mrs Menzies used to know my next-door neighbour quite well.'

'In America?' He frowned, and I had to repeat the whole story. 'Ah. I see. Well, then, I won't keep you, Mrs Menzies. I just dropped in to see if you have any more of that green yarn my wife bought the other day. She thinks she won't have quite enough to finish the shawl for our new grandson, and as he's due to make his appearance very soon, she's anxious about it.'

'I have some, but I'm not sure it's the same dye lot, and greens are hard to match.' She rummaged in a bin of fine, soft baby yarn. 'Here, take this, and if it's not right, tell her to bring it back and we'll find something in a nice contrast for a border. No, don't pay me now. We'll sort it out later.'

He took the yarn and, leaving, held the door open for four women entering. 'Oh, Judy, I'm sure this is the right place! See, there are those darling little sweaters for little girls that Eunice told us about, and just look at the gorgeous yarns!'

The American tourists swarmed over the shop, and Ruth turned to me and shrugged. 'It'll probably be like this the rest of the day. I don't close until six-thirty in summer, but would you like to come over for a drink after that? I'll ask some of the other women, and we can sit and talk to your heart's content.' She gave me directions to her house.

'I'd love to. Thanks for the invitation.'

'Oh, and bring your husband, if he wants to come to a hen party and will promise not to behave like a policeman.'

'I'll tell him.' Ruth bustled away to deal with the tourists, and I spent a little time trying to decide which yarn Jane might like best. She is rather large, and dresses in subdued colours herself, but most of her knitting is for friends. I finally hit on a blue heather mixture with flecks of green in it, and caught Ruth's attention long enough to ask her to set aside enough of it for a generous cardigan. 'I'll come back later for it,' I promised, and she nodded and turned back to one of the women, who was wavering between two sweaters costing a king's ransom.

I left the shop congratulating myself on the first real stroke of luck we'd had in Orkney. Ruth was now firmly enrolled on my side, and would certainly pass along any information that came her way. And that meant I now had a finger on the pulse of the village. But oh! How I wanted to know how she'd planned to end that sentence. 'He was the one who killed . . .' Carter? The cat? Both of them? Someone or something else entirely? Maybe some project had been shelved because of some action or protest by Norquist. Something to do with the museum?

Speculation was fruitless. I'd have to wait until this evening. Meanwhile, I had the whole day ahead of me, with neither husband nor dog to consider. What should I do with those precious hours?

I wandered aimlessly on down The Street. I half-remembered seeing, tucked away somewhere around here . . . ah, there it was!

Like a homing pigeon, I had found the bookstore.

For a booklover, finding a bookstore one has never visited before is like coming upon a pirate's cave full of treasure. The first reaction is bedazzlement. Where, in the midst of such riches, shall one begin to delve?

This shop was small, but jammed floor to ceiling with shelves. There was scarcely room for two people. The proprietor, one Mr Brown according to the sign over the door, was seated on a stool wedged into a corner behind the desk. He looked up when I came in, smiled, said, 'Let me know if I can help you find something,' and went back to the book he was reading.

I wasn't looking for anything in particular, so I perused the shelves happily, greeting old friends, finding intriguing new possibilities. I pulled down a volume of poems by George Mackay Brown who was, I knew, Orkney's most famous poet (and wondered if Mr Brown the bookseller was any relation). I looked over several books about Orkney and chose three, and was amused to find an Orcadian dictionary. 'I haven't noticed that Orcadians speak any differently from people in the Highlands,' I commented to Mr Brown.

'That's because we speak Standard English to strangers. But amongst ourselves, we use our own words. There are a lot of Norwegian derivations, you know, because we're nearly as close to Norway as to Scotland, and many of our forebears came from Norway. The Vikings?' he said, as if questioning whether I'd ever heard of the Vikings.

'I do know a little about the Vikings, though not a lot. I understand Mr Carter, the man who was killed, thought there might be Viking treasure buried at High Sanday.'

Mr Brown smiled. 'Anything's possible, I suppose.'

'But not very likely?'

'Not very. If the Vikings had buried any treasure there – and why would they? – it would have been one of the first things discovered, thousands of years newer than what they're digging up now. No, I fear Viking gold is a pipe dream. I could be wrong, of course.'

'What did Mr Norquist think of the idea, I wonder?' I had spoken in the past tense without intending it, but Mr Brown didn't appear to notice.

'Charles Norquist,' he said with precision, 'finds any modern intrusion into the ancient sites to be sacrilege, and in his mind, the Vikings definitely were modern. He lives and moves and has his being several millennia ago. It used to be a harmless obsession. Now I fear he has become, in your parlance, a crackpot.'

'But he's a member of the Friends, isn't he? And they support and encourage archaeological activity all over the islands.'

'He is a member of the Friends as a political necessity. They control the museum, and he values his association with the museum above life itself. His own or anyone else's,' he added, almost to himself. 'If he were stronger, physically, I'd suspect him of smuggling the artefacts back into the earth, a few at a time. He feels they belong there.'

'They'd just be dug up again.'

'Not if he chose a place that had already been thoroughly excavated and filled in again. But I'm talking nonsense. Norquist couldn't dig so much as a flower bed for petunias. His heart, you know.'

'No, I had no idea. He has heart trouble?'

'He's had several heart attacks. He ought to have surgery, but he says it's against his religion. I personally think he doesn't care about prolonging his life. He's willing, even eager, to join the Company of the Immortals.'

'Whatever he conceives that to be. Mr Brown, where do you think he is now?'

He frowned and looked at his watch. 'At the museum, of course. It opened an hour ago.'

'But it didn't. He isn't. Didn't you know? He seems to have vanished. Nobody's seen him since Saturday.' At the look of disbelief on his face, I added, 'Truly. The police are looking for him. Or actually, they've deputized my husband to do that, given the terrorist scare. Alan is a retired policeman, you see, and the police want Norquist to be found. They're worried about his state of mind.'

'As well they might be. He seems to me to have stepped over the edge some time ago. But I wouldn't have thought a disappearing act to be typical of him. He likes to demonstrate his disapproval in more dramatic ways.'

'Like, for example, a ritual sacrifice?'

'The cat?' Mr Brown pondered. 'It's true that he hates and fears cats. But I doubt we can lay that particular crime at his feet, for the simple reason that cats are quite recent imports to these islands. Recent in his terms, that is. If he wanted to sacrifice something, it would more likely be a bird of some sort, perhaps a gull, or a small mammal. Authenticity in all things, you see. But again, I doubt he'd have the strength to catch such an animal. He certainly could not have subdued that old orange tomcat, whom I always suspected of being Beelzebub in disguise.'

'Hmm. But then who did kill the cat? And where's Mr Norquist?'

'About the cat, I fear I have no idea. As for Norquist, if he doesn't turn up soon, I'll begin to fear an accident. He isn't strong, as I said, and if he were on a beach and was caught by a strong wave, I doubt he'd be able to swim away.'

'If he's drowned, they might never find him.'

He nodded sadly. 'These seas don't always give up their dead.'

I sighed, gathered up the books I wanted, paid, and left the shop, mulling over what Mr Brown had said.

I had moved only a few steps down the street when the rain began. It was the devious kind of fine drizzle that falls with almost no fuss but can soak you through in seconds. I hadn't thought to bring my umbrella. Clutching my books to my breast, I ran for the nearest shop, which happened to be the pharmacy.

There were several others seeking shelter like myself, and among them I recognized the woman from the cat charity. 'This place,' I said to her ruefully, 'has the most changeable weather I've ever seen. The sun was shining brightly with not a cloud in the sky when I set out this morning.'

'That's why I always carry a brolly,' she said. 'We've some for sale cheap at the shop, if you left yours at home.'

'Thank you, but mine is back at the flat. I was just too optimistic to bring it with me.'

'Come back with me, anyway, and I'll lend you one. Mine is big enough for two.'

The shop wasn't far away. Nothing is far away from anything else in Stromness, which is one of its great charms. The woman's umbrella didn't really provide much protection from the persistent rain, but I couldn't get much wetter anyway, and I was happy with the gesture of reconciliation. I had apparently been well and truly acquitted of felicide.

She found me a faded and decrepit umbrella with one broken rib and a chipped handle. 'Here, take it. Someone left it behind years ago, and no one will ever buy it. It'll help a bit, and you can put it in the rubbish when you've finished with it.'

I expressed suitable thanks, and then bent to pet a cat that had rubbed up against my legs. 'Poor baby, you're going to get all wet. My slacks are soaked through.'

'Oh, her fur is so thick, she won't even notice. She's just hoping for a hand-out. She tries that on with everyone who comes in.'

'And from the look of her she must be successful.' The cat was a lovely long-haired tortoiseshell, but so fat that her belly nearly rubbed the floor. She mewed pitifully as I stroked her head.

'Don't you dare give her anything! I've put her on a diet, but she'll never lose weight if she keeps on cadging treats out of everyone. My name is Isabel, by the way. Isabel Duncan. You're Dorothy Martin, and I understand you're coming to Ruth's little drinks party this afternoon.'

'I am indeed. You'll be there then?'

'Half the town will be there. Ruth serves good drink, and everyone is panting to meet you and decide for themselves about you.'

I laughed a little uncertainly. 'Well, thanks for warning me. I'll be on my best behaviour.'

'And bring your dog, if he's good around other dogs. There'll be several there, and most of the women trust people who own dogs.'

'Watson's very well behaved. He's only a mutt, but I wouldn't say that in his hearing. He's a sweetheart, and I say that as a life-long cat lover. I never thought I'd fall in love with a dog, but he's been a great joy to Alan and me ever since he came into our lives.'

So then I had to tell the story of how he came to our holiday cottage during a raging thunderstorm when we were vacationing in the Cotswolds, walked in, shook muddy water all over the room, and made himself at home. 'We were worried about how our two cats would react when we took him home, but they became the best of friends in nothing flat. I suppose everyone thinks their dog is the best in the world, but ours really is.'

Isabel laughed, and the tortoiseshell rubbed against my ankles more forcefully. Enough talk, she seemed to say. Feed me.

'No, beautiful. Your mistress would never forgive me.' She gave me a look that reminded me of the old saying about dogs having owners, while cats had staff, and left me for a couple who had just entered the store. The pickings might be better there.

'I'll see you later, then.' I waved and went out into the rain, which was pelting down harder than before. I was glad, after all, of the bedraggled umbrella. It at least kept the worst of it off the books and my glasses, as I headed for the flat.

Alan hadn't returned yet, so I luxuriated for a while in a lovely hot bath, dressed in dry clothes, and made myself some tea. I'd wait for Alan for a little while before I scrounged some lunch.

Meanwhile I decided it was time for another list. This time I thought I'd adopt the method from Dorothy L. Sayers's *Have His Carcase*, where Harriet and Lord Peter listed 'Things to be Noted and Things to be Done'.

There were several new Things to be Noted:

1. The whole town thinks Norquist is crazy. There are three theories about where he is:
   a. Dead by suicide
   b. Dead by accident
   c. In hiding somewhere off the island either because he stole from the museum, or simply because of his unbalanced mind
2. The bookseller thinks that he didn't kill the cat, because:
   a. He didn't have the strength, with his heart trouble, and;
   b. If he was crazy enough to think a ritual sacrifice a good idea, he wouldn't have chosen a cat.
3. Ruth thinks that he killed someone or something. (I mean to find out more about that this evening.)
4. His mother frightened at least some people in the town, talking strangely and brandishing her cane like a weapon.

I put my pen down and looked over my list. There were a few suggestive points, but nothing that could be considered a real lead. I sighed, considered heating up some soup, and decided to wait a little longer for Alan. I headed a second sheet 'Things to be Done':

1. The cocktail party. Ask about both Norquists, and the cat, and Carter, and anything else that comes into my head or Alan's, if I can persuade him to go.

2. Go and visit Mrs Norquist. She may be crazy as a coot,
   but even the craziest people sometimes make a kind of
   sense.

I chewed on my pen and tried to think of anything else Alan and I
could do that would be in the least productive. I finally added:

3. Check on Norquist's heart condition. The first principle
   of good investigation is verify, verify, verify.

I couldn't imagine why Mr Brown would make up something
that was so easily checked, but I'd check anyway.

Except that the police might already have looked into that – or
no, probably not, with the current crisis taking all their attention.
Oh, well, it wouldn't hurt to check it out anyway. Because he
could have had a heart attack somewhere and be lying helpless,
out in this weather, waiting to be rescued . . .

I shook my head, hoping to clear it. I was beginning to feel
sorry for the man again. What I needed was some lunch, or
coffee, or something to get my mind working properly.

I had just heated up some canned soup and made a grilled
cheese sandwich when Alan and Watson came home. I ran for
a towel. 'Don't let that dog in here till he's dried off,' I called,
but it was too late. He pushed into the kitchen, shook himself,
and padded with muddy feet over to his water bowl.

'Why did we ever want a dog?' I asked.

'I can't imagine. I'll clean up, if you'll make a sandwich
for me.'

Once we were seated around the reasonably clean and dry
table and had a little food in us, I asked, 'OK, who goes first?'

'After you, madam.'

I pulled my notebook over to make sure I didn't miss anything.
'Let's see. I didn't learn a lot, but the most interesting bits are
that Norquist has, or had, a serious heart condition and couldn't
do anything at all strenuous. And he was a stickler for authenticity
with respect to anything ancient, so he wouldn't have killed the
cat.' I gave him the bookseller's reasoning. 'And Alan, I hate to
say it, but I think that makes sense. I was so sure he did it, but
now I'm almost certain he didn't. I'm even beginning to feel

sorry for him again, because absolutely everybody in town thinks he's totally out of his mind, and the woman at the knit shop, Ruth Menzies, thinks he killed someone or something. She was interrupted before she could finish saying who or what.'

'"What" as in a cat?'

'I don't know. We think of a cat as a "who", but not everybody does. I was thinking more of a plan or a project or an idea, that sort of thing. People do sometimes refer to those things being killed. But we'll have a chance later today to hear what she meant. We've been invited to a little party at her house. Because, listen to this, Alan, she knows Jane Langland!'

'Good heavens!'

I explained. 'So once we had established that, I was firmly enrolled in her good books, so she invited me, or us if you want to, to come round to her house after she closes the shop, and talk to a bunch of her friends. I'm told the drinks will be good, but the other guests will all be women, I'm afraid.'

'And when have I ever been known to quail before a monstrous regiment of women? Of course I'll come with you. It'll probably be more productive than my morning.'

'Tell.'

'The news is almost entirely negative. No trace of Norquist. He didn't leave Orkney by any of the commercial carriers; we already knew that. Neither he nor his body has been found anywhere. There's been very little in the way of official search, but the word has got round, and you'd be surprised how many people have been looking, in a casual sort of way. Nothing.'

'Even the official police couldn't cover every square foot of every island! It'd take months, and he could dodge around, and they'd never find him.'

'That thought has not escaped anyone,' said Alan drily. 'But volunteers have searched the more likely Neolithic sites and the obvious caves. A divers' club has even sent people down at some of the more popular suicide spots, like the Churchill barriers.'

I shuddered at the concept of popular places for suicide, but had to ask, 'And what are the Churchill barriers?'

'Great chunks of concrete dropped in the water during the Second World War to stop the Germans bringing submarines in to Scapa Flow to destroy our fleet. I'll have to show them to you before we leave Orkney. There's quite a touching little chapel nearby, put up by the Italian prisoners of war who built the barriers. But that's another story. The point is, Norquist wasn't there, or anywhere else they've tried. Frankly, the only good theory left is that he used a private boat, because people at the private landing strips swear themselves blue that no unlogged departures have taken place in the past few days.'

'Well, they would, wouldn't they, if they're ever involved in anything like smuggling.'

'Of course, but the neighbouring farmers keep a pretty close eye on the planes, and they say the same thing. It's very quiet at night in the Orcadian countryside. They'd have heard a plane taking off, and no one did. But a small boat can be rowed out quite a good way before they start the motor.'

'But Alan! If Norquist didn't steal anything and didn't do any killing, as Mr Brown would insist he couldn't, then why would he run away?'

'It goes back, doesn't it, to your pet theory about motivation. Because he was afraid of something.'

'Hmm. Or someone.'

'But who? And why? I do really believe that the man's dead, either by accident or by his own hand, and they'll find his body eventually.'

'Mr Brown said that sometimes these seas don't give up their dead.'

On that sombre note we finished our lunch, tidied up the kitchen, and went up for well-deserved naps.

SEVENTEEN

We woke in time to give Watson a bath before taking him to call on the ladies, and then of course we needed showers ourselves, so it was nearly seven before we presented ourselves at Mrs Menzies' door. We hadn't been sure we'd found the right house, as it was up a flight of stairs off The Street and round a couple of bends, but the sounds of female voices inside reassured us.

'The door's ajar. Shall we just go in?'

'I imagine that's why it's been left open. They'd never hear a knock, anyway.'

Alan pushed open the door and gestured me in, with Watson firmly on his lead, and we were greeted first by an assortment of polite but very inquisitive dogs, from a minuscule Yorkie to an Old English sheepdog roughly the size of a Volkswagen. Watson, fortunately, is as friendly with other dogs as with people, and entered into the mutual sniffing with no hint of anxiety.

'All right, dogs, that's enough.' Ruth came into the hallway and spoke commandingly, and the assembled multitudes dispersed, presumably back to their mistresses. 'Good to see you, Dorothy. And this must be your husband.'

They introduced themselves, and she led us into the sitting room, where there wasn't a lot of sitting going on, mostly because there weren't a lot of places to sit.

'Everyone, this is Dorothy Martin and her husband Alan Nesbitt. I'm not going to give you everyone's names, you two, because you'd never remember, but you'll get them sorted out in time. Get yourself a drink – they're over there – and something to nibble, and I'll find you some chairs.'

Alan poured himself some Highland Park and me some white wine, and someone shooed a reluctant dachshund out of an armchair. I sank into its embrace and Alan perched on the arm, and Ruth said, 'Well, now. You're wondering why I called this meeting.'

'No, we're not,' said the cat lady – Isabel, that was her name – amid the general laughter. 'Alan is a retired copper, and Dorothy is Miss Marple, and they're wanting to find out what, if anything, we all know about the goings-on around here.'

There was more laughter, and Alan said, 'That's actually a very fair summation, Mrs . . .'

'Duncan. But call me Isabel, everyone does.'

'Thank you. However, I'd characterize my wife more as Sherlock Holmes and Peter Wimsey rolled into one. You need to understand that she's the brains of this partnership. I'm Constable Plod, finding clues for her to interpret – brilliantly, I might add.'

Well, of course after that they were eating out of his hand. Alan can charm a bird out of a tree without half trying, and this time he was trying. If I'd won Ruth over because of the Langland connection, Alan's self-deprecation and deference to me pulled in the rest of them.

'All right then,' said a woman I didn't know, 'you've come to the right place. Between us, we know most of what goes on in Stromness.'

'And most of Mainland, if it comes to that,' said another. 'What do you want to know? We'll help if we can.'

'Do any of you,' asked Alan, serious now, 'have any idea, however far-fetched, where Charles Norquist might be? Inspector Baikie is extremely concerned.'

'You've heard the rumours that he's scarpered, I suppose,' said a woman I recognized from behind the counter at the pharmacy.

'We have. And I can say quite definitely that he did not steal anything from the museum. Nothing is missing from the museum. The police have checked thoroughly.'

'When?' demanded a grey-haired woman with a formidable bosom who had just come into the room.

'Oh, dear,' said Ruth under her breath. 'I might have known she'd turn up.'

'I beg your pardon?' Alan asked the newcomer.

'When did the police check?' she said impatiently.

'Yesterday, as soon as it became apparent that Norquist was among the missing.'

'Ah. Then they'd better check again.'

Ruth quieted the babble that arose. 'Alan, Dorothy, this is Janet MacKenzie, who is a volunteer at the museum. Janet, I think you'd better explain yourself.'

'It's clear enough, I'd think. The police had better check again. Because I walked past the museum on my way here. I'd intended to go in and do a little work on the records, but someone's changed the lock. Shiny new Yale. Classic case of locking the stable too late.'

'Janet, what *do* you mean?'

'I mean I looked in the windows, and the case closest to the door is empty. Someone's rifled the place.'

Stunned silence, then pandemonium. 'But who . . . how could anyone . . . why would they . . . who . . . how . . . why . . .?'

Alan rose and spoke to Ruth. 'I'll have to ask you to excuse me. I must get in touch with the police, and I may have to go to Kirkwall.' He was pulling out his mobile as he spoke. Signalling me a 'stay here' with his eyebrows, he left the room. Watson stirred at my feet and looked at me for instructions. I patted him, and he settled down.

'Still so sure Norquist didn't steal anything?' the volunteer called after Alan, with a cackle.

I tried to follow the discussion that ensued, but with everyone talking at once, it was difficult. I gathered only that there was considerable difference of opinion, with about half the room laying everything including the weather at Norquist's door ('Who knows but what he does rain dances in those weird rituals of his?') and the other half claiming he was just a harmless nutter who hadn't the physical strength to do anything more violent than utter imprecations.

I gave up trying to sort it out after a little, and tried to think. This rather abrasive woman was evidently the chief volunteer, the one who had a key to the old lock. Whoever stole from the museum had to have a key to the new lock. Unless the woman had done it herself, before the lock was changed. But why would she have done that, and then called our attention to it? And who had changed the lock? Larsen, as president of the Friends? The police? And when? And when exactly had the theft taken place?

If it was a theft. I was more and more doubtful that anyone would steal the artefacts in order to sell them. The money they'd bring would scarcely be worth the risk. Norquist might have had some crazy idea about 'saving' them. But save them from what, or whom? And in any case, he'd disappeared before the artefacts did.

Maybe someone had simply moved them. A rearrangement of the museum, now that it would certainly be taken over by a new curator. That would seem possible, if hardly likely. Undoubtedly the police would be in touch with Larsen about that. Eventually.

I turned my attention back to the gathering, which had now reached a different topic of disagreement: where was Norquist?

The strident tones of the volunteer rose to drown out the others. 'I say he's hiding somewhere on this island, and has been the whole time.'

I ventured to speak. 'But where, Mrs . . . um, I've forgotten—'

'MacKenzie, and it's Miss, thank you very much. How should I know where? Some cave, probably. He dotes on caves.'

'The police have searched all the likely ones and found no sign of him.'

'Well, then, they'll just have to search the unlikely ones, won't they?' She stood. 'The rest of you may have time to sit around and tittle-tattle all the evening, but I have not. Good day.' She strode for the door, heedless of the paws and tails in her path, and slammed it on her way out.

'Well!' Isabel, the cat lady, said with an expressive gesture. 'I've always said that Janet MacKenzie is the rudest person I've ever known, but this is too much!'

'I didn't invite her, you know,' said Ruth, 'but of course she knows everything that goes on in this town.'

I cleared my throat. 'Is she . . .?' I began nervously. 'That is . . . does she . . . er . . . take liberties with the facts?'

'Is she a liar, do you mean?' That was Isabel the forthright again. 'I've never known her to tell a lie. "Tell the truth and shame the devil" is her motto. She especially enjoys spreading unpleasant truths about other people.'

The others nodded. A quiet woman I didn't know at all said, 'Her other favourite expression is "I thought you ought to know". What follows is always something nasty. "I thought you ought to know that your husband's seeing a lot of that new woman at the co-op" or "that people are talking about that short skirt you've been prancing about in" or "the things they're saying about that cake you brought to the last fête" or . . . you can supply others.'

'But is it always true?' I persisted.

'It's always true that people are saying what she passes on. Of course it's usually just ill-natured rumour with no basis, but on occasion she hits the nail on the head.'

'The one about the woman at the co-op?'

The women looked at each other. Finally Ruth said, 'I suppose we can tell you. They've all left now, and you don't live here. Yes, a new couple moved to Stromness from . . . Aberdeen, was it?' She looked around, and there were nods. 'A young couple. He came to work on the construction they're doing down at the harbour. She wanted something to do herself, so she got a part-time job at the co-op. She was very pretty, in a flashy sort of way. Lots of hair, lots of make-up, tank tops a size too small, you know the sort of thing.'

I groaned. 'And her husband was working long hours and leaving her alone a lot. I see where this is going.'

'And spending a lot more time and money than he should at the pub after he finished work for the day,' said one of the other women. 'So, of course, she was bored and went looking for other amusement.'

'She didn't have to look very hard,' said Isobel. 'Half the men in town had their eyes on stalks from the time she first sashayed down The Street. Most of us know how to keep our menfolk home nights, but – I'd better not say her name – the librarian was a strait-laced sort who didn't . . . well, anyway, she was a plain woman, poor thing, and hardly ever at home, and her husband—'

'Had a taste for candy,' Ruth finished. 'He started doing all the family shopping. And his wife thought he was being considerate of her, taking some of her work off her shoulders.'

'She should have known,' someone snorted. 'First time he'd ever volunteered to do anything for her.'

'But she was a trusting soul, and never suspected a thing. Everyone else in Stromness knew, but we weren't going to tell his wife. And then Janet told her one day. After chapel, too, right in front of everyone. She didn't believe it, but she wasn't a stupid woman, and she started paying attention. He admitted it in the end, didn't even act guilty about it.

'And then the other husband, the young man, came and told him . . . well, said he'd better get out of it or he'd be sorry. And all of them moved away, and I don't know what happened to poor Anne.'

'And the saddest thing of all is, it all would have blown over if it hadn't been for Janet's meddling.' That was Isobel again. 'You can't tell me that young trollop would have kept her eyes on a middle-aged man like Jack for much longer. She'd have found greener pastures soon enough.'

'Miss MacKenzie doesn't seem to be a very popular person in the village,' I ventured.

'Oh, the woman is pure poison,' said Ruth, 'but we're used to her. And she does work hard at the museum.'

'And we're all afraid of that tongue of hers,' said Isobel, with that call-a-spade-a-spade frankness. 'She's a snoop and a meddler and we all know it, but we don't dare cross her. Everyone has a few secrets.'

'That reminds me,' I said, snapping my fingers. 'Ruth, this morning at the shop, you were about to say something when the vicar came in. Something about Norquist killing . . . but you stopped there, and you've been killing *me* with curiosity ever since.'

One of the other ladies laughed. 'You must have been thinking of the hen, Ruth.'

'Oh, yes!' She laughed, too. 'I suppose it really wasn't funny, but it was just so typical of the man. It was in the spring sometime, April, I think—'

'May,' said a woman, 'because, don't you remember, it was all about May Day.'

'So it was. You see, May Day is a very old festival, with pagan roots. And people on these islands have all sorts of religious beliefs. I suppose it's natural, coming from different backgrounds as we all do, and with the Neolithic influence so strong. At any rate, quite a number of different groups celebrate May Day every year. May poles, bonfires, that sort of thing.'

'But surely,' I interrupted, 'the roots don't go back into prehistory.'

'No. And that's what Charlie Norquist kept saying. He used to get livid about the people who insisted on having their rites at some of the standing stones. Called it sacrilege.

'So, when one of them was going to sacrifice a white cockerel at one of the rites, he went absolutely spare, and stole the poor creature he thought they were going to use.'

'Stole it from his next-door neighbour,' said Isobel with relish. 'And wrung its neck before they could get the chance.'

'Only, you see, it was a hen, not a cockerel.' Ruth took up the tale again. 'A good layer, too, and the neighbour was furious. Made Charlie pay for it. He denied he'd done it, but everyone was sure he was the one. And of course no one let him forget his mistake. There was a good deal of joking about the man not knowing the difference between a hen and a cockerel.'

'And some of it wasn't very kind,' said the quiet woman, in a gentle voice. 'Not everyone in this community is tolerant of anyone who's different. They suggested there were reasons why he still lived with his mother. That sort of thing.'

'Most of us don't give a hoot whether a man is gay or not,' said Isobel, 'but Charlie was so peculiar in every way, I'm afraid he came in for a lot of teasing, or worse.'

'You know,' I said, 'I didn't like Mr Norquist much when I met him, but I'm beginning to feel quite sorry for him.'

'If you'd ever met that mother of his, you'd feel sorrier.' That came from a gruff-voiced woman with cropped grey hair who reminded me a bit of Jane Langland. 'Talk about peculiar! She belonged in an asylum long before they put her in one, and I for one hope they see she stays there. She's a public danger.'

'And so, ladies, will my husband be if I don't get home soon and put a meal in front of him.' The woman who stood started a mass exodus, everyone stopping to nod or shake my hand and make polite noises. Isobel, Watson, and I were the last to leave.

'Your husband seems to have vanished,' she said. 'Do you know how to get home? Round to your right till you come to the stairs, then straight down will take you to The Street. Mind how you go. This passage needs repairing. Here, I'll come with you.' We negotiated the somewhat treacherous stairs together, and reached The Street safely. 'Now, your way lies to the left and mine to the right. Did you get what you needed from the meeting?'

I paused to think about that for a moment. 'It raised a lot of interesting questions, at least. I'm not sure there are any answers hidden in there, but one never knows. And I'll be very wary of Janet MacKenzie.'

'You do that. Good night.'

EIGHTEEN

Watson and I made our way home, and as I walked I replayed the evening in my mind. I couldn't wait to get home and make notes of all I'd learned. I hoped I could remember everything.

That was an odd story about the hen. The oddest part about it, which no one at the meeting had seemed to recognize, was that Norquist had denied killing the bird. I could see him being embarrassed about the mistake as to its sex, but given his obsession about historical accuracy, I'd have thought he would, before the mistake was bruited about, have made a dry little public statement about doing his duty to the ancients, or some such thing.

That was odd.

And there was something else tugging at the back of my mind, trying to get my attention, but for the life of me I couldn't bring it out into the open. May Day . . . pagan rituals . . . sacrifices . . .

It irritated me like a half-remembered tune that one can't quite complete, or a face one can't place. I tried talking to Watson about something else, hoping that ignoring it would bring it forward, but it wouldn't come, and I decided to stop forcing it. It would surface eventually. Meanwhile the women's mass departure from the meeting had reminded me that I had to do something about dinner, and I wasn't sure there was anything much at the flat.

I thought about stopping at the bakery to see if any of their small stock of meat and cheese and groceries looked appealing. I thought about swinging past the museum to see if there was any police activity there. But neither was on my way home, and the few extra steps seemed just too much. Despite my afternoon nap, I was exhausted. 'I am,' I told Watson, 'getting old.'

He whined in what I swear sounded like sympathy.

Alan was back at the flat, and he had, bless him, brought in some Chinese take-away. 'I didn't think you'd feel like cooking.'

'You're right about that, and I'm not sure there's anything to cook, anyway.'

'You look just about done, my love. Sit down and I'll pour you a drink and heat up the food.'

'Thanks, but I've had plenty to drink. You could make some tea to go with dinner if you wanted.'

He wouldn't talk about our problem until we'd eaten. Then he poured himself a small measure of Highland Park, sat back, reached in his pocket absent-mindedly for the pipe he hadn't smoked in years, and said, 'This time I get to go first.'

'I hope it's riveting, dear heart, because I'm about to fall asleep.'

'I know. I'll keep it short. I called the police, as you know, and managed to reach Baikie, for a wonder. They haven't found any bombs at the terminal, so for the moment that scare is damping down, and he was back in the office. He knew nothing about any theft at the museum, but he sent some of his people to check. I met them at the museum, and it's true enough. I can't say I cared much for Mrs MacKenzie—'

'Miss,' I said. 'She makes a big point of it.'

'Ah. For Miss MacKenzie, then, but she was quite right. The odd thing is that it's only the one case that's been emptied. And the lock wasn't forced. It was quite obviously unlocked with a proper key.'

'And they didn't find any of the things? I had a vague idea that someone might simply be preparing to rearrange the exhibits.'

'Not a sign of them anywhere in the museum.'

'What were they, anyway?'

'Pots, mostly. Quite important ones, I was given to understand. Larsen came with us and said they were very fine examples of Unstan ware, which is unique to Orkney. He was quite upset about their disappearance.'

'But they wouldn't be of any particular commercial value?'

'Not unless someone had a link to a collector of Orcadian Neolithic pottery. Which is of course possible. Baikie will check, I'm sure, when he can. He has quite a backlog of work to catch up on just now.'

I sighed, and Watson came over to sit on my feet. He wants his people to be happy, and thinks keeping them warm is one means to that end. 'Alan, we just don't get anywhere with this mess. We're going in circles. Strange things keep happening, and we learn little bits and pieces, but nothing seems to lead anywhere.'

'I've been thinking about that, love. And it makes me wonder. Often, when I was in active police work and that sort of thing happened, it was because someone was making it happen, was creating blind alleys and red herrings to distract us from the main point. Once we worked that out, the murky waters usually cleared and we could see our way.' He chuckled. 'Have I mixed enough metaphors for one evening, do you think?'

'Enough for a week, at least. Do you think someone's manipulating events in this case?'

'I do, but I don't know who. Let's leave it for the moment, and you tell me what happened after I left that rather odd little gathering.'

'I haven't sorted it all out yet, but I did learn what Ruth meant when she said she thought Norquist killed something.' I related the story about the hen.

Somewhat to my relief, Alan didn't laugh. 'Poor chap,' he said. 'Even if he did do it, the village reaction was cruel. And if he didn't, then someone else did it to make him look foolish, and that's crueller still. He really couldn't seem to do anything right, could he?'

'You're speaking of him in the past tense.'

'And you think he's still alive.'

'I don't know.' I sighed again, and Watson looked up at me. I reached down to pat his head. 'It's all right, dog. Mama's puzzled, that's all. It doesn't seem fair, somehow, to assume he's dead when we don't know that.' Watson realized the last comment wasn't addressed to him and laid his head back on his paws. 'However. There was one other thing that struck me, or raised some vibrations somehow, only I can't pin it down. I think it had to do with May Day, but . . .' I raised my hands in the classic gesture of frustration.

'May Day. May pole. Dancing. Ribbons. Morris dancing?'

'No, nothing like that. Ignore me. It'll come, or it won't. I think the only other thing that mattered at all was that Janet MacKenzie is apparently heartily disliked by almost everyone in the village, because she spreads rumours.'

'That's interesting. She fabricates stories, does she?'

'No, actually not. The woman said that all the things she passes along are things she has heard, but she never bothers to verify anything, and she spreads the stories maliciously, where they'll do the most harm. She was the one who spread the story about the hen, for example. I didn't ask who started it, but one almost never knows where such things start.'

'That's the damnable thing about rumour. It can do so much harm, and the guilty person usually gets off.'

'That's so true. There was one other bit of gossip she spread that did a lot of harm, only in this case the whispers were true. The husband of the village librarian, I think it was, was having an affair with a much younger married woman, and everyone except the librarian seemed to know about it. The women at the meeting thought it would have ended soon with the wife none the wiser. They'd actually sort of conspired to keep her from knowing. But then Janet MacKenzie "thought she ought to know", and that blew it wide open.'

'What happened to the people involved?'

'No one seems to know. They left Orkney, all of them.' A thought struck me, and I sat up straighter. 'Alan, you don't suppose it could be Janet MacKenzie who's behind the . . . I don't know what to call it . . . the manipulation of this case? It's the sort of malicious thing she might do. Oh, and remember what she said just as you left?'

'I don't think I heard her.'

'It was a taunt. I don't remember the exact words, but something about Norquist stealing the artefacts. And it occurred to me that she could have stolen them herself, just to make him look bad! She's a volunteer at the museum. She'd have keys to the display cases, or know where they're kept.'

'But not a key to the new lock on the door,' Alan reminded me. 'The Friends had those put on the day Norquist disappeared, and Baikie told me there's only the one key.'

'Oh.' I sank back into the chair. 'Another perfectly good theory bites the dust. I swear I'm going crazy over this one.'

'What you need, my dear, is a good night's sleep. Go to bed. I'll take Watson for his walk.'

'The dishes . . .?'

'Will wait until morning. Go on, then.' He gave me a kiss and a little pat on the fanny, and I trudged up the stairs and knew no more until morning.

'Well?' said Alan the next day, when I'd absorbed enough caffeine to be almost human.

'Mmm?'

'Did you receive any startling illuminations in your sleep last night?'

'Sadly, no. I don't think I even dreamed, or if I did, I don't remember anything. How about you?'

'Nary a glimmer. I did, however, think about what we need to do today.'

'And what's that, Hercule? I'm totally out of ideas, myself.'

'Have some more coffee.' He filled my cup. 'As I see it, there are two people to be interviewed who might give us some fresh information. Neither conversation will be pleasant. I thought we might toss a coin for the honours.'

I gave him a look. 'All right. I'll bite.'

'Mrs Norquist is one.'

I groaned.

'And *Miss* MacKenzie is the other.'

'I think I'll go back to bed.'

'No, you won't. You can never resist a challenge. Which shall it be, a barmy old lady or a venomous younger one?'

'Oh, dear. Alan, I do hate to stick you with la MacKenzie, but I don't think I'd get anywhere at all with her. Mrs Norquist couldn't be any worse and might be a whole lot better. Do you really not mind?'

'I really do not mind. Who knows, Miss MacKenzie might fall victim to my celebrated charm.'

'Women do rather tend to fall at your feet, don't they? I'd better watch out, or rumours will start flying about you and some twenty-year-old floozy at the co-op. Which reminds me, before we do anything else today, I need to lay in some provisions. There really isn't anything edible in the house, and I don't feel like subsisting on take-away for several days.'

'Would you like me to drive you up to the co-op? Are you going to buy enough to need help with carrying it back?'

'Yes to both questions, and I'll risk the floozy. No, Watson, darling, we can't take you. Next time.'

We came home laden with bags, probably more food than we'd need, and of course Watson had to check out everything that smelled good, and then we had to give him a treat or two as we were putting everything away, and then he had to go out, so it was well past mid-morning before we were ready to sally forth to the distasteful tasks we had assigned ourselves. 'I have no idea where Miss MacKenzie lives,' I said to Alan, 'nor what she does when she's not at the museum or meddling in other people's business.'

'I'll go round to the knit shop and ask Mrs Menzies,' he said. 'After I drive you to Sinclair House. That's the home where Mrs Norquist lives.'

'My will isn't up to date,' I muttered, but not loud enough for Alan to hear me.

Once more we had to leave Watson behind, to his obvious disgust. We put him out in the little patio where he could at least see and smell the great outdoors, and ignored his whines of distress.

I felt a qualm when Alan left me at the door of the nursing facility. Mrs Norquist was, after all, reputed to have violent tendencies, and I didn't know how old and feeble she might be. The insane are also said to have strength, sometimes, beyond what might be expected.

Pull yourself together, Dorothy, I admonished myself. There will be attendants and nurses around. And there's a CCTV camera up there over the door, and I'll bet there are more inside. What could happen?

NINETEEN

What could happen was nothing. I girded my loins, walked in the door, and asked to see Mrs Norquist. 'I'm sorry, madam, no one can see her.'

It was like preparing to take the first step up a stairway, only to have one's foot come down on empty air. 'Oh,' I said. 'Oh, dear. Is she – um – ill or something?' I hardly knew how to ask if she was crazier than usual today.

'She has requested no visitors.'

'But I made a special trip out from the village, and my driver has gone. Couldn't I just speak to her for a moment?'

'No, madam.' The woman at the desk was pleasant, but quite firm. 'We always honour our residents' requests of that kind. She wishes to see no one.'

'But she doesn't even know me! I mean, it isn't as if I'm someone from the village who might upset her in some way.'

'I'm sorry.' She smiled and turned away.

I didn't know what to do. Alan had arranged to come back for me in an hour. I certainly didn't want to cool my heels in the reception area for that long, but there seemed to be no way I could see Mrs Norquist.

Reluctantly I pulled out my cell phone. Alan wouldn't even be halfway back to the village yet. He could come and pick me up, and either take me with him to see the redoubtable Miss MacKenzie, or drop me at the flat. I punched in his number and pushed Send.

Nothing happened. I probably tried three times before I noticed the message on the screen: No Signal.

We've grown so used to the idea of instant communication that I simply stared at the miserable thing, willing it to come alive and do my bidding, but of course it lay there in my hand, inert and useless.

'Mrs Martin?' The voice was soft and gentle. I turned around to see one of the women from last night's little gathering. 'We haven't met properly, but I was at Ruth Menzies' meeting last night. I'm Leonora Tredgold, but everyone calls me Nora. The vicar at St Mary's is my husband. You seem to be in difficulty. Is there any way I can help?'

'It's very kind of you, but I . . . the truth is, I'm at a bit of a loose end. I came to talk to Mrs Norquist, but they won't let me in. I guess she isn't seeing visitors. And I don't have a car here, and my husband is on his way back to Stromness, and my mobile won't work, and . . .' To my horror, my voice began to quiver, and I closed my mouth abruptly.

'Then I'm so glad I saw you. I'm quite free this morning, and I'd be happy to take you any place you like. Stromness, or Kirkwall, or anywhere at all.'

Suppressing an absurd desire to say 'Sherebury', I swallowed the lump in my throat and said, 'If you really have the time, I suppose I might as well go back to our holiday flat. It's on the harbour road in Stromness.'

'Yes, dear, I know. The car's this way.'

I had my voice under control by the time we had got away from the home. 'This really is very kind of you. I had so hoped to talk with Mrs Norquist, and when I couldn't, I didn't know quite what to do.'

'I imagine you wanted to talk to her about her son. You might not have learned anything, you know.'

'I've heard she's not always lucid.'

'That's not quite how I'd describe her. She's only mad nor'-nor' west, and I sometimes have the feeling she's pretending to be less capable than she is. That's just my own idea, mind you. My husband would reprove me for saying this, but she's not a very nice person, and I do think she gave her son a frightful life. It's rather a mercy he doesn't have to look after her anymore, but the respite may have come too late for him.'

'You think he's dead, then?'

'I don't know what I think, but that's not what I meant. You know, when a caged animal is suddenly set free, sometimes it won't come out of the cage. It doesn't know how to cope on its own, and fears freedom. I think perhaps Charlie Norquist was in subjection to his mother for so long, he no longer knows how to make his own decisions, fashion his own life. He can't shrug off the bonds.'

'Mrs Tredgold—'

'Nora.'

'Nora, what do you think has become of Mr Norquist? I've heard so many theories, and I know so little about him that I can't begin to guess which might be true.'

She was silent while negotiating a rather complicated roundabout. (Et tu, Orkney, I thought ruefully. I hate roundabouts and hadn't thought to find them here, back of beyond.)

'I don't know what to tell you,' Nora said slowly. 'I cannot feel that he is dead, though I know that seems the most reasonable explanation. I can think of no reason for anyone to wish him dead, and I can't imagine he would have enough resolution, if that's what's required, to take his own life. You see, Dorothy – may I call you Dorothy?'

'Please.'

'Charles Norquist has been told what to do all his life. His mother decided, after his father died, that they would move back to Orkney. His mother decided he should work at the museum. His mother decided what he would wear, what he would eat, probably what he would think. She imposed her own religious beliefs on him, and her own moral values.'

'I've heard his beliefs were – are – somewhat peculiar.'

Nora laughed, rather bitterly. 'That's one way to put it. She was an out-and-out pagan, and directed her son in the same way. I don't mean simply a non-Christian. That's common enough in these days, more's the pity, but Theodore and I can deal with that. Non-believers are usually pleasant and kind people, and we always cherish the hope of leading them into more life-giving paths. But pagans have their own set of beliefs that are not simply un-Christian, but quite definitely anti-Christian, and I fear sometimes quite nasty.'

'Including sacrifice?' I murmured.

'Sometimes including sacrifice, and nothing like the sacrifice of the Eucharist. I am extremely worried about Charlie Norquist, Mrs Martin. I think his life may be imperilled, and I fear even more for his soul. Theodore and I pray for him daily. Now let me see, is this your flat?'

'Yes.' I started to struggle out of the small car, and then sat back. 'Nora, would you like to come in for a cup of tea? Unless you have to be somewhere.'

'That's very kind of you. I'm always ready for a cup of tea. I'll just park across the street in the ferry lot. No one bothers much about the rules unless the lot is full.'

We went into the flat, and I let the dog in. He was voluble in either welcome or recrimination; I wasn't sure which. I calmed him and turned on the kettle.

'This is quite nice, isn't it?' she said, looking around. 'One never knows about holiday flats, but this one's been done up beautifully.'

'It's well equipped, too. Mr Fairweather was telling us about a holiday he and his wife once spent in Cornwall in a cottage with no pots or pans. They couldn't cook at all. It's always tricky in someone else's kitchen anyway, isn't it?'

'Indeed. But Dorothy, you didn't ask me in to talk about kitchens.'

I do like a person who comes to the point. 'No, I didn't. I'll make the tea, and phone Alan to tell him where I am, and then I want to talk over this whole situation.'

Alan didn't answer. I considered worrying and then decided not to. He was probably talking to Miss MacKenzie, or more likely listening to her. She wouldn't take kindly to being inter- rupted by a phone call. Or anything else. I left a voicemail and sat down at the table with the tea tray.

'Now,' said Nora in business-like fashion. 'How can I help?'

'For a start, tell me why Mrs Norquist won't talk to anyone.' I had only just realized how odd that seemed to me. 'Is she usually so reclusive?'

'First you must realize that she's inconsistent. The mentally ill usually are, and when dementia's thrown into the mix, one can never be quite sure what to expect. Having said that, I have to say that I was very surprised to be stopped at the door to her room. I visit several patients there at least once a week. Theodore visits too, of course, but that's parish visiting. I go as a friend. Mrs Norquist is a difficult woman, as I've said, and one who likes to be in control. I think she's immensely frustrated in her present situation. Charlie isn't there to be ordered about, and the staff, though patient and kind, don't take orders from the patients.'

'Of course not. So she doesn't have anybody to boss around.'

'That's it. I understand she had one or two temper tantrums

when she was first sent there, but as they didn't get her what she wanted, she soon decided not to waste her energy. She's not a stupid woman.'

'But if she wants someone to issue orders to, you'd think she'd want visitors.'

'Oh, yes. She usually welcomes me with open arms, though they do rather resemble the open arms of a large carnivorous animal. She tells me all the sins of the staff and demands that I do something about it.'

'She's that much in command of herself?'

Nora nodded. 'Mind you, most of what she says is sheer fabrication, but she expresses herself quite clearly. Forcibly, in fact. I must confess that I'm sometimes a trifle intimidated. She's quite strong physically. Her body seems to have strengthened as her mind has deteriorated. It's rather a pity, really, though I shouldn't say so. If ever someone's death would be a blessing, hers would. To all concerned. Don't you ever dare tell my husband I said that last bit.'

I couldn't help smiling. 'He'll never hear it from me. But does she ever talk about her son?'

'Oh, my dear.' She put her cup down and I refilled it. 'He is her other subject of lament. Sometimes she talks as if he's still about three and running her ragged. At other times she's living more in the present and grumbling about his neglect of her. Really, I'm afraid I do find it hard to be patient with her.'

'I think you're a saint even to go and visit. So this is the first time she's sent you away?'

'Yes, and she was almost hysterical about it. You see, I'd been visiting other patients, so I was in the residents' area. I always keep her visit for the last, though I suppose I should get it over first. But when I came to her door it was shut, which is unusual, and an attendant was sitting beside it. He knows me, of course, and when he said I couldn't go in, Mrs Norquist must have heard him, and she started screaming. Really raving, which I'd never heard her do before, threats and carrying on. It was really quite unpleasant.'

I shuddered. 'It must have been. But it's certainly peculiar. One more peculiar thing. And you know, Nora, one thing I've always believed is that when odd things start happening in a certain . . . constellation is the only word I can find that describes it – the chances are very great that they're somehow related. I've never quite believed in coincidence. There's a reason for most things, don't you agree?'

'Of course I do. God does move in mysterious ways.'

'And not only God! Alan thinks—'

'What does Alan think? Oh, I'm sorry. I thought you were on the phone.' Alan had come in unnoticed and now stood in the doorway to the kitchen. 'I didn't mean to interrupt, but I didn't know we had a guest.'

I introduced them. 'Nora was at Ruth's meeting last night, and I ran into her this morning at Sinclair House. Alan, I didn't want you to leave you a long message, but they wouldn't let me in!'

That entailed a long explanation about Mrs Norquist's atypical behaviour, which Alan thought as odd as Nora and I did. 'And I was just about to tell Nora your theory that someone is manipulating these oddities for his – or her – own devious ends.'

'It would,' said Nora, in the most uncharitable tones I had heard her use, 'take a world-class manipulator to force Lillian Norquist to do anything she didn't want to do. I would have said it was impossible, save for her conduct this morning. Something has moved her out of her groove, but I'm afraid I have no idea what.'

'Or who,' said Alan.

'Or who,' she agreed, and looked at her watch. 'I'm very sorry, but I'm afraid I do have to get home and make some lunch for my husband. He forgets to eat if I'm not there to remind him. We'll talk again?'

'Absolutely.' I stood. 'I'll let you know if anything interesting comes up.'

'And I'll do the same. And please, both of you, be careful. Something evil is abroad in these islands. I fear more people will be harmed before it is vanquished.'

TWENTY

'That,' said Alan when he had showed her out, 'is a remarkable woman.'

'I like her very much,' I said. 'What would you like for lunch, dear?'

We decided on thick, American-style hamburgers. There was a small grill on the patio and we'd bought some charcoal, so they ended up tasting almost as good as the ones I used to make back home, long ago. Different, because the beef was different, but not bad at all.

While we ate, Alan and I exchanged notes. I told him all I'd learned about Mrs Norquist, and he regaled me with his encounter with Janet MacKenzie.

'The woman toyed with me, Dorothy! You know I used to be pretty good at interviewing witnesses, but this one defeated me.'

'It's a pity you have no police authority anymore.'

'I don't think it would have made a hap'orth of difference. She's a malicious woman with an acid tongue, and she despises men.'

'Maybe I should have gone to her after all, but I confess I quailed at the thought.'

'I think she despises women, too. She's the sort that likes to pin butterflies to a board for the fun of watching them struggle to escape.'

'But did you learn anything?'

'If your sources are correct, that she doesn't lie, then I learned a couple of not very useful facts. One is that she doesn't have keys to the display cases, nor are they kept at the museum. She insists that Norquist has the only keys, and that he was pernickety about them. Shorn of her vituperative prose, the story is that he kept them on his key ring and would let no one else so much as handle them. If a case had to be unlocked while the museum was open, which would have been extremely unusual, he did it himself. Most of the time, he did any necessary maintenance after hours, by himself. The keys, she insists, never left his person.'

'But Alan, that makes no sense at all! Those artefacts disappeared after Norquist did. If he's dead, that would mean someone stole his keys and then stole some objects of almost no intrinsic worth. If he's alive and hiding someplace, it means he came back, stole a few objects over which he had custody anyway, and then disappeared again.'

'And got into the museum through a door locked with a new lock. Don't forget that part.' He took a large bite of his hamburger.

I put mine back on the plate. 'I've figured it out!' I said dramatically.

'Oh?'

'We've got into Looking Glass Country, where everything is backwards. The faster we run, the behinder we get. Or maybe Wonderland, with Janet MacKenzie as the Queen of Hearts shouting "Off with their heads!" Would you like some beer?'

'What I'd like is a bottle or so of Highland Park, but I'll settle for beer. A half, please.'

When we'd finished and cleared up, we brewed a pot of coffee and took it up to the sitting room with us. The bedroom was perilously close, calling me to a nap, but I stoically sipped my coffee. I knew from experience what was about to ensue.

'I am reminded less of Alice,' he said, 'than of Don Quixote, running madly in all directions and tilting at windmills.'

'We have, in short, been dancing quite nicely when our strings were pulled.'

'Precisely. It's time to sit back and think properly about what's been happening, instead of merely reacting.'

'So many things have been happening,' I objected. 'It's hard to make them fit into any sort of pattern.'

'Then forget about the many things and concentrate on the most important thing. What's the big piece in this jigsaw puzzle we've been trying to work?'

'Carter's death. Do you know, I'd nearly forgotten about him with everything else that's been going on.'

'I think that's exactly what our puppet master, whoever he or she is, intended. I think that's what all these other little mysteries have been meant to do, distract attention from Carter's murder and hence from his murderer. So let's forget about the rest of the puzzle for a little and think hard about the big piece. One way of understanding an action is to observe its result. What is the net result of Carter's death?'

'The Friends get a whole lot of money, and the dig can continue, forever, as far as I can tell.'

'And who benefits from that result?'

'Almost everybody except Mr Carter. Orkney, the Friends, the kids who're working on the dig . . . oh.'

'Yes. Who gets what amounts to a job for life, given the time that excavation requires? Who gets to make the decisions about the project, the critical decisions like how far down to go, how much of the late history to destroy to reach the earlier levels? Who ends up with enormous distinction in his field as director of the most important archaeological discovery of the century?'

'And who,' I asked, 'has the only new key to the museum?'

'I don't know,' said Alan, massaging the back of his head. 'That MacKenzie woman claimed not to know. I'll bet she does know, but she wouldn't tell me. I'll ask Baikie; he'll know.'

'Was it the police who put the new lock on?'

'I think they saw to it, but at the Friends' instigation. And we need to find out who holds the key at this point. But there's only one answer to the rest of the questions.'

'Fairweather.' I finished my coffee and poured some more. 'We suspected him right at the first, but then . . . I can't remember why we forgot about him.'

'The cat, remember?'

'Oh, yes, poor old Roadkill. He died and then Norquist disappeared, and we thought Norquist must be responsible for at least one of the deaths.'

'Misdirection, in short. And remember who found the cat at the dig?'

'Fairweather, of course.'

I drank coffee and pondered. 'So why hasn't Baikie gone after Fairweather, now that the terrorism business has abated a little?'

'He's a prominent figure, for one thing. He's doing a great deal to bring sorely-needed money to Orkney. Baikie is going to want a good deal of solid evidence behind him before he tries to make a case, and there's none. We can build a great hypothesis, but it's as fine as spider's silk.'

I shuddered involuntarily. I'm terrified of spiders.

'Sorry, love. Insubstantial as a butterfly's wing. Is that better?'

'Much. All right. How do we go about turning that butterfly's wing into handcuffs – no, the metaphor doesn't work. How do we build a case against Fairweather?'

'I don't know if it can be done. I think Norquist was the vital witness, and I think Norquist is dead.'

'Well, I don't. Think he's dead, I mean. I can't tell you why, but I just cannot make myself believe it. So I think the first thing that we need to do is find Norquist.'

'My dear woman, what have we been trying to do for days now?'

'You've been trying to find his body. There's a big difference. A dead man stays in one place. A living man might not. Assume he's living, and then try to think where he might have gone and why.'

Alan was silent for a while. He didn't, I could tell, entirely buy my theory, but he was willing to test it.

'The why part isn't hard,' he said at last. 'He's hiding from Fairweather.'

'Of course. If we've worked out that he's a danger to Fairweather, because he knows something – we don't know what – Norquist would have realized it much sooner. And he would know exactly why. The man may not be quite on the same planet as the rest of us, but he's not stupid. He'd want to get off Orkney entirely, but he might not have had enough time, or he might have been afraid that Fairweather could trace any of the commercial carriers. For whatever reason, I don't think he left. I think he's right here. And I think all the searchers have been wasting their time going to caves and ancient sites, because those are exactly the places where Fairweather would look.'

'Given all that, and it makes a certain amount of sense, where would you suggest they look?'

'I haven't the slightest idea, but I know who might.'

'Mrs Tredgold.' He didn't make it a question.

I pulled out my mobile.

She answered on the second ring. 'Nora Tredgold.'

'This is Dorothy Martin, Nora. I'm sorry to bother you again so soon, but Alan and I have been doing some thinking.' I took a deep breath. 'You may find this hard to believe, but we think we know who killed Henry Carter. That was what started this chain of events, Carter's death. I say we think we know, but we haven't a shred of actual evidence, just speculation. And we believe Mr Norquist may have the evidence needed to bring the murderer to justice. Now Alan still thinks he may be dead, but I don't and I don't think you do, either.'

'No, I don't, though I can't give you sensible reasons for that belief.'

'Nor can I. That doesn't matter. What does matter is that if Mr Norquist is a crucial witness, he would know that he's in danger, and would go into hiding. It's terribly important that the police find him before the murderer does.'

'Yes.'

'The thing is, police and volunteers have searched what they believed to be the most likely places. So he's hiding in some *un*likely place. He hasn't left Orkney, at least not by any commercial plane or ferry. Does he have friends with a plane or a boat who might have taken him to Scrabster or some such place?'

'He has very few friends, really no one who's at all close. I find that notion very far-fetched.'

'So do we, but we wanted to have our ideas confirmed. That means he's still in Orkney somewhere, probably on this island. You know him well. Do you have any idea where he might have gone?'

There was quite a long silence before she said, 'If I knew where he was, I would tell you. I don't. But I do believe his hiding place will have something to do with the two ruling passions of his life, his worship of the ancient peoples and their ways, and his fear of his mother.'

'Fear? Not love?'

'The two are so intermixed in his mind that they have become one. Indeed, he has almost become his mother, so completely has she absorbed him. She is the sort of mother who eats her young, you know.'

'That's . . . horrible.' I swallowed. 'How can you endure your visits to her?'

'I try to keep remembering that every human creature needs love, and she has no one to love her.'

'No one *could* love her!'

'Exactly. So I try. I very seldom succeed, but I try. Sometimes I can manage genuine pity, which she doesn't at all welcome, but which is akin to love. And on the days when all I can do is wish I could bop her on the head,' she added, and I could hear her faint smile, 'I try to think of her as my cross to bear.'

'Well, I think you're a saint, but I still can't work out where Norquist might be. Of course I know almost nothing about these islands, except for the major Neolithic sites. I'm not sure where else we might try.'

'There are quite a number of burial places not known to the general public. Even Inspector Baikie and his men might not know of them. Charlie excavated some of them himself. Unfortunately I can't tell you where they all are, but Mr Larsen would undoubtedly know. Those might be possibilities, though they're hardly big enough to stay in for any length of time. Nor would they provide any degree of comfort.'

'But they're Neolithic?'

'Oh, yes, quite certainly.'

'Then we'll talk to Mr Larsen.' Here at last, I thought, was something positive to do. 'I'm not sure it matters that they're small and uncomfortable. Norquist wouldn't have had to stay in the same one the whole time, if they're not too far apart. He could be hopping from one to another, trying to evade pursuit.'

'Surely that would increase his risk?'

'In one way, but not in another. If he stayed in one until he had some reason to believe someone was seeking him there, he could move to another and then come back to the first, on the principle that it had already been searched and thus was safe.'

'Perhaps. These cairns have not yet been mapped, you understand, and may be quite hard to find.'

'Yes, and that poses a problem. If we take a large party, Larsen and the police and all, we might as well hire a brass band. We'll be trumpeting our objectives and could lead the murderer straight to Norquist. On the other hand, if we go alone and quietly, with just Larsen as guide, we could end up in a peat bog somewhere.'

'I'll trust you to do the sensible thing. And Dorothy, please find him. He's such a sad little man, and so disturbed, and so helpless. Theodore and I will be praying for you.'

Alan had been listening to my end of the conversation. 'And why are we taking a brass band into the peat bogs?'

'We're not. We're hoping to avoid the peat bogs, and we're taking just ourselves, and Mr Larsen, and Watson, who may be the biggest help of all. We're looking for ancient burial places, cairns or tombs or whatever they're called. Nora thinks Mr Norquist may be hiding in one of them, and the police wouldn't have looked there, because they don't know about them. Almost nobody does, except for Norquist, who discovered them, and Larsen, the overseer of all Orkney's ancient sites.'

Alan looked grim. 'There's no way to find these tombs except with Larsen's help?'

'Nora says not.'

'I don't like it, Dorothy. I know we've decided that Fairweather is much the most likely villain, but Larsen certainly had some interest in Carter's death, too. Are we proposing to lead the fox to the chicken coop?'

'I know. I feel exactly the same way. But what else is there to do? We don't know for certain that Fairweather knows nothing about these places, and we've got to find Norquist first. And we can't do it without Larsen. We can tell Inspector Baikie what we're going to do, so if something drastic happens he'll come after us.'

'And much good that would do anyone, if we're all lying dead out there on the moors. And in any case we can't tell him, dear heart, because he's probably still buried in other matters. And if not, he'd certainly insist on making the search himself, or send a platoon of police to do it, and there's your brass band laid on. We're in a cleft stick.'

'No, we're not, Alan. There are the Tredgolds! When we're ready to start out, we'll tell them approximately where we're going. They're utterly trustworthy, and if anything happens, they'll know what to do. Besides, they're praying for us.'

'I wish I found that a little more reassuring than I do. However, you're right. We have to make the attempt. I'll phone Larsen.'

His voice mail answered with a complicated message about

his teaching schedule. Alan rang back twice to get it all. 'He has a lecture until five, and then a seminar all evening. If we're going to catch him, it will have to be between five and seven, or we'll have to wait until tomorrow. What message shall I leave?'

'I don't think it can wait. I suppose I'm being silly, but I have this terrible sense of urgency. Let's not leave a message at all. Let's go over to the university and catch him when he comes out of his lecture.'

Rather surprisingly, Alan agreed. 'I thought,' I said tentatively, 'that you supposed Norquist to be dead.'

'I did. I've not entirely changed my mind, but you're taking this very seriously, and so is Mrs Tredgold, whom I've come very quickly to respect and trust. If you both think it's urgent, it may very well be. You'd best phone and tell her where we're going, in case we're wrong about Larsen's innocence.'

I did that, relegated Watson to the patio until our plans were firm, and we set out.

TWENTY-ONE

We got a little lost on the way to the university in Kirkwall as Alan didn't know the way, and medieval cities, even small ones, can be very confusing. But we arrived a little before five, parked in an illegal spot, and rushed into what seemed to be the main office. Of course the building where Larsen was lecturing was at the far end of the complex, but we walked it as fast as two people our age could be expected to walk and arrived, out of breath, just as Larsen was walking out the front door, chatting with a student.

Alan strode up to him. 'Mr Larsen, a word, please.'

Larsen was a little startled at the interruption, which was just plain rude, and entirely unlike my courtly husband. But the student waved and went on her way, and Alan said, 'I'm truly sorry, sir, but there is a matter that is extremely urgent. Will you walk back to our car with us and let us explain?'

Larsen was slightly annoyed. 'I'm afraid I haven't much time. I've a seminar at seven—'

'Yes, I know. I do apologize, but this won't wait.' Alan looked around. There was no one nearby, no one paying any attention to us. 'It concerns Mr Norquist, who is still missing, and whom we believe to be in considerable danger.'

Larsen stopped walking. 'Norquist? Surely the man's dead? Suicide, I thought.'

'We don't think so, Mr Larsen,' I chimed in. 'We believe he's in hiding, and we think we know where he might be. We need your help to find him.'

'My help? But my dear lady, I haven't the slightest idea—'

'We think he might be in one of the unmapped tombs, or cairns, or whatever you call them,' said Alan. 'I understand you and he are the only ones who know where they all are.'

'That's quite true,' said Larsen thoughtfully. 'The Friends have been trying for some time now to get them mapped, but it's an expensive proposition, and the dig at High Sanday has been taking all our time and money and attention. The cairns are not at all spectacular, nothing like Maes Howe. They're tiny. What makes you think Norquist might be there?'

'We think he'd go to a place that's important to him, and that means one of the Neolithic sites.'

Larsen nodded. He no longer seemed to be in a hurry. 'That man doesn't live in the twenty-first century, you know. His clock is set somewhere around 2500 BC. He's only happy when he's communing with Stone Age people, and I quite honestly believe he thinks they're still here.'

Well, so do you, almost, I thought, *and so in a way do I.* But this wasn't the time to go into it.

'So you could be right,' he went on. 'If he wanted to go into hiding, he might think the new cairns – newly discovered, I mean – a perfect place to go. But why would he want to go into hiding?'

I had the answer to that one worked out. 'A great many unpleasant things have been happening of late,' I said. 'Mr Norquist is not a strong man, and he is, as you say, a little unbalanced on the subject of the Neolithic peoples. All of these events might have disturbed him to the point that he felt he had to get away and "commune" with the ancients, as you put it. And he isn't at any of the big important sites, or even the smaller but reasonably well-known ones. So when we learned about these secret ones—'

'Ah, yes. And just how did you learn of them? They're not exactly secret, but very few people do know about them.'

'Do you know Mrs Tredgold, wife of the vicar of St Mary's?'

'Ah. I understand. A good woman, that, and how she finds out everything that happens in these islands I'll never know. She doesn't snoop. She just knows. A bit frightening, actually. Well, now.' He looked at his watch. 'I have a seminar in not much more than an hour, and I'd hoped to get a bite to eat and look over my notes beforehand. But you feel this matter is urgent?'

'Don't you?' We had arrived at our car. I put my hand on Larsen's arm. 'If that poor man has been out there for two or three days in all weathers, he could be ill by now, and in any case he's probably frightened and disoriented. He must be found.'

Larsen nodded. 'You're right. I'll just ask the secretary to put a note on the door saying the seminar is cancelled for this evening, and then I'll go to my office and get my rough sketch of the cairns. It'll be light for hours yet; we can make a start, anyway. I'll meet you here in ten minutes.'

We got in the car and Alan started it just in time. A traffic warden was approaching with blood in her eye, but Alan explained that we were just waiting for someone, and his charm did its work. She allowed us a few minutes.

Larsen was away longer than he had estimated, and I began to worry. 'Alan, what if he's gone off to hunt that poor man down? What if he really is the one?'

'He'd hardly do that and leave us here. We're witnesses. If he intended . . . but here he comes.'

He had a light pack with him. 'I took the time to change, and I brought a few tools. You'll want to change, as well. The cairns aren't nice and tidy, and the entrances are less than three feet high. You have to crawl.'

Crawling is not something my artificial knees enjoy at all. And I could feel my claustrophobia kicking in at the very thought of crawling into an ancient tomb in the middle of nowhere. But if it had to be done, I'd grit my teeth and do it. I remembered Alan's late wife, Helen. I'll bet she'd explored similar places without a qualm, and I wasn't going to show myself a coward by comparison.

We went back to the flat and changed into jeans and sturdy shoes, and then I took a few minutes to slap together some sandwiches. 'It won't help Mr Norquist if we starve, and I've made some for him, too, in case he hasn't been eating.'

'And bring walking sticks if you have them,' said Larsen. 'We'll run out of road rather soon.'

It took a moment to remember where we'd put them, but in a very short time we were off, Watson quivering with the excitement he'd caught from us.

We headed west and north, to a part of the island I hadn't seen. It began to be very hilly, and the road very narrow. We munched on sandwiches, getting food into us while we could, though my stomach was so full of butterflies it was a wonder there was any room for bread and meat. What were we getting ourselves into? Would we find Mr Norquist in this apparently deserted countryside? Or would we find . . . something else? Was this apparently pleasant man leading us to our doom? Surely not. We were three against one, after all, if you counted Watson – who had demonstrated his protective instincts. And Larsen was a decent man. Wasn't he?

I cleared my throat. 'I hope this isn't just a wild goose chase,' I said. 'It was Mrs Tredgold who put us onto it, as we said. She was pleased to hear we were going with you to search.'

Alan recognized my motives in mentioning that someone else knew what we were doing. He also recognized my unspoken anxiety. 'Steady on, old girl,' he murmured, patting my hand.

'The road comes to an end just up here,' said Larsen from the back seat. 'You can leave the car anywhere you like. No one comes up here except the odd farmer. From here we walk.'

Well, we were committed now. Alan got our walking sticks from the boot, and Larsen pulled on the small pack he had tossed in the car. I very much wondered what was in it.

He saw me looking at it and obligingly offered me an inventory. 'Map, compass, torch, my folding stick, and a few other oddments like trowels and brushes. One never knows what might turn up.'

I wasn't altogether reassured. 'Oddments' might easily include things like a hammer. I moved a little closer to Alan and grasped Watson's lead firmly, and we set out.

'Watch your step,' said Larsen cheerily. 'This is a pasture, you know.'

'For cattle or sheep?' Alan asked.

'Both.'

'But they're not here now, are they?' I asked a little anxiously. 'I mean, I can see they're not, but are they apt to appear soon? Because of Watson,' I added. I didn't intend to admit that large animals with horns terrify me.

'Don't know. Don't know much about farming. I'd think that the beasts would spend most of the summer moving from one pasture to the next, as the grass grows, but I don't really know a thing about it.'

Great. Any time now, someone might open a gate somewhere, and we'd be stampeded by a thundering herd of something or other. That was one of the few hazards I hadn't imagined in dreading this expedition.

I reminded myself that we were trying to save a man's life. If we could accomplish that, my petty fears were of little importance. I tried to focus on Larsen and what he was telling Alan.

'A lot of peat hereabouts, you see, not just here, but a bit farther north, round Evie and Birsay. It's still an important resource. People don't use it for fuel so much anymore, but the distilleries use a lot of it to dry the malt. It's what gives whisky the smoky flavour. Most of what's dug in Orkney goes to Highland Park, of course.'

That was actually interesting, and took my mind off cattle and hammers for a few seconds.

We came upon the cairn with no warning. There was nothing, to my eyes anyway, to mark the little rise as anything special, but Larsen walked around it to the far side, and there, sure enough, was a small opening perhaps eighteen inches wide and high. I'd have thought it the burrow of some biggish mammal, if I'd thought about it at all. A raccoon, say, or a big groundhog. If either of them inhabits burrows.

'It hasn't been properly excavated, of course,' Larsen was saying. 'The entrance was a good deal taller when it was built, and people were shorter. But even they would have had to stoop to enter. We think it was a gesture of respect to the dead, or perhaps to the gods that inhabited the place. There's no telling, now.' He reached in his pack, pulled out a powerful flashlight, and shone it on the ground around the entrance opening. 'Hmm. We can go in if you like, but it doesn't look to me as if anything bigger than a rabbit has been here for some time.'

The ground was soft in front of the entrance, and bare of grass. I could see by the strong slanting light of the torch what the sky light hadn't shown me, the tracks of quite a number of small animals. I recognized only a few, familiar from tracks in the snow back in Indiana. Rabbits, yes, mice, others I couldn't identify.

Alan shook his head doubtfully. 'I'm sure you're right, but we'd best look anyway. I'm not sure I'll fit, but I'll give it a try. I'll need a shoehorn.'

Larsen was the slimmest of us. I knew why Alan preferred to examine the cairn himself.

With some difficulty, he managed to get his head and shoulders through the opening. That was a bad few moments for me. All my claustrophobia kicked in on his behalf. What if he couldn't get out? What if the roof caved in? What if there was something horrid in there? What if Larsen attacked him while he was helplessly on his knees, and then went after me?

He'd borrowed Larsen's torch, and the two or three minutes seemed like hours, during which I scarcely breathed, before he backed out and got to his feet. 'Ptthah!' He spat out bits of mud and leaves and I didn't care to consider what else. 'It's pretty foul in there. And certainly no human has been inside recently, probably not since Norquist discovered it.'

Larsen nodded. 'Right. Shall we go on to the next? We've hours of daylight left.'

I left my fears behind at the third or fourth cairn. I could see them for the foolish fancies they were. I could also see this as an increasingly futile expedition. Some of the cairns were considerably bigger than the first one. I even ventured, briefly, into one myself when Alan pronounced it rather interesting inside. In none of them did we find the slightest evidence of human occupation, at least not in the last few millennia.

'There are a few more,' said Larsen at last, 'but they're even smaller than the smallest we've seen, and the light's fading. You don't want to be out here on the moors in the dark, even the twilight of a midsummer's night. There are bogs, for one thing.'

'You're right,' said Alan. 'We'll have to give up, at least for tonight.'

'Mr Larsen, it's been wonderful of you to give up your time for this.' I shook his hand. 'I'm sorry it's turned out to be a wild goose chase.'

'But it might not have done,' said Larsen. 'If Norquist is alive, and frankly that seems more unlikely every day, this is the sort of place we might expect to find him. If you want to continue tomorrow, I'm quite free.'

We agreed to let him know, and drove back to Kirkwall in sombre silence.

We were dead tired when we dropped Larsen off at the university, and very hungry. Those sandwiches had been a long time ago. But the state of our clothes prohibited a restaurant meal, and after eleven o'clock we probably wouldn't find one open anyway. So Alan popped into a fish-and-chips café we spotted on the way back to Stromness, and we ate our greasy meal sitting in the car. Watson insisted on his share, and we gave it to him. 'It'll probably make him sick,' I pointed out.

'Just now I simply do not care. It may make us sick, for that matter. Never mind. Let's get home to bed.'

TWENTY-TWO

My dreams were uneasy that night. In the morning I remembered none of the details, only the feeling of imminent disaster and my own helplessness to avert it. Alan was still asleep when I fought my way out of an especially awful dream and staggered down to the kitchen for some coffee.

My predictions about Watson had, all too obviously, come true. He was looking shame-faced, his tail between his legs. 'Never mind, dog,' I said wearily. 'It's not your fault. We shouldn't have fed you that junk. I'm not really feeling too well myself. Out you go.' I opened the patio door and he slunk out, still not sure he wasn't in disgrace. I made coffee and took it upstairs to the sitting room. I was definitely not up to that clean-up job until I'd had some caffeine.

The smell of coffee woke Alan, who padded out to the sitting room looking as dishevelled and out of sorts as I felt. 'Watson was sick all over the kitchen floor,' I said by way of cheery greeting. Alan groaned and poured himself some coffee.

We cleaned up the kitchen in grim silence, cleaned up ourselves, and then by common consent put Watson on his leash and headed for the nearby café for breakfast. He had to wait outside, of course, but he was feeling quite a lot better by that time and was happy to receive the admiring pats and coos of passers-by.

We couldn't talk about our problem in the crowded café, which was a real blessing. It gave us time to sort out our ideas and psyche ourselves into better moods. After we'd eaten we took Watson for a long walk along the harbour and then back up along The Street.

It didn't come as any real surprise when we ran into Mrs Tredgold. She smiled, observed our faces, and said, 'There's no need, I see, to ask how you fared yesterday.'

'Badly, I'm afraid,' said Alan in a low voice.

'We can't talk here,' Nora said. 'Come back to the vicarage with me. That is, how does Watson feel about cats?'

'He loves our two,' I replied. 'In fact, the only one I've ever known him to dislike . . .' I trailed off, and she sighed and nodded.

'Entirely understandable. We're up this lane.' She turned into a steep by-way that was signposted 'Khyber Pass'.

Shades of the Empire, I thought, and tugged at Watson, who had located an interesting smell and wanted to linger.

The vicarage was small and cosy. Watson trotted in with no hesitation and set about sniffing out the cats he knew were there. We followed him and our hostess into a sitting room furnished with soft squishy chintz-covered furniture and, sure enough, two soft squishy cats asleep in a window seat. They opened their eyes at Watson's advance, yawned, stretched, and went back to sleep again.

'No trouble there,' said Nora. 'Now tell me.'

We told her, omitting no nasty detail. The mud and excrement in the cairns, the smells, the horrid confinement of the interiors that nearly drove me mad, even when it was Alan venturing in. 'And it was a complete waste of time and effort,' I finished morosely. 'Norquist wasn't in any of them; hadn't ever been there.'

'But it wasn't a waste, was it?' she said. 'You've crossed one possibility off your list.'

'Larsen said there are a few more cairns,' I reminded her.

'But even smaller and less convenient. I think you can say you've eliminated the cairns. And you've eliminated Larsen as a suspicious person.'

'He could have taken us to the cairns because he knew perfectly well Norquist wasn't there,' I said without much conviction.

'He could, but is it likely he'd spend an evening at a fruitless endeavour, an evening, moreover, when he had other responsibilities?'

'Probably not. I suppose not.'

'You're tired,' she said charitably, 'and no wonder.'

'We both are,' said Alan. 'Tired and discouraged. We don't seem able to make any progress at all.'

'You will. The great thing is not to give up. For a start, you may remember that I suggested one other possible hiding place for Charlie.'

'You did? Oh, I remember. You said it would have something to do with his mother. But she's incommunicado right now, and

probably not very helpful at the best of times. I don't mean to
seem ungrateful, but I don't see how that line of reasoning leads
anywhere.'

'Nor do I. At the moment. But bear it in mind. And my dears,
do know that several of us are racking our brains trying to think
of anything that might help. Ruth, Isabel, even Celia Freebody.'

'Oh, has she finally decided I didn't kill Sandy?'

'She's accepted that. I don't say she'll ever be your best friend,
and she certainly isn't a great friend to Charlie, with his fear of
cats.'

'You said he didn't have any real friends.'

'Nor does he. But he's one of ours, and we stick together.
People do, in a village. In any case, nearly everyone feels a
certain sympathy for him, because of what he's had to put up
with from his mother. So you've lots of support in your endeavour,
my dears.'

'I wish,' I said, 'that made me feel much better. We don't
know what to do now.'

'What I think you should do is forget all about it. It's a lovely
day. Go on a sightseeing tour. *Not* the Neolithic sites. They would
keep your mind on your troubles. Have you seen the Italian Chapel?'

'I have, years ago. Dorothy hasn't,' said Alan. 'That might be
just what's wanted. And when we get there, we can take Watson
for a lovely long walkies.'

He thought Alan meant now, and trotted to the door. 'No,
darling,' I said firmly. 'You've had your walkies for this morning.
Later.'

He understood the tone, at least, and walked the short distance
back to the flat in resignation.

When we got there I sank down on a kitchen chair. 'Alan, I
don't think I want to go anywhere. You were polite to Nora, but
I'm just not up to it.'

'Yes, you are. You'll enjoy it. Wash your face and brush your
teeth, or whatever you need to do, and come along.'

I was nettled. Alan almost never tries to force me into anything.
'Look, I'm tired and depressed and *I do not want to go!*'

'Dorothy.' He ran a hand down the back of his head. 'I understand exactly how you feel, and of course you're free to do as
you like. But this might be our only opportunity to see the Italian

Chapel, and it would be a great pity for you to miss it. And Nora is quite right. It'll be good medicine. If you stay here all by yourself you're just going to brood.'

There are times when an understanding husband can be a great trial. I remember once, as a child, when I was furious about something and had a temper tantrum. With me a tantrum consisted not of screaming and kicking, but of sulking. My two older sisters tried to snap me out of it by making me laugh. They succeeded, against my will, and then I was madder than ever, because I *wanted* to sulk.

Today I wanted to brood and wallow in gloom. Alan had no right to walk into my mind, figure it out, and try to amend matters.

Tight-lipped, I followed him to the car, got in the back seat with the dog, and sat in utter silence as he drove east, toward Kirkwall.

I had to fight to hang onto my bad mood as we drove, in silence, through the countryside. It was truly a glorious day, the hills warmed and gilded by the sun, the sea diamond-sparkling. The very sheep seemed whiter and fluffier than usual, the grass greener, the birds more melodious. All nature was inviting me to rejoice, and I wanted to sulk.

Alan began to talk. 'We've talked a little about the Churchill Barriers. It was during the Second World War. Most of the British fleet, what there was of it, was berthed at Scapa Flow, the large basin southwest of Kirkwall. When the Second World War began, it was thought that the ships were safe from U-boats, because a good many German ships had been scuttled there at the end of the Great War, and were lying on the bottom creating a hazard to underwater navigation. However, the pundits were wrong. A U-boat got through and sank a ship, killing hundreds of men. So in 1940, I believe, Churchill ordered barriers built to shut off the eastern approaches, underwater walls from one island to the next, as it were. As most British labourers were serving in the military, someone had the bright idea of using the Italian prisoners of war, housed on Orkney, to do much of the work.'

I opened my mouth to comment, and shut it again.

'It was probably very hard work, but apparently the men had some time on their hands, because the beauty-loving Italians began to beautify their camp. Their most urgent wish was for a chapel, because of course they were Catholic and the local churches were either Church of Scotland or Church of England. So the officials, who seemed to have been reasonably sympathetic, gave them two extra Nissen huts.'

Quonset huts, I mentally translated. 'Must have been a pretty ugly chapel.'

'It happened that one of the prisoners was an artist, and he and the others set out to make a place of worship worthy of its purpose. They lined the walls so the corrugations wouldn't show and then painted them in trompe-l'oeil fashion to look like carved marble and vaulted brickwork. They made an altar and altar rail of concrete. One of the men was good at metal-work, so he made candelabra and a beautiful wrought-iron rood screen. The artist in charge painted a beautiful image of the Virgin and Child over the altar, flanked with saints and angels.

'And then something happened. The war ended. The prisoners were free. But the artist hadn't quite completed his work. He was given permission to remain behind and finish the font.

'But that wasn't the end of the story, either. Harsh weather conditions and the nature of the structure combined to allow serious deterioration, but local interest was strong and money was raised for repairs and restoration. And in 1960 the original artist was brought back, at local expense, to supervise the repairs and do some of the repainting himself. At the rededication service, some two hundred Orcadians crowded in to the tiny space to pay tribute to the dedicated and gifted men who built it.'

Alan brought the car to a stop. 'And there it is.'

Somewhere in the middle of the story I'd forgotten why I was annoyed with Alan. Now I forgot everything except what was in front of me.

The site was austere and windswept. In the fields on either side livestock moved slowly, oblivious to anything except their food. But the chapel . . .

It was simple. Painted brilliantly white, with red trim, it reminded me a little of the adobe mission churches of the American southwest. A tiny porch, flanked with two narrow windows, was decorated with a bas-relief head of Christ, with his crown of thorns. 'Made by the prisoners?' I asked. Alan nodded. And we went inside.

I found I couldn't say a word. Tears welled in my eyes as I looked, and looked, and looked some more.

The workmanship was flawless. I had to touch the walls to convince myself that they were not, in fact, brick and carved stone, but a flat, smooth surface. The vaulted roof, the glorious vault of the chancel – all paint. All done with such skill, such love and devotion. And all by men being held prisoners in a foreign land, among people who didn't speak their language, didn't worship as they did.

'Several of them came back,' said Alan softly. 'About twenty years ago. The lead artist wasn't well enough, but some of the others came and spent several days here. There were Masses and celebrations. And when the artist died a few years later, there was a requiem Mass for him here, and everyone who could crowd into the chapel came. There is great love between the Orcadians and those POWs.'

I swallowed the lump in my throat. 'It's hard to imagine, isn't it? Love between prisoners and their captives? I think of the Americans held in Vietnamese prison camps, or for that matter the Japanese-Americans held in our internment camps, and try to visualize any of them coming back to break bread with their captors. This must be unique in the world.'

'I don't know if it's unique, but unusual, certainly. A tribute to everyone involved, I'd say.'

'And to the human spirit.' I wiped away another tear.

'Feeling better?' he asked.

'Much. You were right. This was just the medicine I needed. I'm sorry I was so snarky about it.'

'You're tired. We both are. Let's leave the car here and take the pooch for a nice long walk.'

We had, of course, left Watson in the car, but now we invited him out, put on his leash, and started down the road.

We walked in companionable silence for a while, letting him off the lead when we were reasonably sure he was going to behave.

The weather was perfect. It had forgotten how to rain and blow, how to make humans miserable. Blue skies, not too hot, a gentle breeze, birdsong, bright waves in the distance. It was, in short, exactly the same as a couple of hours ago. The only difference was my mood.

Watson got excited about some small creature and took off after it, straight into a ditch. He emerged covered in water and mud, which he proceeded to transfer to us with a vigorous shake.

'Did you bring a towel?'

I shook my head.

'Nor did I. We're going to have to walk until we all dry off, or we'll never get the mud off the cushions of the car.'

'It's all right with me. We have some thinking to do, anyway.'

'Have you had a brilliant idea?'

'Not the whisper of one. No, but I'm ashamed of myself for almost giving up.'

'The chapel?'

'The chapel. Think of what those guys had to deal with. Enemy aliens, working hard all day, and against their own allies, the Germans. Living in primitive conditions, probably without enough food. Nobody in this country had enough food during the war, did they?'

'I was only a baby, you know. I don't remember much until the war was over, but certainly there wasn't a lot to eat then. My mother had a friend in America who used to send us parcels loaded with food, and we'd get so excited. Real eggs, I remember, instead of the frightful powdered ones. I don't remember now how on earth they packed them to ship them safely such a long way. And there was tinned ham, and Spam. I always liked Spam, actually. I wonder why one never sees it anymore.'

'I'll get you some, dear, and we'll see if we still like it. It was a staple of my childhood, too. But anyway, I'm assuming the prisoners were on short rations like everyone else. So they'd come home at night, dead tired, and instead of falling into bed, work a little more on their chapel. Begging materials, scrounging, making do, and they created a miracle. Two miracles. A chapel, and a bond of friendship with their captors. And here I am, ready to call it quits when a solution doesn't just drop into my lap. And losing my temper on top of it. As I said, I'm ashamed of myself.'

Alan just nodded.

TWENTY-THREE

We were quiet on the way home. I was thinking about the chapel and its lovely story, and then as we passed some of the Neolithic sites my thoughts reverted to our problem. Not so lovely, but requiring our attention.

Watson, too, required our attention when we got home, though he indicated that he would gladly do without the bath we found it necessary to inflict on him. He's not a big dog, but he can certainly fill a room with water and mud. That meant Alan and I needed showers and clean clothes, too, and then we were all three of us hungry. So what with one thing and another, it was mid-afternoon before we sat down at the table with pen and paper to do some serious thinking and planning.

'When I was a working policeman,' said Alan, 'before the chief constable days, I often found it useful to sit down with my team and talk about everything that had happened on a knotty case, even things that seemed irrelevant. Sometimes we found some surprising connections.'

'Let's try that, then, bearing in mind that we're apt to forget some things. My memory isn't what it used to be.'

'And you think mine is? Never mind, we'll reinforce each other. Where shall we start?'

I pulled out a pocket calendar. 'Let's see. We arrived here on a Sunday. That is, I don't think our car trouble in Edinburgh can have anything to do with anything, do you?'

'Nothing except a whopping bill for repairs, I shouldn't think. Which reminds me. I need to call the garage and ask about the prognosis. Make a note for me, will you?'

'Right. So on the Sunday here, we got settled in and then Andrew took us out for dinner.'

'Don't forget the cat.'

Watson was snoozing quietly in a sunny corner, but at the word, or more probably Alan's tone of voice, he looked up and whined.

We smiled at him. 'It's okay, sweetheart. But how could I possibly have forgotten Roadkill? Sandy, I mean. I said I wouldn't call him by that mean name anymore. All right, what's next?'

'Monday Andrew took us to the dig. Did anything odd happen there?'

'Not unless you count my being struck dumb by the mystery of it all. But that evening – was it that first evening – the meeting?'

'And all kinds of fireworks!'

'Andersen's tirade,' I wrote on my pad. 'Carter hustling him out. Norquist's quiet little fuss. That reporter, whoever she was, who challenged Carter, and the ripples that raised. Quite an interesting evening.'

'And don't forget Fairweather, trying to handle it all diplomatically. Now, can we draw any inferences from all that?'

I tried to think back to the impressions I got at the time. 'I was favourably impressed with Fairweather. He acted intelligent and knowledgeable, and I thought he did handle the disturbances well. But he also seemed . . . well . . . maybe a little less disturbed by all of them than he should have been. I can't put my finger on it, but there were hidden agendas. That could just be hindsight, of course.'

'I don't think so,' said Alan. He stood to open a window. It was getting quite warm in the room. 'I'm going to have some beer. Shall I get you some?'

'No, I'll pass, thank you. Why do you think my impressions are real memories?'

'Because I shared them. You're more intuitive than I, but feelings were running high in that room. I knew that, though I didn't understand it all at the time. Not sure I understand it still, or not all of it. But I noticed that Fairweather was rather calm throughout it all, and I wondered why.'

'Of course now we know about the bequest, and know he was already aware of it. That's why he wasn't worried about the funding.'

'And that puts another nail in his coffin, or would if we still had capital punishment. Obvious obstacles came up at the meeting, Andersen for one, and the question of how far down they were going to dig. If I'd been the chap in charge of it all, I'd have been sweating. Not only did the problems exist, they were laid out in public, and with the media in attendance. There'd be no hushing anything up. And yet Fairweather dealt with it as befitted his name. Smooth sailing all the way.'

I shivered. 'Do you think he was planning Carter's murder even then?'

'I'm afraid I do. Are you cold, love? Shall I close the window?'

'No, I'm only cold inside. Darn it all, I *liked* the man. He impressed me. Never mind. Let's go on.'

'Your President Truman is said to have remarked of Stalin, "Damn it, I liked the little son of a bitch." Likeable characters have been murderers before now.'

'I know, I know. Now, did anything else important happen at the meeting? I can't think of anything.'

'Well, we were treated to Andrew's assessment of Carter's character, motives, and lineage.'

'It's a pity Andrew's at the back of beyond right now. He could probably tell us a lot.'

'Heavens, woman, how far away do you think Spain is? As the crow flies, Madrid is quite a lot nearer to Orkney than Los Angeles is to New York, and you Yanks think nothing of flying that every week or so.'

'I hate flying, but I take your point. I always forget how teeny Europe is. Shall we call him, then?'

'The only difficulty would be that I don't have his mobile number. When he called earlier it was from his home. And I have no idea where he might be reached by landline.'

I sighed elaborately. 'Like I said. Back of beyond. To get back to the matter at hand, I think it's important that we noticed how light it was that night. Remember, we went for a walk and I mentioned wishing I could see the stars, and you talked about the summer solstice.'

'With no moon, though. And that leads us directly, though not chronologically, to the question of what on earth Carter was doing at the dig that night.'

'If he was ever there, alive, that is. Is it even remotely possible that he was killed elsewhere and taken to the dig? You thought so at one time, remember?'

'Anything's possible. Given the nature of his injuries, and where he was found, I've just about given up the idea. Moreover, it would be far easier to kill the man in a remote, nearly unpopulated place than in Kirkwall at his hotel.'

'Who said anything about Kirkwall?' I argued. 'Anyway, Kirkwall isn't exactly Grand Central station. And most of the rest of Orkney is pretty deserted, even in the daytime.'

'Very well, for the sake of the argument, let's assume he was killed somewhere on Mainland. You'll agree to that stipulation?'

'Yes, since it was on this island that he was last seen alive.'

'Not only on this island but in Kirkwall, at his hotel.'

'Do we know that for certain? I know that's what Fairweather told you, but we can't take his word for anything.'

'You're right about that, but Baikie confirmed it. I thought I told you. Of course one of the first things he did was check everyone's whereabouts, as best he could. That was before the terrorism business came up, if you recall. The men who live alone have no alibi, as would be expected. But Carter definitely went back to his hotel, had dinner and then a drink or two in the bar, went up, and presumably went to bed.'

I pounced on that. 'Aha! "A drink or two." Does that really mean five or six? Enough to make him easy to bop on the head?'

'Not according to Baikie. They checked the body's blood alcohol level. I don't recall what it was, but it was consistent with what the barman told the police. Two to three ounces of whisky.'

'Hmmm. That wouldn't put him out, unless he was normally a teetotaller.'

'Grasping at straws.'

'You're right. Very well. So he goes up to bed at – when?'

'My dear, the concierge didn't personally tuck him in with his teddy bear. He went up about eleven. No one in the hotel saw or heard anything more of him. The assumption is that he went to bed.'

'But he didn't, Alan. Or at least he didn't stay there. Because when next seen he was dead of a head wound at High Sanday, and had been dead for some time. So we get back to where we started. Who or what took him out there between eleven and – when do they think he died?'

'Probably before two, but you know how cagey the medicos are about time of death.'

'Well, say between eleven and two, anyway. Because it would have started getting light again at around two-thirty. The morning was beautiful and clear; it was only later that it started to pour. Actually, it was still light at eleven, too. So he must not have been killed before twelve or so . . . wait a minute!'

'What?'

'Don't talk! Don't say a word – I've almost got it – yes!' I raised both arms in relief and triumph. 'Alan, you know I've been trying to catch a stray idea, something to do with May Day?'

'If you say so, my love.'

'And I just made the connection! Listen.'

That was one of the less necessary remarks. Alan's attention was riveted.

'All right. It started with May Day, and something someone said about it being a very old, very primitive celebration. And then poor Mr Norquist was accused of sacrificing that hen. That started my brain on a path littered with primitive celebrations and ancient rites, and you know I'd been sort of haunted with the idea of sacrifice anyway. And then just now the summer solstice came up again.'

I waited for him to get it, and he didn't disappoint me. He smacked his forehead. 'Of course! The solstice. Ancient rites, perhaps even sacrifices. Good grief, Dorothy, why did it take us so long to think of it? The people of Britain have marked the solstice in one way or another since well before we called ourselves Britain. And in this land where the ancients are so much in evidence . . . good grief, half Orkney might have been up that night dancing around dolmens or some such nonsense!'

'Mr Norquist wouldn't like you calling it nonsense,' I said soberly.

'Ah. Norquist.'

'Are we back to him, then? Alan, I don't want it to be him.'

'We don't want it to be anyone we know, do we? But let's look again at the facts. Someone sacrificed the cat, at the dig.'

'Someone killed the cat,' I corrected.

'In a ritualistic way, don't forget.'

I shuddered at that. 'Don't remind me. Did the police find out anything about the knife that was used, or didn't they bother, since it was just a cat?'

'They might have done, but they were fully occupied by that time. Anyway, Fairweather had disposed of the poor moggie's body by the time anyone else got there. Didn't I tell you? He said he thought a burial at sea was appropriate.'

I shuddered again. 'I can't stand the idea of a cat, who hates water and hates being cold, tossed into the cold unforgiving sea. Okay, yes, I know he was dead and couldn't feel anything at all. Still, I hope he haunts Fairweather, along with his murderer, if they're not the same person.'

Alan tactfully ignored this and went ahead with the case against Norquist, ready to tick off points on his fingertips. 'As to the cat, Norquist hated cats and believed in ritual sacrifice.'

'But he has a heart condition, remember?' I persisted in speaking of him in the present tense. 'How could he have caught Sandy? I wouldn't want to try it unless I were wearing a full suit of armour and had a platoon of dog-catchers for back-up.'

'There are such things as tranquilizers and sleeping pills, my dear. But in any case, the cat is a side issue. The matter at hand is Carter's murder, and there I think we have a pretty good case. I have a possible scenario.'

He tented his fingers in his lecturing mode. 'It's the summer solstice, a very holy time in the Old Religion. Norquist, whose mental balance is somewhat questionable, has been upset by Carter's behaviour at the meeting. He has already planned a ritual activity of some sort for later in the evening, probably midnight, at one of the ancient sites. He would want a place where he could be alone, without others to profane the purity of his rites. He has chosen, perhaps, one of the cairns known only to him. But as burial sites, they aren't quite appropriate. Then he has a much better idea.'

'High Sanday, with its huge temple. But does he have a boat to get there?'

'No, but he knows who has a beautiful one. And he has the perfect lure. "There will be a sacrifice ritual tonight at the temple. If you will take me there, I will explain to you what is happening." Or words to that effect. He probably phones Carter and arranges to meet him at the boat. Carter doesn't know that *he's* the sacrifice until he gets a building stone swung at his head.'

'Probably he never knows. I'd think he died immediately. Alan, it's horribly plausible, but there are a couple of minor problems. Such as, where did Norquist get the strength to manhandle the murder weapon? And what happened to the boat? And where is Norquist now?'

'That, of course, is the sixty-four dollar question. If he's the murderer, you realize the suicide theory becomes a good deal more plausible.'

'Yes.' I sighed. 'We seem to have talked ourselves into a corner again. I'm still not convinced Norquist is the villain. And I'm not sure it's Fairweather, either. They both had motives, even if the one is pretty crazy. But there's no clear indication either way.'

'No smoking gun? One seldom gets them in cases like this, you know. One builds up a theory based on tiny shreds of evidence, hearsay, and plain intuition. Then one goes hunting for the proof. That can be the sticky part. And that's why there are always a few instances of the villain getting away with it. The police know beyond a shadow of a doubt who did it, but they can't get enough evidence to take the scoundrel to court.'

I stood up and stretched. 'Well, that's not going to happen this time. We're going to pursue this. If the police can't find enough evidence to put somebody behind bars – anybody! – we'll do it for them. Of course the trouble is we don't know who – whom – we want to convict.'

'True. The case isn't good enough against either of them. I don't mean good enough in the police court sense. It isn't good enough to satisfy me.'

'There's something we've overlooked, that's all. Something we've forgotten, or failed to notice properly, or didn't think was important. I think it's time for a drink, and then I'll make some dinner, and we'll forget all about it . . . Was that somebody at the door?'

'Hello!' came a quiet voice. 'Anyone at home?'

'Nora! Come in! We've worn out our brains and were just about to have a little libation. Would you care to join us?'

'For a moment. Theodore has a meeting this evening, so we're eating a bit early, but I was anxious to hear your impressions of the chapel. I don't have to ask if it lifted your spirits.'

'Anyone with eyes to see and ears to hear would be inspired by that lovely place and its amazing history,' I said warmly. 'I can't find the words to talk about it.' I felt tears start in my eyes again, just thinking about the story. 'I'm so grateful to you for suggesting it.'

'Even though you didn't really want to go,' she said with a hint of a twinkle.

'You don't miss much, do you? What can we get you?'

'A small sherry, if you have it. I really can't stay long, but I did want to mention one thing. Thank you, Alan.' She perched on a chair and raised her glass. 'May I offer a toast to the Italians?'

'Long may they wave,' I said fervently, and sipped my own bourbon. 'They certainly cheered me up, as well as making me feel guilty for what my father used to call "bellyachin'", but I can't say they cleared up my thought processes. Alan and I have been going over and over it, and have only succeeded in coming up with too many ideas that don't fit together.'

'Have you any further theories about where poor Charlie Norquist might be?'

'We . . . um . . . we came up with a good reason for him to have committed suicide,' I said with a grimace. 'I can't say I believe it, but it's awfully plausible.'

'And possible, if you mean that he might be the murderer. But nor do I believe it. What I wanted to suggest, if you don't think it unpardonable interference, is that you try once more to talk to Mrs Norquist. I do believe that she might give you a hint about where Charlie is hiding, if she is so inclined.'

'But how can I get in to see her? She wouldn't even see you last time.' Besides, I quailed at the thought of bearding the lioness in her well-protected den. Mrs Norquist scared me, but I wasn't going to admit that if I didn't have to.

Of course Nora the all-seeing knew it anyway. 'I'm sorry, I worded that ambiguously. My idea was that perhaps Alan could attempt the visit. Mrs Norquist fancies a good-looking man, even at her age. He might succeed where either of us would fail. And now I really must be seeing to Theodore's supper. Thank you for the lovely sherry, my dears.' And she let herself out.

TWENTY-FOUR

'I think I need a little more Highland Park,' Alan said after a slightly stunned silence. 'Did that woman actually just give me orders to visit the madwoman of Chaillot?'

'Something like that, my intrepid knight. I don't want to seem hard-hearted, but better you than me. Nora's a dear, isn't she, but very . . . I don't know quite what the word is. Kind, gracious, but somehow it's almost impossible to say no to her.'

'She reminds me,' said Alan glumly, 'of Mrs Thatcher. The Iron Lady. I don't know what you were planning for dinner, my love, but I vote for the Royal Hotel. I require sustenance if I'm to work myself up to my ordeal.'

Well, I'm never averse to being treated to dinner, although I told myself I mustn't eat too much. I fight a constant battle between my appetite and my stern dietary instructions to myself. Appetite usually wins, sad to say. I just plain like food, and when lovely food is in front of me I tell myself I should be grateful that I can still enjoy it. Then when I step on the scale I give myself a lecture about next time.

There was no scale in the bathroom at the flat. And besides, I told myself as I scanned the menu, I'd been walking a lot while I was here. And I was going to walk even more tomorrow. And how often did I get a chance to eat haggis?

After dinner, feeling slightly like a Strasbourg goose, I persuaded Alan to go with me on a long walk with Watson. We strolled along the harbour, watching the lights of the last ferry as it left for Aberdeen. Watson was more interested in the seagulls, some of which seemed nearly as big as he was. 'They don't grow 'em like that back home,' I said, and Alan chuckled. 'Nor in most parts of England. Different variety, I suspect. No, Watson, you must not chase it into the water.'

The dog gave a disappointed woof and looked around for something else he could chase. The gulls were thinning out; night was coming, though the sky still held lots of light. The sounds of the busy little town were quieter, evening sorts of sounds. Somewhere a cat was being called to its supper. Watson stiffened at the answering meow.

'It's all right, pup, that one won't bother you anymore.' Watson picked up both the reassurance and the sadness in my voice and whined questioningly. 'It's all right,' I said again, and gave him a pat. 'Just be glad you're not human. We have much more to worry about.'

Alan took my arm and we walked on till the light was almost gone and we were glad to turn toward home.

Wednesday dawned bright and clear and all too soon for people who hadn't fallen asleep till well after midnight. Alan sat up and blinked at the brilliant sunshine pouring through the uncurtained window.

'I was hoping for torrential rain,' he croaked in an unpractised morning voice. 'Or snow. Or an earthquake.'

'Or a tornado or a tsunami,' I agreed. 'Any sort of friendly weather. Go back to sleep, love. It's ridiculously early. You don't have to face the day's ordeal for hours.'

Watson, of course, had other ideas. He jumped down from his spot in the middle of the bed and padded downstairs. We slipped back into an agreeable doze, but he was back in moments. He whined. He licked Alan's toe and my hand, both of which were poking out from the covers. He barked sharply. He jumped back on the bed, creating something resembling that hoped-for earthquake, and barked again.

'Cats, you know, use a sandbox,' I remarked sourly, as I swung my feet to the floor and felt around for my slippers.

I'd planned to go straight back to bed as soon as I'd dealt with Watson's needs, but I found to my dismay that I was wide awake. The air I'd caught a whiff of when I let him out was so clean and fresh, so full of the cries of gulls and the hoots of the ferry, that I had to admit I didn't want any more sleep. Besides, it was later than I'd thought, nearly seven. That's early enough, in all good conscience, for someone on holiday, but I knew I simply wasn't going to be able to force my eyes shut again. I made myself a cup of coffee, took it and Watson out on the patio, and settled back to wait for Alan to wake up.

I was heartily in agreement with Alan's wishes for a cataclysm. I, too, would rather have coped with almost any meteorological phenomenon than with the harpy who lay in wait for her morning's prey: my poor husband.

Mrs Tredgold was right, though. It had to be done. One way or another, we needed to learn what Charlie Norquist's mother knew about his whereabouts. I just wished there were some way that didn't involve a personal interview, perhaps some sort of electronic suction device attached to her skull, to draw out all the information without pain to anyone concerned. I pictured the device, something Frankensteinian, humming away, humming . . .

I jerked myself awake to find a bee hovering over my coffee cup, and Alan just sitting down with his own mug.

We greeted each other with our usual raised eyebrows, and waited for the caffeine to kick in before embarking on conversation.

'I thought I wasn't sleepy, or I'd have come back to bed,' I said. 'But the sunshine out here was seductive.'

'Mmm. Pouring into the bedroom and shining straight into my eyes, it was insistent.'

'Up and doing with a heart for any fate, are you?'

He grunted. 'Do you suppose if I ran up and down the road for a while I'd have a heart attack?'

'More likely I'd have one, just watching you, and then you'd have to cope with me *and* Mrs Norquist. What would you like for breakfast?'

'Just toast. I'm still feeling like a stuffed goose after that meal last night.'

'Me, too. Sit still. I'll bring it out here. It's far too nice a day to spend indoors.'

We dawdled over our toast and coffee far longer than such modest provender warranted. Watson dozed in the sun for a while, but eventually he reminded us that a dog is a more active creature than a cat, and requires more out of life than a sunny spot for a nap.

I stood up. 'Do you want to take him for a walk while I do the dishes, or vice versa?'

'I'll do the walkies. Gives me an illusion of freedom for a few more minutes.'

It doesn't take long to deal with one coffee pot, two cups, two plates, and assorted silverware. I was finished before my two males returned, and had plenty of time to fret about what the day had to offer. When they got back, Watson with a happy grin on his face and Alan looking glum, I told them I'd made up my mind.

'About what?'

'We're going with you, Watson and I both. No, I know what you're going to say. We won't go in with you, if you say not, but I want to be there. Just in case.'

'My dear woman, I hardly think there's any danger involved. Mrs Norquist sounds like an extremely unpleasant old woman, and I'm not looking forward to the encounter, but she can't eat me.'

'You never know. I want to be there. And Watson does too, don't you, mutt?'

Watson, who had a dim instinct that an outing was under discussion, yipped enthusiastically in agreement.

'You do remember that the blasted woman is more likely to see me alone, according to Nora Tredgold?'

'I remember. I said I'll probably not go in.'

'In that case, why . . . oh, very well. Are you ready?'

'Ready as I'll ever be.' I tucked a scarf around my neck against the probable wind. 'Let's go.'

We rode in silence through a gorgeous day. The air was a bit nippy for late June, by English standards, let alone Hoosier ones, but it was crystal clear and invigorating. I should have been in the best of spirits.

'I don't think that woman has a friend in the world,' I said after we'd negotiated the tricky roundabout. 'How do people end up so sour and unloved? She must have been loved once. She married and had a son, after all.'

Alan shook his head. 'Some marriages have very little to do with love, I'm afraid. We've been very lucky, you and I, to have had not one but two good marriages. Helen and I loved each other very much, as did you and Frank. And when they were gone, we found each other, against all odds.' He reached over and took my hand.

I cleared my throat. 'You've never talked very much about Helen.'

'No need. I'll never forget her, as you'll never forget Frank.

And that's the way it should be.' He said nothing for a little time. We passed a field of barley, slowed, and turned a corner to drive alongside a pasture. 'You know,' he said, 'I had some idea you agreed to come to Orkney because you didn't want to disappoint me, or something like that.'

I sighed. 'You don't need to tiptoe around it. You're quite right. I came because you came here with Helen. There, that's out!'

He smiled and grasped my hand more firmly. 'And I went to Indiana with you because you'd been there with Frank all those years. And we're a pair of fools. It isn't a competition, is it?'

I managed a smile, though tears were close to the surface. 'I suppose we haven't talked about it because there was no need, was there? They do say that more people who have had happy marriages remarry than the others. Well, you know what I mean, even if I didn't say it very well. We found each other, we knew we were right for each other, and having loved before, we knew what love was about. And I'll bet Frank and Helen are both looking down and smiling at us.'

Then I had to blow my nose. When I thought I could trust my voice, I cleared my throat and changed the subject. 'But my question remains. If we are what we are because of our past experiences, what twists a person into a Mrs Norquist? I know she's mentally disturbed, but there are mentally disturbed people who are perfectly lovable, aside from thinking they're Napoleon, or whatever, and then there are the hateful ones. Where does the difference come from?'

Alan pondered for a while. 'I think it goes back to your prime motivating factor, fear. But fear of what, I can't tell you. I imagine it's different for everyone. Fear of rejection, failure, poverty, loss of some sort . . . given the right, or I suppose the wrong, set of circumstances, I'd think an overpowering fear could turn into a monomania, and that could twist a soul into a fearful shape.'

'You're probably right. But I think a seed has to be there from the start. Discontent, jealousy, ambition, anything that can sprout and grow into a monster, given the fertile ground of fear.'

'"Envy, hatred, malice, and all uncharitableness"?' he quoted.

'The Prayer Book hits the nail on the head so much of the time, doesn't it? And I think we're about to meet them all, or at least you are. You turn in here.'

'Yes, love, I remember. And what are you going to do while I go in there and confront all the deadly sins at once?'

'Walk Watson around the building and pray for you. And hope you get something useful out of the ordeal. But we're going to wait right here for a little while. We don't know if she'll even see you.'

'True.' Alan seemed cheered by the thought as he crunched across the gravel drive toward the front door.

TWENTY-FIVE

Watson whined anxiously as he watched Alan disappear inside the house. It's remarkable how he can sense that all may not be well with his people. At such times he wants both of us to be under his watchful eye. 'It's all right, dog,' I said, but I didn't fool him for a moment. He knew I was edgy, too.

My edginess increased as Alan remained in the house. I had assumed, probably hoped, that the disagreeable old woman would refuse to see him, and that would be that. Apparently that wasn't the case.

Watson was growing more and more impatient, so I attached his leash and let both of us out of the car. 'Okay, then, we'll walk it off, my friend. No, you can't go inside. See, they don't allow dogs.' The sign just outside the door was small and discreet, but quite definite. 'Service dogs only, please.' I suppose other animals might disturb the inmates, whose emotional stability was fragile, anyway.

Watson was happy to be moving instead of just sitting and waiting, but he very much wanted Alan to come back. Now that my husband had got himself in there, though, I was hoping he'd get something useful out of the old termagant before she threw him out. That way neither of us might have to come back.

We had made only one circuit of the house, before Alan appeared at the door and walked toward us. I could not, for once, read his face.

'You weren't gone long enough for a real conversation,' I said when he was close enough for speech, 'but too long if she just refused to talk to you.'

'She couldn't refuse,' he said with a peculiar intonation.

'Alan! You don't mean . . .'

'No. Or probably not. The thing is, she's not here.'

I looked at him blankly. 'But that's impossible! She couldn't just walk away. The security is very good. CCTV and all that.'

'Nevertheless, they can't find her. They're in quite a swivet over it, as you can imagine, and they weren't best pleased that I came along when I did. They'd just as soon nobody knew they occasionally mislay their patients.'

'Occasionally! You mean this has happened before?'

'Only once. That they would admit to, anyway.'

'Let me guess. It was Mrs Norquist that time, too.'

'It was. A little over a week ago.'

'Not . . . oh, no, Alan! That really is impossible!'

'I'm afraid it's true. She vanished briefly, sometime the night of the summer solstice.'

I gazed at him, mouth agape, and then suddenly I started to laugh. I had a hard time stopping, in fact, and Alan was, I could see, beginning to get concerned. 'No, I'm not having hysterics,' I said at last, when I could. 'It's just that this is the final touch of madness. Now I suppose we have to consider a crazy old lady as a murder suspect, and it's completely ridiculous, and I think I may go mad myself. Are there some straws around that I can weave into my hair?'

Alan began to laugh himself. 'You're right. It's utterly insane. I can't seriously consider the woman, but her disappearance needs explaining. Both times. And certainly she needs to be found.'

'Haven't they notified the police? I thought that was standard procedure.'

'There's a specified time limit after which they have to do that. They were a bit dodgy about saying how long. They'd much rather find her themselves, as you can imagine.'

'But they haven't, at least not yet. Well, then, what are we waiting for? Let's go in and help them look.'

I brought Watson inside with me. The staff were inclined to be stuffy about that, but I insisted. 'You're conducting a search. You've used your eyes and ears, and have had no luck. I suggest that a dog's nose is a much more powerful search tool than any of our senses. Give him something belonging to Mrs Norquist to sniff, and he may be able to help.'

The manager, or matron, or whatever she was called, frowned. 'Is he a trained search dog?'

'No. But he's polite and well-behaved, and what harm can he do?'

'Some of the patients are terrified of dogs.'

'Then we'll keep him away from those patients, won't we?'

'But it won't do any good. Mrs Norquist is not in the centre anywhere. We've looked. Exhaustively.'

'Then if she's not in, she's out. And how did she get out, pray tell, with cameras at every exit?'

'She can't have got out. Our security—'

'Mrs . . . Mrs Graham,' I said, looking at her nametag. 'Do make up your mind. If she can't have got out, she's here. If she's not here, she's out. On which premise shall we operate?'

'Oh, search where you like!' she said, her temper rising. 'You'll not find her!' She stalked off, and I looked at the other staff members, who had been standing around looking helpless.

'We truly don't want to upset the patients,' I said. 'Can one of you tell us where Watson would be likely to create a panic?'

'There are really only two ladies who are genuinely afraid of dogs,' said a gentle, quiet-spoken young woman whose nametag read Peters, 'and even then, this one isn't a big brute. Does he like people?'

'He's a lovely boy,' I said, hearing in my own voice the doting tone I had so often laughed at in Alan's. 'Oh, dear, I sound like an idiotic parent, don't I? But he really is quite a nice dog, and he almost never barks. I'd think if you'd show me which rooms to avoid, the wary ones would never even know he's here.'

'Most of the patients are in their own rooms at this time of day, but I'll just make sure of the two, and then all the common rooms are at your disposal. Sam, do you suppose you could find one of Mrs Norquist's shoes for . . . Watson, is it? Appropriate name.'

So in a few minutes we were ready to set out, and Alan took over. 'This is an old house, isn't it?' he asked the woman who had been so cooperative.

'Not so very old,' she answered. 'Almost none of the lairds' houses survived from before the eighteenth century, and very few even from after that. This was never a laird's house, though, as you may know. The Sinclairs were lairds here back in the fourteenth and fifteenth century, and the man who built this house was a great admirer of them, so he named his house after them. It's probably not even three hundred years old.'

I hid a smile. Back in Indiana, anything over about fifty counted as old. 'What happened to all the lairds' houses?'

'Weather and war and just neglect. Orkney's been pulled about from one ruler to another for centuries. The Norse and the Scots and the English, coming in to take what they could get and then leaving again. They'd build fine houses and then get murdered in their beds by the next lot, and the houses burnt to the ground, like as not. It's a long and terrible history we have behind us, sure enough, and a hard life for many of us now.'

She said it as if she were reading the weather report. 'This was probably the drawing room of the old house,' she went on. 'It's our common room, though few of the patients ever use it. There's always a draft, for some reason.'

'Hmm,' said Alan. He walked over to the windows. 'These seem to fit well enough. And the fireplace has been blocked up.'

'Yes, a pity, that. There's nothing like a good peat fire, to my mind, and our old folks feel the cold. But it wasn't safe, you see. Some of the old dears can't be trusted around fire.'

'What a shame. I love an open fire myself, though at home we burn wood.'

'Nothing like as warm as peat or coal – but peat's the best. Mind you, there's a knack to getting it started, but then it burns forever.'

Alan and Watson had been prowling the room as we talked. 'Dorothy, let me have that scarf thing you're wearing, will you, love?'

I slipped it off, with raised eyebrows. Alan took it and stood next to the bookcases on one wall, where Watson's attention was centred. 'There's your draft,' he said, holding the scarf by one corner. We could see it flutter.

'Wheeel! Whit a wonder! Who'd hae thowt it!'

It was the first time Miss Peters had spoken broad Orcadian, and I couldn't follow it all, but the astonishment was obvious.

'The house was built in a time of political instability,' said Alan almost apologetically. 'I thought there might be concealed doors and passages, and a bookcase was often used to conceal such features. I'd be very surprised if there isn't a door behind these panels. Would anyone object if I moved a few books?'

Watson was becoming more and more agitated. I snapped on

his leash. 'Hush, now, it's all right,' I said soothingly. 'You're a wonderful dog, but you must stay quiet.' He shook his head impatiently and strained at the leash, but at least he didn't bark. 'Alan, I'd better take him out. He's not going to behave much longer.'

'Yes, fine.' Alan's mind was elsewhere. He was pulling books off the shelves and handing them to Miss Peters, who was stacking them neatly on tables. I wanted to stay and see what happened, but Watson was growing more and more restless. I headed for the door just in time to encounter the starchy Mrs Graham. She looked beyond me into the room. 'And precisely *what* do you think you're doing?' she demanded.

Watson uttered a low growl. I grasped his leash firmly and fled.

'I don't like her either,' I assured my dog. 'Let's go around the outside and see if we can look in the window of that room.'

The house had a sizable foundation, which put the windows too high for convenient peering. Watson wanted to go somewhere else, anyway. He tugged me around a corner, put his nose to the ground, and barked sharply. Once. Then he sat back and looked at me with that silly doggy grin.

'What? What have you found?' I examined the patch of ground that so interested him, and could see nothing extraordinary about it. 'No gold watches this time? No bloodstains? Oh!'

My startled cry was occasioned by the sight of my husband emerging through what I had thought was a solid wall.

'And this,' he said, 'is how Mrs Norquist leaves the house whenever she wishes.'

Behind him, Miss Peters looked scared and Mrs Graham furious. 'But that means she could be anywhere!' said Miss Peters. 'We've got to find her!'

'Yes, of course,' said Alan, 'but it's a job for the police now.'

'The police!' Miss Peters was so white I was afraid she was going to faint, and Mrs Graham was sputtering with rage.

'They have dogs trained for the search,' said Alan before Mrs Graham could get a word out. 'Or at least I presume they do,' he said with a hint of doubt in his voice.

'Calling in the police would ruin us!' said Mrs Graham.

'As would losing a patient,' he reminded her. 'In any case, I believe it's your legal responsibility.'

'Alan, she has a point, though.' Much as I disliked the woman, I had to admit it. 'Police would mean publicity. Anyway, they may not have trained bloodhounds, or whatever. Can't we just let Watson try a little longer? He picked up her scent just outside the door here. At least I think that's what he found. He sniffed at the ground and barked and looked very pleased with himself.'

'Really!' said Mrs Graham. 'A dog is not a person!'

Whose side are you on, lady, I thought but did not say. 'Perhaps you have never had a pet,' I said, the frost in my voice almost matching hers. 'Animals have quite obvious emotions, and display them for any human with any sensitivity. Of course it's a matter of no importance to me whether you allow Watson to search, or call in professionals, but you seemed upset at the idea of the police.'

She turned red. That woman hates to back down, I thought. She'd cut off her own nose to spite her face, but surely she can see the advantage to staving off the police for a little while.

'Very well. Keep the dog quiet, if that's possible, and away from windows. I don't want the patients to know he's here. Already his barking will have disturbed them.' She looked at him, dislike in her eyes. He responded with a low growl.

Attaboy, I thought. So much for animals not displaying their emotions. 'I can't promise to keep him away from windows. He'll go wherever the scent leads him.' Of course, the scent he was following might well be that of a rabbit. I didn't say that, either. 'Alan, do you still have that shoe, so he can smell it again?'

Miss Peters had it. I held it in front of Watson's nose. He sniffed at it ecstatically and then put his nose to the ground in established bloodhound style.

He was not, of course, a trained searcher. He wasn't even a hound, or not by appearance, though there could have been almost anything mixed in with the dominant spaniel. He led us all over the grounds, showing a tendency to chase the gulls or dig for something interesting. Mrs Graham, to my relief, became disgusted after only a few minutes and went back inside. Miss Peters stuck it out, but I could see the hope in her eyes dimming with each passing moment.

Alan was the one who set Watson back on the right path. My husband is, of course, a trained searcher, though he uses mostly his eyes. He caught the trace of a path in a few broken blades of grass, a smear in a small patch of mud. 'Someone's walked this way, and recently,' he said quietly. 'Watson, come here and tell me what you smell.'

The dog came, obediently, and stiffened at what he scented. Then he was off, pulling at the leash and whining.

'Here, let me take it.' Alan took the leash from my hand and lengthened it a bit. 'Let's give him his head.'

This time there was no chasing, no play. This was serious business. He headed straight for an outbuilding of some sort.

'The old dovecote,' said Miss Peters. 'It's not used now, and it's kept locked. Supposed to be kept locked,' she added, as we approached and could inspect the door closely. The padlock was still firmly attached to the hasp, but the screws holding the hasp had been pulled out of the rotting wooden door frame.

Alan reeled Watson in and approached the door cautiously. The dog gave one sharp bark, as he had back at the house.

The door swung slightly ajar, and a face appeared out of the gloom.

'Good morning, madam,' said Alan with utmost courtesy. He would have doffed his hat if he'd been wearing one. 'Mrs Norquist, I presume?'

TWENTY-SIX

'**I**ndeed you do, sir,' she replied, in the best Restoration comedy manner. 'I am not aware that we have been introduced.'

'Alan Nesbitt, at your service.' He came up to the door and offered his hand.

'No! You can't come in! Go away!' All mannerisms had fled. She let out an eldritch screech and tried to pull the door shut.

Alan hadn't been a policeman all those years for nothing. His sturdy foot was in the door, which he wrested from her grasp and pulled fully open.

A form behind her attempted to retreat into shadows, but the room was very small, and the sun was shining brightly.

'Mr Norquist,' said Alan calmly, 'I'm very glad to see you. We've been considerably worried about you.'

The man fell into Alan's arms in a dead faint.

Mr Norquist, we could see once we got him safely into the house, was a wreck. He hadn't shaved or washed for days, and his clothes would probably have to be burnt. His mother, for all her ninety or so years, was in far better shape.

At least physically. She could still wield her cane to some effect. Alan was going to have bruises from the blows she'd managed to land before Miss Peters and I took Mr Norquist from his arms and Watson helped him subdue the mad woman.

For mad she undoubtedly was. Her tirade made little sense, but one could trace the underlying theme of sacrifice and blasphemy, mixed with abuse hurled at an ungrateful and disobedient son.

Abuse in plenty was hurled at us, too, along with the staff who subdued her and took her away from Mr Norquist. 'They need a straitjacket,' I said.

'They probably haven't one. This isn't a home for the insane, merely for the confused. She'll have to be taken to a secure institution.'

'I wonder how poor Mr Norquist will react to that.' For he

had shown fear akin to terror of his mother, but had wept when she was taken away. 'I can't tell whether he wants to escape from her or be with her.'

'He probably doesn't know, himself. It's possible, once he's free of her presence, that a psychiatrist might help him regain some semblance of a normal balance, but . . .' Alan spread his hands. 'He'll still be under her influence. One doesn't erase overnight the impact of sixty or so years of venomous manipulation. It's a pity. He's an intelligent chap.'

'Do you think he'll be able to answer questions any time soon? Because there's so much we need to know.'

'I have no idea. They're sending for the doctor who deals with the residents here. He must know a thing or two about mental disturbance, and of course he knows Mrs Norquist and probably her son, as well, since Charlie visited so often. We'll hope he can restore the poor man to a degree of normality. Meanwhile, let's get out of this place before I go round the bend myself.'

I heartily concurred. So did Watson. He was tired of being looked at askance, and when Mrs Graham hove into site, he couldn't get out of there fast enough.

We took him back to the flat for something to eat, and had a bite ourselves, and then I took my phone out of my pocket and called Mrs Tredgold.

'Nora, this is Dorothy Martin. There's news. Would it be convenient for Alan and me to come round to see you?'

'I'm not at home, dear. I had a little shopping to do. Suppose I come to you. What time's best?'

'The sooner the better.'

I decided it was too early for tea with a capital T, and anyway I didn't have time to make any sort of pastry, but it's never the wrong time for small 't' tea. I was assembling cups and saucers, sugar and milk, when Nora tapped on the door and came in.

'Sit down, and let me put the kettle on. I was just making a pot of tea.'

She smiled at the obvious and put her shopping bag on the floor, but not before pulling out a small box with a picture of a dog on the front. 'I brought Watson a little treat. I hope you don't mind his eating between meals, but I thought he deserved a hero's reward.'

'Oh, then my news isn't news at all. I suppose it's all over the village by now. And Mrs Graham was so worried about publicity!'

'It's hard to keep a secret in so small a community. The fish had called at the home in the midst of the commotion, and of course he brought it back with him.'

After a moment I identified the fish with a delivery person rather than the scaly breed. 'With embellishments, no doubt,' I said, shaking my head. 'We'd better give you the unadorned version, so you can set people straight.'

So we sat and drank tea and told the tale. 'So you see, you were quite right about where to find Mr Norquist,' I concluded. 'In the arms of his mum. A fate, incidentally, I wouldn't wish on my worst enemy. Now that I've actually met the woman, I'm filled with even more admiration for your good offices.'

Nora sighed. 'She's got much worse in the past few months. When she still lived at home, she could be quite entertaining in a mean-spirited way. You know the sort of thing. Ripping everyone up the back, but being funny about it. It got to the point that Theodore wouldn't visit her, because he's too kind a man to listen to her malice. I can't say I actually enjoyed it, but at least it kept her off the subject of poor Charlie and his sins.'

'If I'd been Charlie, I'm afraid one of my sins might have been matricide,' said Alan. 'That's a truly poisonous woman.'

'And she's well and truly poisoned her son. It'll take me some time before I can forgive her for that.'

'Furthermore, she's turned him, at least temporarily, into such a basket case there's no hope of questioning him about any of the recent disasters on these islands.' Alan ran his hand down the back of his neck. 'And until we can do that, I think we're stuck for answers.'

'Are you still seriously considering Charlie as a murder suspect?'

'I don't know, and that's the truth!' Alan spoke as explosively as he allows himself to get. 'Everyone who might have wanted Carter dead has an alibi of sorts, so logically no one killed him. Nevertheless, the man's dead. Am I to believe that one of Charlie's *Them* killed him out of revenge, or for a sacrifice, or . . .?' He raised both arms in frustration, and Watson came over to comfort him.

'I suspect we can leave *Them* out of it,' said Nora with the hint of a smile, 'but what strikes me is that, until you can question Charlie, he's still in great danger. I know you must keep him on your list of suspects, but I quite absolutely refuse to do so. That means that the real murderer has a very great interest in keeping Charlie quiet. Perhaps permanently. Have you given him a police guard?'

Alan smacked the table. 'I never thought I'd have a vicar's wife teaching me my business! By heaven, that ought to have been the first thing I thought of. I don't have any authority to order police protection, but if you'll excuse me, I'll phone Baikie right now and hope to heaven he's in the office.'

He pulled out his phone and went upstairs, and I poured us more tea. 'Poor Alan,' I said softly. 'This has been a pretty strenuous holiday for him.'

'And for you,' said Nora.

'It's different for me. I've gotten to be fairly good at solving crimes, much to my amazement, but it isn't and never was my job. Alan takes it personally when he can't unravel a problem, even though he's not official anymore, and he hates it, just now, that he forgot to take that precaution about Charlie. Though I will say I'd have thought the dragon at the mouth of the cave was adequate protection against most hazards.'

Nora smiled again. 'I don't think Patricia Graham cares very much for her job, and that makes her snappish. It isn't a peaceful place to work, is it?'

'Not exactly, but Miss Peters seems to cope. I think she likes the patients, which must be a big help. Mrs Graham doesn't, and I'm sure they know it. Oh, Alan, what did he say?'

'He was already on it,' said Alan. 'Is anything stronger than tea on offer?'

Oh, dear. Alan was really down in the dumps. And alcohol in the middle of the day would just put him to sleep. Both of us, in fact, since I wasn't about to let him drink alone. And then we'd wake up feeling logy, and more useless than ever.

'I have the very thing,' said Nora, reaching once more into her bag. She pulled out a small parcel and spilled its contents out on the table. 'Marion's chocolate tarts. You know Marion, at the bakery? These are a weakness of mine, and quite sinfully delicious. Everyone knows chocolate is the cure when the Dementors strike, and I would say, Alan, that you're very nearly demented.'

Well, that launched us into a discussion of J.K. Rowling's wonderful books, and that led to talking about our own Harray Potter and how he might be getting along in Spain, and Alan was eased out of his slough of despond.

'And I'll tell you what I'm going to do,' said Nora as she picked up her bag, ready to leave. 'I'll ask Theodore to go and visit Charlie. They've not always got on terribly well, because of Charlie's peculiar theology, but Theodore may be the one person he trusts. Charlie's not afraid of him. Well, no one could be, could they? It could be that Charlie will talk to him. No promises, but it's worth a try.'

'If I weren't already married to you,' said Alan, devouring the last chocolate tart after she'd left, 'I'd marry that woman.'

'In the interest of selfless love, I'd give you your freedom. Especially since you've scarfed all the chocolate. Unfortunately she's already married, too,' I pointed out.

'Drat. And to a clergyman, to boot. Ah, well. What's on the agenda in that case, my dearest love?'

'Well,' I said, going to the front door and locking it, 'I thought we might take a nap. So to speak.'

We were awakened some time later from our contented slumbers by the tootle of my phone. I had a little trouble finding it, but fished it out of a rumpled pocket just in time. It was Nora.

'Dorothy? I hope I didn't wake you.'

Honestly, the woman's a witch, I thought. 'Well, actually . . .'

'I *am* sorry. I hope you had time for a nice nap. That was just what you both needed.'

I had the uncomfortable feeling that she knew exactly how our nap had begun, as well. And then I decided I didn't care. 'It was delightful, thank you,' I said demurely, and made a face at Alan, who was leering from his side of the bed.

'I thought,' Nora went on, 'that you'd want to know right away that Theodore has talked to Charlie.'

'Oh, good! Did he say anything that made any sense?' I turned up the volume on the phone and held it so that Alan could listen in.

'Not a great deal, but Theodore did grasp the idea that the poor man is terribly frightened, and not just of his mother. He had to be reassured again and again that no one could get in to see him.'

'He's still at Sinclair House, then?'

'Yes, it seemed best. There are people to look after him there. Of course his mother is also nearby, which isn't the best circumstance, but she won't be for long, and she positively can't get at him. No one can, except the staff, and of course Theodore. The policeman at the door is very large and about as moveable as the Old Man of Hoy, Theodore says.'

'Well, that's something, at least. Is there anything we can do to move things along?'

'I can't think of a thing, unless you want to put up an extra prayer or two for Charlie's swift recovery.'

'We'll certainly do that. You'll keep us posted?'

'I will. Don't worry too much, Dorothy. It will come right. I can feel it.'

Given her extraordinary ability to see into other people's minds, that remark reassured me considerably.

TWENTY-SEVEN

'Who's the Old Man of Hoy?' I asked Alan after I ended the call.

'What, not who. It's an amazing rock formation on the island of Hoy, very near here. We haven't seen a lot of Orkney, have we, what with one thing and another. Would you like to take a tour of the islands? There are cruise boats.'

'I would love to do that! As Nora says, there's not much else we can do until Charlie is able to talk to us, or at least to Baikie. Let's do it. Are they all-day cruises, or can you do one in an afternoon and evening?'

We walked down to the ferry building and discovered there was a tour leaving in fifteen minutes. There was just time to go back and let Watson out into the patio (a proceeding of which he took a dim view) and grab my ginger capsules before jumping on the boat.

It was a wonderful day. The way to see Orkney, I became convinced, was by water. Our other water trips had been accomplished in a hurry, in iffy weather, and for the purpose of getting someplace. This time the weather was perfect and our object was to relax and see what was to be seen.

The first thing was the Old Man of Hoy, which stands over four hundred feet high and looms over the sea like a primitive cathedral tower. Then we cruised around the Mainland, seeing magnificent beaches and bays, ruins of medieval defences, seals and otters playing on rocks, puffins and so many other birds I couldn't identify. We sailed close to Shapinsay, where I caught a tantalizing glimpse of Balfour Castle. 'We have to come back,' I said over and over to Alan.

We had a sandwich supper on the boat, so when we finally got back to the flat, tired and sated with sun and sea air, we had no appetite for a real meal. 'Cheese and biscuits and some wine?' I offered, and Alan helped me set it out. We sat and munched contentedly.

'Alan, it was lovely to get away from it for a day, and it helped clear my head,' I said when I'd nibbled all I wanted. 'I've been thinking.'

Alan chuckled. 'So have I. You first.'

'Well, it's nothing very spectacular, but it's occurred to me that we have three principal suspects, all of them with at least partial alibis for the presumed time of the murder. Right?'

'Right.' Alan was almost purring. I looked at him suspiciously, but went on, 'But the trouble is, all their alibis depend to some extent on each other. X alibis Y, who alibis Z, who alibis X, in a neat little tail-chasing circle.'

'Exactly.'

I sighed and took another sip of my wine. 'You're way ahead of me, aren't you? So if one of the three is an unreliable witness . . .'

'And that, dear heart, is why we have a police guard over Charlie Norquist. He's about as unreliable as anyone could be. I don't mean that he's untruthful. On the contrary, I think he's almost painfully honest. It's just that his grasp of reality is problematic.'

'And that's throwing roses at it. Alan, I do feel so sorry for that man!'

'As do I. That mother of his has twisted him in to a corkscrew, and I don't know if all the psychiatrists in the world can straighten him out.'

'All the king's horses. Yes.' I stood. 'Have you had all you want?'

'And more than I need.'

'Then let's go for a little walk to work off some of it. There's still nearly an hour of daylight left.' We cleared away, snapped on Watson's leash, and set out.

The village had its own special charm late at night. All the shops were closed and very few people were abroad. What gulls could be seen were perched with their heads tucked beneath their wings, ignoring any humans or dogs that came their way. We startled a cat or two, abroad on the prowl, but they were apparently of a more amenable temperament than poor old Roadkill, and passed by Watson with no more than a disdainful sneer.

I stopped to look in one shop window, where one light glowed softly on a display of paintings. Most of them were Orkney scenes, but one caught my attention. 'Look, Alan. That's one of Penny's, isn't it?'

Our friend Penny Brannigan, a Canadian ex-pat living in Wales, was a talented amateur artist in water colours. She loved painting the Welsh countryside and the occasional castle, and here before us was a splendid view of Conwy Castle, one of my favourites. 'It's great that she's in a gallery here. I wish she were here right now. She's given us valuable hints in the past.'

Alan nodded and yawned. 'Sorry, love. Too much fresh air. Let's call it a day.'

Watson was disposed to argue the point, but he gave in to force majeure and trailed after us, the picture of an abused, unloved dog.

I woke the next morning from a dream of freight trains, wondering if something had gone wrong with my bedside clock. The room was gloomy, about a three-in-the-morning (for mid-summer Orkney) shade of grey, but the clock read eight-thirty. Then I heard the pounding of the rain on the roof, what my dreaming mind had turned into the roar of a train. Neither Watson nor Alan was in the room, and I couldn't hear, above the rain, any sounds of habitation from the kitchen below. I would happily have curled up under the covers again, but I already had that logy, headachy feeling that comes from sleeping too long. I heaved myself out of bed and into the shower.

I felt quite a lot better once I was clean and dressed, and could smell toast and coffee in preparation. Alan greeted me with a kiss and a smack on the rump. 'Glad to have you back among us, Sleeping Beauty. Scrambled, boiled, poached, or fried?'

'Scrambled, please, with some of that lovely salmon if we still have any. Have I mentioned lately that I think I'll keep you?'

'No, but I'm glad to hear it. It's a filthy day.'

'I can tell.' Watson lay in a corner, still damp from his morning outing, with Alan's wet shoes beside him. 'I'm glad we got our sightseeing in yesterday. Oh, that's heaven.' I sipped from the steaming, fragrant cup he handed me. 'I don't know who first figured out that you could take some red berries and do a lot of unlikely things to them and come up with this magic brew, but

I owe them a great debt. Have there been any developments while I was doing my Rip Van Winkle act?'

'Yes, as a matter of fact. I called Baikie this morning. Apparently the terrorist threat turned out to be a tempest in a teapot, a hoax gone wrong. Of course the police are incensed about the waste of time, and are doing their best to find those responsible, but Baikie does have time now to deal with High Sanday matters, and he had quite a lot to tell me. The most important is that Norquist is back in his right mind, or what passes for a right mind in his case.'

'That's terrific! And what does he have to say?'

'That's not so terrific. Apparently he's still so afraid of his mother that he's not talking much. There's something on his mind, but Baikie says he, Norquist, that is, seems to think his mother wouldn't want him to talk about it. So far no one has been able to persuade him that Mum is safely out of reach of her son. He becomes so disturbed when pressed that they've had to stop questioning him. I understand they're seeking medical advice, hoping there's something they can give him to ease his anxiety.'

'I know what I'd take, if I were suffering from anxiety,' I said. I finished my coffee and held out my cup for more.

'What's that?' said Alan with a slight frown. I'm not much for any drugs more exotic than ibuprofen, and he knows it.

'A strong dose of Nora Tredgold,' I said. 'I'm not sure she ever tried it, but I'll bet she could have subdued old Roadkill if she'd wanted. Surely she can calm down Charlie Norquist, for whom she obviously has a lot of sympathy. As soon as we've had breakfast, I'm going to call her.'

Nora was delighted to hear that Charlie was doing better, and agreed gladly to go and try to talk to him. 'You'd like to come with me, wouldn't you?'

'You know I'm panting for the opportunity. What about Alan?'

'Unless he particularly wants to come, I think it might be better not. Charlie might view him as an authority figure, and he rather fights shy of those.'

'As well he might, considering his mother. All right, I'll tell Alan he has to stay here. Given the weather, I don't imagine he'll mind.'

'Good. Now don't you even try to walk up here. I'll pick you up there in ten minutes.'

It was raining harder than ever, with a brisk wind, when Nora's car stopped outside the flat. My umbrella was nearly carried away, which wouldn't have mattered much, since I was pretty well soaked in the few seconds between house and car. 'Heavens, can you see to drive?'

'Not terribly well, but the car knows the way. Close your eyes if you get frightened on the roundabout.'

'How did you know I think they're an invention of the devil?'

She shrugged.

'You know, Nora,' I persisted, 'there's a character in a series of old mysteries to whom, as someone in the books remarks, "the human race is glass-fronted". I think you must be related. How *do* you do it?'

She smiled gently. 'I suppose it comes from living with a priest for so many years. Theodore has to be good at hearing the things people aren't telling him, and I seem to have picked up the trick. As for you and roundabouts, however, I suspect your white knuckles might have been my first clue.'

That made me laugh, and I deliberately relaxed when we got to the devil's invention. I don't think my unclenched hands fooled her a bit.

I was half afraid we'd find some new horror when we got to Sinclair House. Charlie would have been abducted, or Mrs Norquist would have escaped and got into his room, or something equally awful. But nothing of the kind had happened. The policeman on duty outside Charlie's room was plainly bored.

Nora knew him. I wondered if she knew everybody in Orkney. 'Hello, Ian,' she said cheerfully. 'Have you met my friend Mrs Martin? Her husband is Alan Nesbitt, the chief constable who's been helping Mr Baikie with these puzzling events. How's Charlie?'

'Very quiet,' said Ian. 'He's polite when they go in to give him his meals, but otherwise he's said hardly a word.'

'Ah, well, I'll just see if I can cheer him up a bit.' And with that she opened the door and sailed into the room.

I hoped Ian was more efficient with other people he might know who might want to visit Norquist. Nora was safe, but almost anyone else was suspect.

They had put Charlie in an old wing of the house that was empty of other patients, and at the end of that wing, so his large room had windows on all three sides. On a nice day the view must have been breathtaking, endless hills, a loch, birds, wide sky. Today all was greyness and gloom.

Mr Norquist was huddled in a chair in one corner, looking miserable. He cringed at our entrance and tried to make himself even smaller.

'Hello, Charlie,' said Nora with a smile. 'I understand you've been having a bad time. I'm so sorry. I've brought you your favourite chocolates to cheer you up.' She handed him a small bag. He accepted it, laid it on the table next to his chair, and murmured an almost inaudible 'Thank you.'

'You remember Mrs Martin, I'm sure,' Nora went on, sitting in the chair nearest to Norquist. He nodded, but looked away from me.

'We've all been very worried about you, you know, my dear. Where have you been all this time?'

I feared a direct question might distress him, but he simply sat still, saying nothing. Nora waited, and at last he pointed. 'Out there,' he said. 'A sort of shed. Mother said . . .'

'She said you'd be safe there, didn't she? And indeed you were. Not very comfortable, though, I shouldn't imagine. Hardly the sort of place for a man in your position.'

'No.' For a moment the man I had seen before looked out of Charlie's eyes. 'It didn't suit me at all, but Mother said . . .'

'Charlie Norquist, tell me something. How old are you?'

He looked surprised. 'Sixty-two.'

'And where did you go to university?'

'University of Exeter. I wanted to go to Cambridge, but Mother needed me at home.'

'What did you study, Charlie?'

'Archaeology, of course. I never wanted to do anything except study ancient peoples and their civilisations.'

'I think I remember your telling me that you received a first-class honours degree.'

'Yes.' He straightened a little in his chair. 'Yes, I was at the top of my year. I was offered a teaching position then, but Mother needed me at home.'

Nora wisely didn't pursue that recurrent theme. Instead she looked out of the window. 'Not a good day for an archaeologist, is it?'

Charlie straightened still more. 'No. I hope they've covered the High Sanday excavation properly. Stone that's been buried for millennia is very vulnerable to wind and water damage. They are not careful enough. But they won't let me help.'

'That's a great pity, Mr Norquist,' I put in. 'You are certainly knowledgeable about such things.'

He gave me a look that was almost his old pedantic one. 'I am, indeed. I know a great deal more than those students. Arrogant young pups! They know nothing about the ways of the people, their beliefs, their practices . . .' He trailed off, suddenly uneasy.

'Ah, yes, their practices,' said Nora. 'I know there's a good deal of controversy about whether or not their practices included sacrifice. Of course most of the ancient religions did regard sacrifice as extremely important. Even the Hebrews, forerunners of my own religion, thought God required sacrifices. In the very early days, of course. Abraham and Isaac . . .' She trailed off artistically.

I thought she was treading on dangerous ground, but Norquist steadied. 'Barbarism! Human sacrifice! The Aztecs and Incas, yes, perhaps. But never the Neolithic peoples of Europe.'

'What would their sacrifices have been, Mr Norquist?' I asked ingenuously.

'Purely symbolic,' he said. 'Usually grain, perhaps a small mammal or a . . . a bird.' He swallowed hard, but went on bravely. 'Here in these islands, although their food supply was adequate, it was not so plentiful that they could afford to give valuable food to the gods. And never, never, never a human, no matter what my mother . . .' He stopped, a look of panic in his eyes.

'What a pity we can't talk to your mother about it,' said Nora smoothly. 'But you know she's become quite ill and has been taken to hospital. I'm sorry, Charlie, but I'm told they won't let anyone visit, even you. She's going to be fine, but she may be there for some time, so you need to work on recovering fully yourself, so you can get back out to the dig. You haven't been for several days, have you?'

We could see Charlie processing the information about his

mother. Concern and relief chased across his face. 'You'll tell me when I can visit?' he said.

'The very moment, I assure you. Meanwhile she's getting the best of care and doesn't need a thing, so you're not to worry.'

'Well, then.' He took a deep breath. 'What day is it?'

'Thursday,' I replied. 'The first of July.'

He got agitated again. 'But that's dreadful! I've been away for days. And the museum! Who's been looking after the museum?'

'It's all right, Mr Norquist,' I said soothingly. 'They've closed it since you went away. They know no one else could run it properly, you see.' I thought we'd better not tell him about the missing artefacts until we had to.

'Who closed it?' he asked sharply. 'No one had the right to do that.'

I was somewhat taken aback. 'I suppose it must have been Mr Larsen, as president of the Friends. They're the trustees, aren't they?'

'Yes, but I must tell him . . . I must . . .' He tried to get out of his chair, but fell back, clutching his chest.

I didn't have to be told to ring for a nurse.

TWENTY-EIGHT

'They say it was a minor heart attack,' I told Alan hours later. Nora and I had accompanied Mr Norquist to the hospital and endured the harsh words of the doctors. I, for one, felt we'd earned them. I had forgotten about Norquist's heart condition. Now I was back at the flat, sitting by the fire with Alan, trying to sort out what I'd learned. 'It was too much for him, all that stress on top of those awful days in the shed. We should have known better. It's really a wonder it wasn't worse. He must have a stronger constitution than meets the eye.'

'Don't blame yourself too much, love. How were you to know what would upset him? You say it was about the museum?'

'Apparently. There was something he felt he had to tell Larsen, something about the museum or the trustees, or maybe the collection. I have no idea, really. I just know he tried to get out of his chair, and then he turned sort of blue and collapsed, and I was scared to death. I thought we'd killed him, and we sure got a tongue-lashing from his doctors.'

'You can just be glad his mother wasn't there. She might have given you a cane-lashing.'

'Oh, that reminds me. Aside from whatever bothered him about the museum, there was one very interesting thing that turned up. We got him talking about the ancient rites, and sacrifice, and all that, and he went into some detail about what the sacrifices might have been. Well, he didn't say might, but . . .'

'He was probably as authoritative as he could be, which is considerable. Go on. What was so interesting about it?'

'He got into a bit of a lather about the idea of human sacrifice, and said that Abraham was a barbarian, or something like that, and then he said that the Aztecs and the Incas might have practised human sacrifice, but never the Neolithic Orcadians, never, never – and this is the interesting part – "no matter what my mother" and then he broke off and got all panicky, and Nora had to assure him that the witch couldn't come and get him. She didn't say that in so many words, of course.'

'"No matter what my mother says." You think that's how he would have ended it?'

'I'm nearly certain. Because he was obviously terrified at the idea of contradicting her, even when she wasn't nearby, lest somehow she find out. I think he thinks she's a seer, or a witch – a real one, I mean.'

'And I'm not so sure he's wrong,' said Alan. He adjusted his position in the chair, trying to ease pressure on the various welts Mrs Norquist had inflicted back at the shed. 'I trust they're going to see that she's kept from doing any more harm to anyone.'

'Especially her son. Alan, that poor man hasn't been able to call his soul his own for . . . well, probably ever.'

'I hope,' said Alan soberly, 'that he still has a soul of his own. A mother like that can destroy a person so utterly that he can never be healed.'

'That's what Nora said. Remember? She said she's the sort that eats her young. But he still has that spark of rebellion. That gives me hope that he still may have a persona of his own. He wouldn't agree with her about sacrifice, even though the dissent terrified him.'

'Well, we just have to hope that the doctors can get him to the point that he can make a cogent statement. We still don't know why he was in hiding, and that's what matters most just now.'

'And,' I said, 'if we're to be in on it, it needs to happen soon. We have this flat for only a few more days.'

'Our holiday hasn't worked out quite the way we'd planned, has it, love?'

'But then,' I said, smiling at Alan, 'they seldom do, do they? We do seem to attract trouble wherever we go. At least it isn't dull. And Alan, I want to come back here one day. There's something about this place . . . I don't know, it's got a grip on me.'

'Probably some of your ancient forebears lived at Skara Brae. Didn't you say you have some Scandinavian in you?'

'My mother was an Anderson,' I admitted. 'Spelled with an O, though, so Swedish, not Norwegian.'

'Or changed by time and/or your Ellis Island authorities.' He yawned.

I yawned in response. 'Do you want to take Watson out, or shall I?'

'I think I'll let him out, rather than taking him, given the weather. If I can persuade him to go, that is. You go on up to bed.'

'I'll do that, after I pray for a miracle of healing for poor Charlie.'

I was asleep before he came upstairs.

The miracle came just as we were finishing breakfast the next day, and it was typical of the perversity of my nature that I didn't welcome it.

The weather was no better than the day before. Watson was getting short shrift in the matter of exercise. I'd been first out of bed, so I'd let him out onto the patio for his hygienic necessities. He would much rather have stayed in, had it not been for the urgency of nature's call, and he answered it as rapidly as possible and whined to be let back in. If he could have spoken in English, I'm quite sure he would have had some opinions about indoor plumbing for dogs.

'I agree completely, old boy,' I said, shivering in my bathrobe. 'Here, let's dry you off, and then we'll get some breakfast into you, and some coffee into me, and we'll both be happier.'

Alan came down shortly after that, and we lingered over our oatmeal. 'For,' I'd said, 'it may be the beginning of July, but it feels like the middle of winter, and I want something hot and sustaining inside me.' Alan, like a true Brit, called it porridge and took it with just salt and milk. I loaded mine with brown sugar and raisins, and would have indulged myself with cream if we'd had any.

We were just thinking about getting showered and dressed when my phone made those peculiar noises that meant a call was coming in. It irritates me. Old fogey that I am, I think a ringing phone ought to sound like a ringing phone. 'Yes?' I said into it, in a snappish tone.

'I'm sorry if this is a bad time, Dorothy, but can you both come straightaway?'

'Nora? Come where?'

'The rectory.' She lowered her voice. 'Charlie is here, and I think you need to hear what he has to say.'

I looked out the window. I could barely see the huge ferry at the dock, so blinding was the rain.

'Oh, dear. I mean, that's wonderful news, but we slept late this morning, and we're not even dressed yet.'

'I think it's important,' she replied. She sounded as calm and serene as she always did, but there was a hint of steel in her voice. She Who Must Be Obeyed was speaking.

'We'll be there as soon as we can,' I said, and clicked off.

'You know,' I said to Alan as I got to my feet and began to clear the table, 'As much as I want to get to the bottom of this mess, I'm getting just a little tired of crises having to do with Charlie. That was Nora. She wants us to go to the rectory right away. I can't say the prospect of more alarums and excursions thrills me.'

'Have another cup of coffee, and then go get dressed,' said Alan. 'I'll wash up.'

I grumped upstairs. Charlie Norquist was developing into a prime pain in the neck, and for once I didn't want to see Nora, either. I wanted to stay home and nurse my bad mood.

I remembered what had happened the last time I'd felt sulky. Nora had sent us to the Italian Chapel, and I'd been shriven. As contrary as I was feeling just now, she was likely to have the cure. I sighed, finished my coffee, and headed for the shower.

Alan has put up with my moods for long enough that he knows better than to try to jolly me out of a really good snit. He spoke very little until I was finally ready to go, and then said only, 'We'll drive up.'

'That's ridiculous! Where on earth will you park?'

'Don't know.' He opened the door to the attached garage. 'In you go.'

It took longer to drive up to The Street than it would to walk. Traffic on the narrow street was awful, even though, or perhaps because, very few pedestrians had ventured out. Alan stopped in front of the steep, narrow passageway leading to the rectory. 'You'll have to walk from here, I'm afraid. Here's my brolly; it's bigger. I'll be with you in a tick.' He all but shoved me out of the car and drove on before I could argue.

Despite the big black umbrella, I was very wet indeed when I rang the bell and opened the door of the rectory. Nora came to meet me. 'My dear, I know you'd like to strangle me, but this really is necessary. Did Alan not come with you?'

'He drove me up. He's trying to find a place to put the car.'

I was trying not to sound the way I felt. I dropped the umbrella in the stand with rather more force than was necessary and shook my raincoat with extra vigour, spraying rainwater around the entry almost as efficiently as Watson. My hostess only smiled and offered me a pair of slippers. 'I'm sure your feet must be soaked.'

They were, in fact. I slipped out of my shoes and into the slippers, beginning to feel ashamed of my ill nature. What *was* it with me these days, anyway? Nora took my coat with no care against getting herself wet and hung it on the rack. 'Charlie's in the sitting room,' she said softly. 'I talked them into releasing him from the hospital into my care. They've given him something to calm him down, and he's really quite himself, but they couldn't say for certain how long the effect of the drug will last. I wanted you to hear what he has to say while he's still . . . well, you'll see.' She turned toward the sitting room.

'Nora, wait.' I had, I thought, figured out what was really wrong with me. 'I need to know what I'm getting into. Can Alan and I ask him questions without sending him into another heart attack? Because I don't think I can take much more drama. I . . . you see, my first husband died of a sudden heart attack, and . . . actually, I didn't realize until this minute why I was so loath to come and see Charlie.'

'I understand, and it's all right. I mean, your reaction is reasonable, but it will be all right to say anything you like to Charlie, as long as you're gentle about it. Just now he's eager to tell his story. You'll see why. Ah, here's Alan.'

Alan was as wet as a man can well be, short of drowning. 'You had to go back to the flat, didn't you?' I said accusingly. 'And without your umbrella.'

'I won't melt,' he said. 'Dinna fash yoursel', lass.'

His Scottish accent was a lot better than his American, but it still sounded strange coming from his very English lips. I smiled almost in spite of myself, and he stepped toward me and then backed off. 'I'll not give you a hug, my love. You're reasonably dry. Let me just rid myself of this coat, which weighs approximately fifty pounds, and I'm at everyone's service.'

Charlie was looking much, much better than the last time I'd seen him. His cheeks weren't exactly rosy, but they were back to his normal colour, and his expression was the normal prissy one. 'Good morning, Mrs Martin, Mr Nesbitt. I hope we can get this over quickly. I am exceedingly concerned about the museum. It's most irregular for it to be closed at the height of the tourist season, and there is much I must see to.'

'I believe some of the volunteers have been keeping it at least partially open, sir,' said Alan. 'In any case I doubt there'd have been many visitors today. The weather is not conducive to a pleasure outing.'

'All the more reason why I should be there. I have no doubt there are things that have been left undone since I have been away. However, I wished to acquaint someone with several important details about the recent disgraceful events surrounding High Sanday. Mrs Tredgold tells me you have the ear of the police, and I would rather deal with you than with them.'

He'd have to deal with them eventually, but I saw no reason to tell him so right away. 'We're eager to hear your story, Mr Norquist. We'd both like to know why you went away.'

'That's soon told. I went away to avoid being murdered by Mr Fairweather.'

'I expect you'd like some tea,' said Nora into the sudden silence, and slipped away.

Alan was the first to recover his aplomb. 'And why did you think that Mr Fairweather intended to murder you, sir?'

'I assure you, it was not a matter of "thinking". I knew quite well what he intended. I was a danger to him, you see. But perhaps I had best begin at the beginning, though I hate to take the time.'

'Please do.' Alan sat back with the air of one who had all the time in the world, and I tried to assume the same manner.

'It's somewhat difficult to know where the beginning really began, if you follow me,' said Charlie in his dry, pedantic way. 'I suppose it really goes back to when Mr Fairweather was hired to direct the dig. I was not in favour of his appointment, for he seemed to me to lack the requisite single-minded commitment. An endeavour such as this one can become a life's work, and Mr Fairweather did not, I thought, quite understand that. However, I am not an influential voice in the Friends, though one would think I ought to be. I voiced my objections. I was overruled. Mr Fairweather was hired.'

Nora came in with a tea tray, poured out for us all, and sat down noiselessly.

'The trouble actually began when Mr Carter interested himself in the dig.' Charlie sipped his tea nervously, pausing after every sentence to refresh himself. 'He was not a sympathetic character, and I could see at once that his motive was self-aggrandizement rather than the furthering of knowledge. Again my objections were ignored. Archaeology is expensive. He had money. He was embraced by Mr Fairweather and, to a lesser degree, by Mr Larsen. Might I have a bit more tea, Mrs Tredgold?'

None of this was new information, of course. I was impatient for Charlie to get the point of being an almost-victim of murder, but a look from Alan made me bide my time.

'I could see,' Charlie went on, 'that Mr Fairweather was growing more and more disenchanted with Mr Carter, as was I, and really, everyone who knew him. He was a most unpleasant man. He thought he could buy everything and everyone, and he knew nothing, nothing at all, about archaeology. He became obsessed with digging deeper and deeper at High Sanday, without regard to what might be destroyed in the upper layers. He was foolish enough to think he would find gold, Viking gold, when the Vikings were of an entirely different period, much, much later than the dwellings we were finding. They were finding, I should say. I, of course, was simply an observer.'

There it was again, his not-so-veiled irritation at being shut out of the inner circle. How much of his statement now was motivated by that envious anger?

'The night of the meeting was when it all came to a head. Mr Fairweather seemed to handle himself well, but I knew he was beside himself. He was so upset he did something he had never done before. He invited me out for a drink. He said he needed to calm down, and said he thought I could use what he called "a little tranquilizer" myself.

'Now, I am not a drinking man, but I did not feel I could turn down an invitation from my superior in the Friends. He was, in a way, my boss, though of course Mr Larsen as President of the Friends is really the head of the museum. At any rate, Mr Fairweather took me to a pub. I was at the time grateful that it was in a rather remote village, where I might not be recognized. My mother . . . that is, I should not have wanted anyone I know to see me drinking.'

'Mr Fairweather mentioned that you and he had a drink or two,' I said. 'He told us in confidence, you understand, to help us in making sense of Mr Carter's death.'

'And did he tell you the extraordinary proposition he made to me?'

Alan and I looked at each other, then shook our heads. I realized I was sitting on the edge of my chair, and scooted back. Charlie didn't notice, but went ahead with his narrative.

'He told me he was going to the dig that night at midnight. It was the solstice, you remember. He said he had heard that there might be some activity at the site. "Goings-on" was the term he used. I wasn't altogether sure I knew what he meant by the term, but I didn't care for any of the possible meanings. He suggested that I might care to go with him, in order to prevent what he called "blasphemies". I told him I would think about it and let him know. I would have had to go with him, as I do not own a boat. He quite urged me, and bought me several drinks. I do not have a strong head, as I am unaccustomed to spirits. At last I managed to break away. Fortunately, we had driven separately, so I was able to make my way home, and I have to say that I am grateful I met with none of the constabulary on the way home, for I was certainly in no condition to drive. And that is virtually all I remember until I was awakened the next morning with the news of Mr Carter's death.'

'You did not go to the dig that night?' Alan asked, wanting to be certain.

'I did not. I was not feeling at all well, and I did not care for the idea of a boat trip with a man I disliked in the middle of the night. I went to bed and woke with a dreadful headache the next morning. You may remember I was feeling ill when we went to the dig.'

'Mr Fairweather said he took you home and put you to bed, at around midnight. I believe you agreed with that statement earlier. Is that not what happened?'

'No. I agreed because I couldn't quite remember, and I . . . didn't want to upset Mr Fairweather. But I drove myself home, and it wasn't even ten o'clock. I'm quite sure, now that I've had a chance to think. It was still light outside when I went to bed, and my car was there in the morning, as it would not have been had someone else taken me home.' He sounded quite certain.

'Who woke you in the morning, Mr Norquist?' I put in. 'I suppose someone phoned you with the dreadful news.'

'Mr Larsen. I fear I wasn't very courteous when I answered. I was feeling like nothing on earth. I must say, I fail to understand why some people drink themselves to a stupor, when the after-effects are so dire,' he added, with the first sign of an ordinary human reaction I had seen from him yet. 'I beg your pardon. That is not germane. You know what happened next. I could not imagine what had brought Carter to the dig in the middle of the night, unless he had been part of the "goings-on" Mr Fairweather mentioned. But Mr Fairweather seemed to have no idea what Carter was doing there, either, and I thought it best not to discuss his own proposed midnight trip to the dig, since he did not bring it up. It was, I thought, possible that he had abandoned the idea of going, since I had not seemed enthusiastic about going with him.'

He picked up his teacup, took a sip of the rapidly cooling liquid, grimaced, and went on.

'That was on the Tuesday, the twenty-second. The rain prevented any work at the dig, or any effective police work, either. The next day, the Wednesday, they arrested Andersen, and I assumed that was that, and went about my business.

'But then I went to see my mother, and of course I told her everything that had happened. She was . . . quite upset. She said I should have gone with Mr Fairweather on the solstice. She said I should have made a sacrifice, as she did, herself, near the home. She said . . . I don't remember everything she said.'

He was clenching his hands spasmodically. His lips seemed dry; he kept licking them. Mrs Tredgold took away his tea cup and poured some for him from a fresh pot. He seemed not to notice.

'Mother told me I needed to atone, needed to placate *Them*. That's why I went to the sites on Saturday. Were you there, too?'

'Yes, Mr Norquist,' Alan said, very gently, as though to a wounded animal. 'We saw and talked to you at Skara Brae and High Sanday. Do you remember?'

'No . . . I . . . and then Mr Fairweather told me about the dead cat and said everyone was blaming me, and I'd best go away, and I knew I'd never killed a cat, and he tried to put me in his car, and I ran away and went to ask Mother what to do, and she . . .' His hand motions were entirely out of control now. His right hand flew out and knocked the tea cup to the floor, where it shattered.

Mrs Tredgold simply looked at us, and we nodded. Plainly the meds were wearing off, or else the frightful memories were too much for Charlie to cope with. We stood. 'Thank you, Mr Norquist,' said Alan. 'You have been a great help. We'll leave you now to get some rest.'

TWENTY-NINE

We stood in the entry for a moment, trying to decide what to do next. Nora had stayed with Charlie, to try to calm him a bit, and probably to give him another pill. The rain had almost stopped, or at least had paused. 'Shall I bring the car around?' asked Alan.

'Don't be silly. We'll walk. We can change when we get back to the flat. And then . . . Baikie, do you think?'

'Right. I'll phone him straightaway.'

The conversation was brief. Inspector Baikie agreed that Fairweather had some explaining to do. 'Though of course,' Alan said when he'd ended the call, 'the police will have to talk to Norquist at some point.'

'Not now, Alan!'

'No, not now. He's in no shape to stand up to that sort of thing, the condition he's in now. I hope they can pump enough drugs into him to get him relatively balanced soon. If Fairweather knows Norquist has talked to us, he'll also know he's under grave suspicion. That alibi he gave for the night of the murder is now no alibi at all, unless Norquist is lying his head off. And frankly, I don't think the man is capable of formulating a lie at this point.'

'He's barely up to speaking at all, if you ask me. That mother of his . . . anyway, is Baikie going to let you talk to Fairweather, too?'

'He gave that impression. He'll phone when he's located the man.'

I spent the rest of the morning on pins and needles, tidying up the flat to have something to do. Alan took Watson for a walk, never getting far from the flat, in case the inspector called. He was back, pacing the floor while I tried to think what to have for lunch, when the call came.

'Nesbitt here. Yes. Yes? You've tried the museum? Yes. Certainly. As soon as we can get there.' Alan clicked off. 'They can't find Fairweather. He's not answering his phone, and they've tried his home and the museum and all the places he's known to frequent. Baikie's going out to the dig, in case he's there. The mobile reception isn't good on Papa Sanday.'

I nodded. 'I think that's the place to try. It's the centre of all that's happened, isn't it? The dig is at the heart of the matter, I'm sure.'

'Well, get a move on, love. We're to meet Baikie at the Tingwall pier.'

'It's all right for me to come too?'

'I didn't ask,' said Alan. 'Better bring rain gear. It's clear now, but who knows? And don't forget your ginger capsules. And we'll take Watson. He might be needed.'

If Inspector Baikie was surprised when Alan appeared at the boat accompanied by wife and dog, he made no sign. He greeted Watson with grave courtesy and ushered me aboard with some courtliness. He also gave me what looked like an ancient steamer rug for warmth. It was needed. The police launch was a fast and efficient boat, but it was built for utility rather than comfort. The sea was rough, but either I'd become inured or the ginger was doing its work, or else I was simply too absorbed by what we might find at High Sanday to think about being seasick.

It was raining again when we got to the island, not the deluge of the early morning, but hard enough to make us all thoroughly miserable in a few minutes. There was no sign of another boat, though Baikie'd had his pilot circle the island before we landed. 'Doesn't look promising to find him, but we might as well have a look, now we're here,' Baikie said. 'He might have spent the night here and sent someone back with the boat, to fetch him today. The wee dog might find him, maybe?'

The wee dog had had just about enough of Orkney weather. He wanted to go back to the boat, where it was, if not warm, at least dry. Failing that, he wanted to explore a shed near the pier. He dragged at the leash and finally had to be spoken to sharply by Alan, who was better than I at discipline. I could see the dog's point and was in hearty agreement with it, but I plodded along with the rest, sniffling. I was pretty sure my cold was coming back.

There was no sign of any human anywhere we looked, at least near the dig. We thought about going as far as Andersen's place, but the thought of our probable reception kept us away. We could think of no reason why Fairweather would be there, and Andersen was the sort of man who would pitchfork first and ask questions later. The other crofters lived at the far end of the island, much too far to walk.

'I'll send for a ferry with a car if we canna find him elsewhere, but it's no weather for a ferry today.'

Indeed, the sea was looking rougher every moment, and the wind blowing harder, though the rain had slackened a bit. There was no sign of Fairweather. 'He should be here, though,' I said through chattering teeth. 'He should be here with a crew to put the place to rights. The rain isn't doing the site a bit of good.'

Big plastic tarps which had, I presumed, been positioned over parts of the excavation had blown free and were snapping in the wind. The paint shop was getting soaked. 'Just look at that, Alan! All those pigments are going to be ruined. It's a crime.'

'Not the only crime the gentleman's committed, if we're believing Mr Norquist,' said Baikie grimly, becoming more Scottish by the minute. 'I doot we'll no find him on Orkney nae mair.'

'I agree it's becoming more and more likely he's done a runner,' said Alan. 'We might as well go back to the boat. We'll not find him here, at any rate.'

We were nearly back to the boat, Watson now trying to pull the leash out of my hand in his eagerness, when he suddenly stopped dead, stiffened, and growled.

I was freezing, fed up, and mightily annoyed with the dog. I tried to pull him along, but Baikie held out a restraining hand and bent to Watson's level. 'What's troublin' ye, noo?'

Another growl. A step backward. Watson's eyes were fixed on a large, beat-up wooden box in front of the shed near the pier.

'There's something in that box,' I said in a voice I could barely make function. It was big enough to hold a man, or perhaps the remains . . . I willed my brain to stop working.

Baikie moved slowly to the box and reached for the lid. Watson's growls grew louder. Baikie raised the lid.

'Why, it's a wee moggie!' And he lifted out a thin, wet, bedraggled rag of orange and dirty white fur, with one nicked ear and fire in its eye.

'Alan!' I said with a gasp. 'It's Roadkill!'

THIRTY

I would not have recognized the sorry specimen as the belligerent Lord of The Street. The colouring was more or less right, and the battered ear and the attitude were familiar, but this cat was thin. Or perhaps it was just that his wet fur clung to his bones.

Watson knew, though. Appearances don't fool a dog. This animal smelled like his nemesis.

'You'd better be careful,' I said. 'I know that cat, and he's not got the best reputation. Unless that's his ghost. The latest bit of his reputation is that he's reputed to be dead. Robert Fairweather said he found him with his throat cut, about a week ago, and he spread the rumour that Mr Norquist had killed him.'

'Ah. So this is the puir wee beastie. Well, he's not eaten for a good while, and I've seen cleaner cats, but he's verra much alive. Aren't you, lad?'

Baikie held the cat close in his arms and tickled him behind one ear. A sound as of cast iron being crushed in a meat grinder filled the air.

I looked at the oddly matched pair in disbelief. Roadkill was purring.

Watson could hardly believe that he had to share a smallish boat with That Cat all the way back to Tingwall. He cowered behind me, trying to make himself invisible. There had been nothing on board that was really suitable for a cat's meal, but the starving beast devoured a muesli bar with no trouble and washed it down with several small plastic containers of coffee cream poured into the lid of a coffee can. After his repast, Roadkill sat on Baikie's lap washing himself with great thoroughness, every now and then giving Watson a thoughtful look that made the poor dog whimper and try to scooch farther into the corner.

'So that was another of Fairweather's lies, that he'd found Roadkill dead,' I said. 'Why did he go to all that trouble?'

Alan answered that one. 'Probably to give credence to the idea that Norquist was well and truly bonkers and had killed Carter

for some mad reason. Things weren't looking too good for
Fairweather at that juncture, if you recall. Andersen had been
released from jail, and Fairweather must have been sweating. He
and Larsen had the best motive for Carter's murder, and, his,
Fairweather's alibi depended on Charlie. And poor old Charlie
had been acting very odd. Really, he gave Fairweather a beautiful
opportunity for a spot of framing.'

'And it all tied in with that unfortunate incident of the hen in
May. I wonder who actually did kill the hen?'

'I dinna like to pour cold water on your theories,' said Baikie,
roused from his preoccupation with Roadkill, 'but we've no proof
of Mr Fairweather's guilt. Likely enough he's lied about this,
that, and the other, and provided himself with an alibi that's no
good, if Mr Norquist's to be believed, but I'd be happier if we
had one single piece of evidence I could take to the chief
constable.'

'As would I,' said Alan.

'Well, we've got Roadkill, alive and kicking,' I pointed out.

'That's evidence of a lie, Dorothy. Or perhaps merely a misun-
derstanding. Fairweather could have confused another cat for this
one. Well, it's possible,' he added, seeing my look. 'We need
something airtight. A smoking gun, to hark back to your American
Watergate scandal.'

'Hmmm.' There wasn't much more to be said, and as Roadkill
seemed inclined to take fresh interest in Watson, I gave my poor
dog an absent-minded pat now and then, and mused all the way
back to Tingwall.

Watson was greatly relieved to be removed from the cat's
vicinity, and would have been even happier if he'd been able to
understand that Baikie was taking him back to the police station.
'For he's in want of proper attention, the puir wee thing, some
good food, and a good rest, and mayhap a trip to the v-e-t.' He
looked a trifle embarrassed at that remark.

'We always spell that word in front of our animals,' I hastened
to assure him. 'And we used to spell the one that means taking
a constitutional, but Watson's figured that one out. I'm so glad
you're looking after Roadkill, Inspector, and if I were you, I'd
give him a new name. He might be a nicer kitty if he had a nicer
name, and if some of his . . . um . . . personal attributes were

removed. A woman in Stromness seems to think a good deal of his behaviour stems from too much testosterone. But before you go . . . do you have a search warrant for Mr Fairweather's lodgings?'

'We do. And of course we searched his room, earlier today.'

'You searched it for him, or for some indication of where he might be. Did you find anything else of interest?'

'Nothing that was reported to me. What are you hinting, Mrs Martin?' He had dropped most of the accent and was sounding very official.

'It's just that I thought there was something else you might find. And if you did, and if you could find Fairweather and confront him with that evidence, and with the cat, the two things together might rattle him into a confession.'

'And what would we be looking for, then?'

I told him, and he nodded, saluted, and strode to his car, the cat purring in his arms and giving one long last look at Watson.

'Are you going to tell me what you said to him?' Alan asked.

I told him, and added, 'I hope they find Fairweather soon. I'd hate to go home with all this unresolved.'

'There's one thing that's resolved, at any rate,' said Alan, opening the car door, which he had left unlocked in conformity with established Orcadian practice. He had, however, taken the keys with him, defying the local custom of leaving them in the ignition. 'In you get, dog.'

'And what's the thing that's resolved?' I got in the back beside Watson, who badly needed some cuddling.

'That cat's fate. Call him Roadkill, call him Sandy, call him anything you like, I'm calling him Baikie's cat. I would not have believed that canicidal monster could have settled down into a purring pussycat.'

'Yes, I do believe he's found a home. Maybe Celia was right, and all he needed was a little love.'

'More likely he's decided that he's lost three or four of his lives and had best preserve the ones that are left.'

It was far past lunchtime and we were all starving, and there wasn't much to eat back at the flat. We'd been trying to use up our groceries, since we were going home in a day or two. So we stopped at a café in Kirkwall where we got a very satisfying meal and an extra roast beef sandwich for Watson, which he wolfed down in the car. Alan sighed over the mess he left on the floor. 'I hate to think what we're going to have to pay in cleaning fees for this vehicle.'

'I'll do the best I can with it before we drop it at the airport. Which reminds me. We'll have to take the ferry back, I suppose, or else call our nice pilot.'

'I have to phone in any case, to check on the status of our car. And how we're going to get home if it isn't ready, my love, I do not know.'

'We'll manage, by rail if we have to. We've made use of virtually every other form of public transport known to man on this little jaunt. A nice civilised train wouldn't hurt us.'

All of us were ready for a nap when we got back to the flat, but I slept with one ear open, figuratively speaking. No call came, however, and after Watson had wakened us and we'd taken care of his needs, I began to be impatient. 'They should have found him by now,' I said to Alan. 'They've enough evidence, surely, to warrant a full-scale search.'

'They'll find him,' said Alan serenely. 'Are you hungry enough for supper?'

'Not really, but eating would be something to pass the time. Beats pacing the floor.'

'Then how about a drink, and some cheese and biscuits? We can stretch that out for quite a while, if we put our minds to it.'

We had barely settled down with our drinks and our snack when Alan's phone tootled. I put my drink down.

'Nesbitt here. Ah, you did. Good. And . . . well done!' He gave me a high sign. 'And you'd like us . . . of course. When and where?' He listened for a moment longer and clicked off. 'You've gathered what that was about.'

'They've found what they were looking for, and they've got Fairweather.'

'And Baikie is kindly allowing us to be in at the kill. So to speak. I'd save that for later, love,' he said, nodding at my bourbon. 'Best, perhaps, to approach this in a godly, righteous, and sober state.'

The venue Baikie had chosen in a moment of brilliance was the Ancient Orkney Museum. All the lights were shining brightly when we arrived. Mr Norquist was absent, for which I was grateful. Mr Larsen was present, however, along with Baikie and Fairweather. Baikie sat in a Windsor chair, his voluminous and rather shabby raincoat draped over the back. I thought about Columbo.

Fairweather was inclined to be bellicose. 'I demand to know why I have been brought here! Mr Nesbitt, I asked you to look out for my interests. I have to say you've done a damn poor job of it!'

'On the contrary, sir, you asked me to investigate the murder of Henry Carter, which I have done, or rather which my wife and I have assisted Inspector Baikie in doing.'

'Then why hasn't someone arrested that fool Norquist? He's nutty as a fruitcake, but he's also a killer.'

'I don't believe so, sir,' said Baikie calmly. 'You are, I think, aware that he has emerged from hiding, and has told us a number of very interesting things.'

'And you believed him. I thought better of your intelligence than that. He's a raving lunatic, I tell you.'

'So you do, sir, repeatedly. Everyone here will, I believe, concede that Mr Norquist has been severely disturbed, and is still in rather a fragile emotional state, but there is nothing whatever the matter with his memory. We believe his account of the night of the murder, an account which leaves you, sir, without anyone to verify your whereabouts.'

'I've told you. How many times! I had a drink or two with Norquist, who has a remarkably low tolerance for alcohol, namby-pamby that he is. He became drunk and incapable. I took him home and put him to bed, and then went home to bed myself, after midnight.'

'No, sir, you did not.' Baikie's manner had sharpened. 'You left Mr Norquist before ten. You then went to High Sanday with Mr Carter, on some ruse or other, and killed him. It seems probable that you then took the time to bury his watch in Mr Andersen's pasture, hoping to incriminate him, and then took Mr Carter's boat back nearly to Kirkwall harbour, where you scuttled it and swam to shore.'

'You should write fiction for a living, Baikie, but you need a little work on the plots. This one doesn't quite hang together.'

'Oh, I think it does, sir. When you realized Mr Andersen was not going to be charged with Mr Carter's murder, you tried very hard to confuse the issue with several ploys that, while ingenious, were not well thought out. For example, you tried to incriminate Mr Norquist by stealing some of the museum's artefacts, but you did that after his disappearance, and after the lock on the door here had been changed. Poor planning, Mr Fairweather.'

Larsen spoke. 'I left my key in my office at the college, fool that I am. Of course I never lock my office door. He must have "borrowed" it and had a copy made.'

'One moment, sir,' said Baikie, as Fairweather began to speak. 'You see, we found this in your room today.' He pulled out a pottery beaker in the distinctive Unstan Ware style. 'There were a good many other such items, as well. I'm happy that your scientific training would not allow you to destroy them, but it was a mistake from a criminal point of view.

'Even before that,' he went on, again riding over Fairweather's attempt to speak, 'you spread the tale of the sacrifice of a cat at the dig, and laid the blame at Mr Norquist's door. Leaving aside the unlikelihood of such an action – Mr Norquist being deathly afraid of cats, and a cat being unsuitable as a sacrifice, from the point of view of the ancient Orcadians – how do you explain this?'

He opened the box under his chair, the box that had been hidden by his raincoat. With a hiss worthy of a Shakespearean actor responding to his cue, Roadkill leapt out of the box, straight for Fairweather's face.

'Did he scratch you badly, love?' Alan and I were sitting with our belated drinks and a somewhat more sustaining snack, seeing as how it was now well past supper time.

'I had taken the precaution of leaving my gloves on, anticipating such a scene,' Alan said placidly. 'The copper who was hidden in the corner had gauntlets, so between the two of us we managed to capture the cat without serious injury. To ourselves, at least. Fairweather's face won't be the same again for a while, but he'll recover. An amazing memory that cat must have.'

'An amazing capacity for holding a grudge,' I amended. 'He had every right, though. I suppose the fool man must have intended really to kill him, but Roadkill managed to get away. I must say he made an effective inducement to confession.'

'I'd have confessed nearly anything, if that cat had been attacking me.'

'And there's the flaw in the whole thing, of course. Interesting, isn't it, that it was fear, along with greed, which led to the murder, and in the end, fear prompted the confession. A good lawyer will work that for all it's worth. The case is solid, though. I don't think he'll get off. What will happen about the inheritance? Does Fairweather's guilt nullify that?'

'That's another thing the lawyers will have to work out, but I shouldn't think it will make any difference. The bequest was to the organization, Friends of Ancient Orkney, not to Fairweather individually. Assuming he does not, in fact, manage to "get off". And speaking of getting off. I did find time today to phone the garage in Edinburgh. The car is ready and waiting for us, and for something less than a king's ransom. His brother's plane is engaged for the next few days, but for a small additional fee MacTavish will drive the car to Aberdeen and meet us at the ferry. I said I'd phone and tell him when we'd be there.'

'Not by the first ferry in the morning, Alan,' I said sleepily. 'There are people to say goodbye to.'

There were many people to say goodbye to next day, Nora Tredgold, and all the shopkeepers on The Street, and even Celia Freebody. I told her what had become of Sandy.

'I hope you won't mind too much,' I said. 'He and Chief Inspector Baikie just hit it off, and I think he's found a good home.'

'I'll miss him,' she said, 'but if he's happy, that's the main thing. Mrs Martin, I'm sorry I suspected you of killing him. I've worried about him for a long time, and . . .' She made a vague gesture.

'I understand. It's all right. I love cats, too.'

Then, on the drive to the car rental return, we stopped to say goodbye to Orkney. We took the longest way, with many detours, and even so we couldn't see everything I wanted to see. The ferry didn't leave until quite late, so we had plenty of time to stop and gaze at the Ring of Brodgar and the Stones of Stenness. We watched the gulls quarrel over titbits, watched the sheep and cattle make their leisurely way across pastures. We looked at the great over-arching sky and felt the ever-present wind in our faces.

'We're coming back,' I said firmly. 'With no alarums and excursions next time. I never got to see Andrew's pottery – his workshop, I mean – and you still haven't shown me the castle, not properly.'

'Ah, the castle,' said Alan when we were aboard the ferry and settled in for the night journey. 'I'll tell you about the castle as you fall asleep. There's an enchanted wood, you know, and a maze, and a formal garden with a pond . . .'

I was asleep almost before my head hit the pillow.

stains on edge SV/LU 04/05/22